Homeco

Suddenly, unexpectedly, like the cry of fire in a crowded room, there he was. McKenzie's vocal mechanism froze, and she stood for endless seconds as she stared at him.

Eight years. Had it been eight years since Jeb had stormed out of her life? Now that he was here it seemed more like an eternity. Her heart tripped a time or two as she looked at him full in the face.

Physically he hadn't changed—at least, not much. He was perhaps a little thinner, and had his smoky green eyes always had that steel edge to them?

The tight-fitting jeans showed off trim hips and long legs, and the powerful muscles of his upper arms and shoulders moved with his every twist and turn. He looked as dangerous and lazily attractive as ever.

"Taking inventory?" he drawled.

Dear Reader,

When two people fall in love, the world is suddenly new and exciting, and it's that same excitement we bring to you in Silhouette Intimate Moments. These are stories with scope, with grandeur. These characters lead the lives we all dream of, and everything they do reflects the wonder of being in love.

Longer and more sensuous than most romances, Silhouette Intimate Moments novels take you away from everyday life and let you share the magic of love. Adventure, glamour, drama, even suspense— these are the passwords that let you into a world where love has a power beyond the ordinary, where the best authors in the field today create stories of love and commitment that will stay with you always.

In coming months look for novels by your favorite authors: Maura Seger, Parris Afton Bonds, Elizabeth Lowell and Erin St. Claire, to name just a few. And whenever you buy books, look for all the Silhouette Intimate Moments, love stories *for* today's women *by* today's women.

Leslie J. Wainger
Senior Editor
Silhouette Books

Price Above Rubies

Mary Lynn Baxter

Silhouette Intimate Moments

Published by Silhouette Books New York

America's Publisher of Contemporary Romance

SILHOUETTE BOOKS
300 E. 42nd St., New York, N.Y. 10017

Copyright © 1986 by Mary Lynn Baxter

ISBN: 0-373-07130-2

First Silhouette Books printing February 1986

America's Publisher of Contemporary Romance

Printed in the U.S.A.

MARY LYNN BAXTER

owns and manages the D & B Book Store in Lufkin, Texas.
Romances have been her favorite books for years, and she
sells more romances in her store than any other kind of
book.

To Peggy Thomas
Thanks for everything

Who can find a virtuous woman?
For her price *is* far above rubies.

Prologue

Sonofabitch!"

Eating another mouthful of dirt, Jeb Langley dived to the ground as another bullet whizzed past his head. He should have known better, he cursed again silently, than to roam the streets of San Salvador at this ungodly hour of the morning. But he'd been restless, deciding to bid an eager farewell to the city.

Now, minutes later, he was lucky he hadn't gotten his damn head blown off. Slowly, he rose to his knees and looked around. All quiet. Too quiet. Knowing from experience those shots were a warm-up for what was to come, Jeb jumped to his feet and ran across the street to his hotel room.

After closing the door behind him, he crossed the room to the bed, where he eyed a suitcase covering the tattered spread. He reached down and slammed it shut, the sound zinging off the walls, reminiscent of the sound of the gunshot that had just skimmed over his head.

Thank God, he was going home. At last. A silent smirk ghosted his firm lips. The prodigal son was returning, but certainly not to dine on the fatted calf. Just the opposite, he told himself bitterly. Would his old man ever forgive him? And what of McKenzie? Had he actually committed a crime that night so long ago? No. He thought not—just an error in judgment, letting the heat in his loins overrule his head.

The smirk still in place, Jeb unceremoniously dumped the baggage on the floor and moved to the window. He slung aside the poor excuse for a drape and stared out at the terrain. El Salvador. A tropical land of mountains, cone-shaped volcanoes, green valleys and scenic lakes.

He'd been in this stinking hole far longer than he cared to remember. And its tropical beauty was deceiving as hell. It did little to cover up the bloody war going on between the U.S.-backed government troops and the leftist guerrillas. He was sick of it. He was tired of traveling, tired of hotel rooms and tired of his own company. As a free-lance journalist, he'd covered his last senseless war—at least for a while, he cautioned himself. Hadn't he learned the hard way? Never say never.

Suddenly, a loud knock on the door jarred him out of his reverie. Not bothering to turn around, thinking it was the taxi driver, he called out in fluent Spanish, "Come in. My bags are on the floor."

There was a moment of silence; then Jeb heard a shuffle of feet behind him. Instantly alert, he whipped around, confronting a barefooted peasant boy staring at him with large haunted eyes.

"*Señor*, I have a message for you," the boy said in his native tongue. Then his arm shot out, a yellow envelope dangling from his fingers.

With a sinking feeling in the pit of his stomach, Jeb took the telegram and tossed the kid a coin before he turned and scooted out the door.

Reluctantly, Jeb ripped it open and stared down at its contents. The words on the paper glared up at him:

PLEASE COME HOME AS SOON AS POSSIBLE YOUR FATHER HAD A STROKE LIFE THREATENING LOVE.

RACHEL

"Damn!" Jeb muttered, wadding the paper up in his large hand, which he noticed was not quite steady. This brought on a string of expletives, finally halted by another rap on the door.

A few moments later, his luggage loaded in the rear of the taxi, Jeb paused and took one last look around him. Then with a shrug, he got into the vehicle.

So much for his unexpected homecoming, he thought ironically, the telegram now a tattered mess in the palm of his hand....

Chapter 1

This had better be important."

A short stocky man with graying sideburns framed by a strong jaw stood up and grinned. "Ah, come on, McKenzie, give me a break," he pleaded, coming around to pull out the chair opposite his. "Have I, as a fellow reporter, ever led you on a wild-goose chase?"

McKenzie Moore rolled her eyes, though an answering grin softened her full lips as she took the seat offered her. "More times than I care to remember, John Riley," she quipped. "But we'll let that slide, since it's obvious I fell for your line again—and on a day like this, too."

McKenzie shivered, momentarily focusing her attention on the wide expanse of glass adorning one end of the quaint downtown Austin restaurant. On this November afternoon, the rain splashed against the panes, reminding her of thousands of sparkling diamonds. It was an unusually cold day, and she'd hated leaving her snug cubbyhole at the newspaper office.

John's voice suddenly broke her train of thought. "What would you like to drink?"

"Just a cup of coffee, please," she said to the waitress hovering at her side. Then she turned back to John. "Okay, let's have it. What's up?"

John wrinkled his rather substantial nose and grinned smugly. "Actually, what I have to say would be better said in the presence of your stepfather, but since he's unavailable..."

McKenzie barely managed to curb her impatience. "John, will you please get to the point."

"Okay, okay. Here's the scoop," he said, only to pause again while the waitress brought their drinks. After a moment, he continued. "This morning I checked into an accident at the site of the Cedar Plaza Mall. A construction worker was killed."

Only a mild flicker of interest showed on McKenzie's face. "And you think there's more to it than meets the eye?"

"Positive. And the rumors have been flying to boot." He leaned forward. "Here's this small company spending millions of taxpayers' dollars for months now and nothing much to show for it except a man's death." He shook his head. "There's no way you can convince me someone doesn't have his hand in the cookie jar."

"Proof, my friend. You'll need proof. And it'll be hard to come by since the project has the backing of the mayor—*and* everyone's scrutiny."

"My gut instinct tells me I'm on to something."

McKenzie's brows furrowed. In spite of his outward tomfoolery, John Riley was a crackerjack at his job. "All right. You have my attention."

He shrugged before replying, "I snooped around and nothing appeared ordinary to me. My old man was a carpenter, taught me about building. I know a faulty, overloaded elevator when I see one. When that cable snapped, it was lights out for that fellow. He had as much chance as a snowball in hell getting off that lift alive. Then Jeff Dillard, who owns the construction company, made his presence known.'' He stopped, seeing the look on McKenzie's face. ''You know him?''

''No, but I've heard plenty about him.''

''Well, he strutted up like a tight-legged bantam rooster, all primed to jump me if I acted like I was going to blast his company on the front page of the paper.''

McKenzie grinned. ''And that made you dislike him on the spot?''

''That, and the way his eyes kept shifting. When a man won't look at you, you can bet he's got something to hide.''

Suddenly, McKenzie felt a sense of excitement. Was it possible that this was the break she had been waiting for? Cedar Plaza was the project of the mayor's, Jackson Witherspoon, who had aspirations of becoming the next governor of Texas, and was her stepfather's sworn enemy.

The shopping center was being built in a deprived section of the city for the purpose of not only upgrading the area but also giving the local residents a chance to purchase high-quality goods at low prices. It was hailed as a first of its kind.

Riley, seeing the light in McKenzie's blue eyes, smiled and took a sip of his coffee. ''Think this little tidbit was worth battling the elements for?''

''Well, it's certainly worth telling my stepfather, and knowing him, he'll want me to get on it right away.''

Her stepfather, Carson Langley, had founded the Austin *Tribune* years ago and had remained both its owner and publisher. He was determined to unseat Witherspoon and topple the city government as well.

McKenzie had always been a part of the family-owned paper, but had worked her way up from the bottom to become both an investigative reporter and editor. She was good at her job and took great pride in what she had accomplished.

"It could be dangerous, you know."

McKenzie pursed her lips. "I doubt that. But even if it is, I'll just have to be careful, won't I?"

John raised his hands in mock defense. "Whatever you say."

McKenzie grinned, watching John sign a tab for their drinks. "Thanks, Riley, I'll return the favor."

"I'll hold you to that. Now run along and tell the boss."

As McKenzie skillfully maneuvered between the posts that guarded the drive leading to her stepfather's plush home in old west Austin, she could barely contain her mounting excitement. Opting to bypass the garage in the rear, she wheeled the sedan up the circular drive and brought it to an abrupt halt.

For a stolen moment she allowed herself the luxury of looking at the house she was so fortunate to call home. The house itself was a three-story white frame with white columns spaced across a wide porch. It was lovely, never failing to remind her of Scarlett O'Hara's Tara in *Gone With the Wind*, as it sat elegantly amid its many landscaped acres. But for herself and her stepfather, so much space seemed obscene.

Having dallied long enough, McKenzie scrambled out of the car and made her way up the long walk and through the front door. Immediately she knew something was wrong. She didn't know what exactly, yet she sensed it with every fiber in her body.

"Rose," she called, addressing the housekeeper who had been with the family forever. "Is Dad home?"

Silence. That was it, she told herself. The silence. The house seemed like a tomb. No Rosie. No Carson. More noticeable now than ever was the absence of her stepfather's favorite brand of tobacco. More times than not, Carson would beat her home, and the moment she stepped through the door the smell of vanilla would tantalize her nostrils. But not today.

Trying to ignore the icy feeling of apprehension, McKenzie trotted farther into the entryway, where she paused to shed her raincoat and umbrella. Then she quickly darted across the foyer and down the hall toward the family room in the rear of the house, completely oblivious to the beauty surrounding her. The heels of her shoes tapped briskly across the parquet floor. She halted just inside the door.

Instantly, her blue eyes clouded with anxiety and the bottom seemed to drop out of her stomach. Rosie was pacing the floor, a shredded tissue hanging limply from her hand. McKenzie had eyes only for her, unaware of the other presence in the large room.

Before fear could completely paralyze her throat, McKenzie whispered, "For God's sake, Rosie, what's wrong? Where's my...my father?"

"Oh, child, thank heavens you're home," Rosie wailed as she moved toward McKenzie, tears streaming unchecked down her rounded cheeks. "Something...something terrible has happened."

"It's all right, Rosie," a man's voice said. "I'll take care of Ms. McKenzie."

"Yes, sir," the housekeeper murmured before squeezing McKenzie's hand and exiting the room.

McKenzie turned wild-eyed, her heart in her throat, and faced the man moving from the shadows into clear view. "Daniel, what on earth...I mean, what are you doing here?" The last person she had expected to see was her fiancé, Daniel Evans, managing editor of the *Tribune* and her stepfather's protégé. "I...I thought you were out of town."

"I...I was, but I was called back," he said, his eyes filled with sympathy—and something else.

McKenzie felt her face drain of every ounce of color, and it was all she could do to keep her lower lip from trembling. "It's...it's Carson, isn't it?"

Daniel shook his head while closing the distance between them and enfolding her in his arms. "I'm afraid so, my dear," he whispered consolingly. "He's had a stroke...."

"Oh, God, no!" McKenzie cried, clutching at the lapels of his sport coat, tears momentarily blinding her. *It couldn't be. It just couldn't be. Not her stepfather. Not the mainstay of her life. Nothing could happen to him!*

"He's in intensive care at Seton Hospital. Rachel's with him now, waiting for us."

McKenzie couldn't stop shaking. "When...when did it happen?" she asked, finally moving out of Daniel's arms, taking deep breaths, trying to get control of herself. She dared not let her stepfather see her like this. She had to be strong for both of them.

"He had the attack sometime around lunch, I believe," Daniel answered, slipping into his coat. "I called around, but no one seemed to know where you were."

McKenzie blinked back her tears as she made a mad dash for the door, Daniel close behind. "I was checking out a story that I thought would be important to Carson." She paused and slipped into her own coat. "Only now I won't even be able to tell him about it," she added on a choked note.

"Sure you will," Daniel assured her. "He's a tough old fellow; he'll pull out of it, you'll see." After telling Rosie they were going, he followed McKenzie out the door. "Let's go in your car. Mine's parked in the back driveway."

"Please, hurry," McKenzie whispered, handing him the keys.

As they rolled down the drive, McKenzie sat mummi-
fied, biting down on her lower lip, failing to notice the taste
of blood on her tongue. *Oh, God,* she prayed silently, *please
don't let him die.*

The offensive odor of the hospital met McKenzie with
nauseating force the minute she scurried through the
swinging doors. Even Daniel's arm securely around her
waist failed to ward off the impending threat of doom that
hung over her like a black cloud.

Rachel was the first person McKenzie saw as she rounded
the corner of the seventh-floor intensive care unit. Her aunt
stood outside the door, waiting, her face anguished. She was
tall, like her brother, but pencil thin, with clear, concise
features. Her soft gray hair hugged her well-shaped head,
enhancing her regal beauty.

McKenzie practically ran headlong into her adoptive
aunt's arms and clung to her for dear life. They held each
other for a long moment, sharing their fears in silence, before breaking apart.

"How...is he?" McKenzie asked in a strangled tone.

Rachel shook her head. "Not good, I'm afraid."

McKenzie held back a sob. "Have you talked to the
doctor?"

"I'm expecting him any moment."

"Were...you with Dad when it happened?" McKenzie
asked.

Rachel swallowed hard. "We were to have a late lunch
together and were just walking out the door, when all of a
sudden he made this horrible sound..." For a moment she
couldn't go on, she was shaking so. "Then he just pitched
forward, and I screamed for help. When Dr. James exam-
ined him, he told me he'd had a stroke." She sighed. "I've
been waiting ever since."

"Do...you think we'll be able..." This time it was McKenzie who faltered as she dug deep in her purse, searching for a tissue. Tears darkened her lashes.

"To see him?" Rachel finished for her. Again she sighed. "I certainly hope so, but my patience is wearing a mite thin."

McKenzie saw the dark circles under Rachel's eyes and the added wrinkles to her beautiful skin. Carson was all Rachel had left and, for brother and sister, they were extremely close.

Fighting back another onslaught of tears, McKenzie asked, "Is there a waiting room close by?"

Rachel straightened her sagging shoulders. "There's one down the hall, I think. I'm sure Dr. James will find us there." She paused, looking to her left. "By the way, didn't I see Daniel come in with you?"

A guilty flush stained McKenzie's cheeks as she whipped around. "Yes...somewhere." She couldn't believe it, but she'd almost forgotten about Daniel.

As though on cue, Daniel glided toward them, concern tightening his lean, solemn features. "Can I get either of you a cup of coffee?" he asked, falling in step with them.

"No...thank you," McKenzie said, almost gagging at the thought of food or drink. If only she could see her step-father, then maybe she could control this gut-wrenching fear gnawing at her insides.

Rachel also declined with a wan smile as they reached the waiting room. Thank God it was deserted, McKenzie thought, hating the thought of strangers' eyes tracking her every move.

Instead of joining Rachel on the couch, McKenzie wandered to the nearest window and stared outside. Although Daniel was silent, she knew he was close by. Why couldn't she lean on him, draw strength from him? She knew he wanted to share her worry and pain, but for some unexplainable reason she could not accept it.

When she'd poured out her misgivings to her stepfather about accepting Daniel's proposal, he'd laughed at her. "Don't worry, honey, love will come. You just wait and see if I'm not right. Just trust me."

As always, she'd listened to him, but the human joy of falling in love with Daniel had continued to elude her. Could she settle for second best? she'd asked herself over and over. Companionship instead of love? Of course she could. After all, one broken heart was enough for anyone.

Out of the corner of her eye, McKenzie watched Daniel sit down next to Rachel and awkwardly try to comfort her. He was an attractive, masculine-looking man—tall, well-built, broad chest and shoulders. He parted his dark hair down the middle and wore sideburns, and he smiled easily—too easily.

Suddenly, he raised his eyes and caught her studying him. Ignoring the light she saw spring into his eyes, she turned away abruptly, embarrassed at being caught red-handed. *Where was the doctor?* she cried silently.

Forcing herself to concentrate on the scene below her, McKenzie watched the bustling traffic on one of the medical center's busy thoroughfares. But nothing helped. Her insides continued to feel as though they were in a shredding machine.

Finally, with a grim set to her mouth, McKenzie turned and closed the distance between herself and Rachel. Looking down at her aunt, she touched her lightly on the shoulder. "I'm going to the nurses' station and have them page Ed. I can't stand not knowing another minute."

Rachel reached out and took McKenzie's hand in hers, giving it a tight, encouraging squeeze. "Please do," she whispered, her bottom lip quivering.

McKenzie reached the door, only to come to a sudden halt. Ed James's short, wiry thin frame came barreling across the threshold, exhaustion evident in the stoop of his shoulders. He was dressed in surgical green, and when he saw McKenzie he yanked off his matching green cap. A weary smile touched his lips.

McKenzie's eyes widened anxiously, "Oh, Dr. Ed," she began.

He grasped her cold, trembling hand in his strong one and said, "He's holding his own, my dear. In fact, he's resting as comfortably as can be expected."

A deep sigh of relief filtered through McKenzie, and it was only by sheer force of will that she kept her legs from caving in beneath her. "Thank God," she cried, motioning for Rachel and Daniel to join them. But there was no need; they were already standing behind her, and judging from the look on her aunt's face, she'd heard the doctor's news.

Dr. James cleared his throat, his eyes taking in the three of them. "Let me say how sorry I am I kept you waiting so long, but I had an emergency surgery which proved to be more complicated and took longer than I expected." He paused. "Now back to Carson—"

"When can we see him?" Rachel interrupted. She was nervously clinching and unclinching her fingers.

"I'll let you and McKenzie go in now for about ten minutes. But there are a few things you need to know before you see him."

"He's going to die, isn't he?" McKenzie asked in an emotionless tone. *Why did something bad always have to happen to the ones she loved?*

The doctor bypassed Rachel's muted cry of pain and looked severely at McKenzie. "No," he stressed, "he's not going to die. However, he is paralyzed on his left side and his speech is somewhat impaired."

McKenzie swallowed the panic that was building inside her. She could not afford the luxury of crumbling now, as much for her own sake as for Rachel's. If only Jeb... she thought fleetingly. *No! Don't even think it, McKenzie Moore. Don't you dare think about him!*

"What's... what's his prognosis?" McKenzie forced herself to ask. Anything, she told herself, to keep her mind off thoughts that were definitely taboo.

The doctor began to massage his own neck to relieve the tension in his muscles. "At the moment he's stable. That's about all the encouragement I can give you." He paused. "Though in all fairness, I'll warn you that if he does recover, it will be an uphill battle, taking months of physical therapy."

"Just tell us what we need to do," Rachel chimed in, her voice suddenly much stronger and self-assured.

McKenzie couldn't help but smile. When there was a job to be done, Rachel was the one to tackle it. Not only was she a great organizer, but her love for Carson and his family made her irreplaceable in time of trouble. Ever since McKenzie's mother died, she had gone to Rachel for comfort and guidance. She adored her and trusted her judgment completely.

"McKenzie."

Rachel's soft voice brought McKenzie back sharply to the moment at hand. She turned toward her aunt.

"Ed said we can go in now." Rachel's voice was gentle.

McKenzie took a deep breath to try to clear her mind. "I'm ready."

The cubicle where her stepfather lay was as quiet as death itself. When she and Rachel tiptoed through the opening, McKenzie bit down hard on her lip to keep from crying out loud. She dared not look at her aunt. The nurse beside the bed nodded and then left the room.

Carson Langley's eyes were closed, but McKenzie sensed he wasn't asleep.

"Who's there?" he whispered, his words slightly slurred.

"It's Rachel and me, Dad."

Carson extended an unsteady hand.

Rachel stood while McKenzie latched on to his outstretched hand and lowered herself gently onto the side of his bed.

McKenzie blinked back the tears as she took in his appearance. As long as she could remember, she had always thought Carson Langley to be larger than life. He was a tall, robust man, well over six feet and two hundred pounds, with shrewd blue eyes and steel-gray hair. But at this moment he looked nothing like his old self—the gruffly self-confident, highly acclaimed newspaper entrepreneur.

The grayish tint of his skin and his cold, lifeless hand made him seem fragile and much older than his seventy years, to say nothing of the intravenous bottle hanging from the rack above his head and the air tube positioned at the base of his nose. But even more than that, it was his sudden vulnerability; it broke McKenzie's heart to see him like this.

"What are you staring at, girl?" Carson demanded, his words slurred and hard to understand.

"You, Dad. I'm staring at you." McKenzie smiled through her tears, thankful that at least his spirit was not broken. Not yet, anyway. She slowly lowered his hand onto the bedcovers.

"Dry up those tears now, do you hear me?" he whispered weakly.

Rachel moved closer to the bed. "Oh, Carson, we've been so worried. We..." Her voice broke.

"Shhh." He paused, as though having difficulty forming his next words. "I... I may be down, but I'm not beaten."

McKenzie quickly turned away, unable to bear the thought of her beloved stepfather lying helpless in this room

for days, maybe even months. Suddenly, her heart gave another twist. What about the *Tribune*? Who would run it?
Make the important day-to-day decisions? She certainly
wasn't capable of assuming that responsibility.

Feeling a caress as light as a feather on the side of her
cheek, McKenzie swung her head back around to meet
Carson's watery gaze. Unconsciously, she tracked the tiny
lines of exhaustion marking the edges of his eyes and the
weary droop of his mouth. "I'm...going to be...all right."
He was again struggling to speak. "Don't you worry."

She cupped his hand against her cheek, then stood up just
as her stepfather switched his eyes to his sister.

The silence lingered. If possible, his face had grown a
shade paler and his eyes heavy-lidded; it was apparent he
was fighting to stay awake. McKenzie knew they should
leave, but she was loath to do so.

Then after a moment, she heard him whisper, "Jeb."

Rachel leaned closer. "What . . . what about Jeb?"

"Want to see him."

"He's coming," Rachel soothed. "I've already gotten in
touch with him. You don't worry about a thing. Just rest."

Suddenly, the nurse appeared in the doorway, signaling
their time was up. Rachel took the hint, bent down and
kissed her brother lightly on the cheek.

McKenzie couldn't move. It was as though someone had
just jerked the rug out from under her, leaving her stunned,
unable to cope. *Jeb. Jeb. Jeb.* The name raged through her
like an arrow piercing her heart, sharp and deadly, damaging every nerve, every cell in her body. She simply stood
there, her brain refusing to function.

"McKenzie, we have to go. The nurse..."

"Yes...I know," she said at last, straining to speak, her
throat starting to close, her eyes stinging with the need to
cry.

As McKenzie left the claustrophobic confines of the unit, the pain around her heart was increasing, and trying to force herself to be calm only made it worse. Oh, God, why now? Why after all this time did he have to come back? She'd been expecting this, knew it had to happen. Why, then, did she feel so devastated, so destroyed, so frightened?

"McKenzie, are you all right?" Rachel's soft inquiry was almost her undoing. They were standing just outside the door, and for the moment they had the corridor to themselves.

Misty blue eyes sought her aunt's. "I . . . I still can't believe he asked for Jeb."

Rachel sighed. "Something told me to contact him, that Carson would want to see him."

"It . . . it doesn't seem possible . . . that's all." The quaking in McKenzie's voice was almost imperceptible. "Especially after all that's happened."

Sympathy shaded Rachel's eyes as she reached out and gave McKenzie a quick hug. "I know what Jeb's return will mean to you, but Carson is gravely ill. He's had the scare of his life. It's only natural that he'd want to see his son and make amends." She paused thoughtfully. "Now that you're grown up and plan to marry Daniel, I'm sure there'll be no problems."

"I don't think he'll come."

"I know Jeb, and I think he will."

No! Oh, God, please no. She couldn't handle seeing him again, especially not now. Her breath stuck jaggedly in the center of her chest, and her hands were damp with perspiration.

"Oh, please, McKenzie," Rachel pleaded, sensing her distress. "I don't know all that transpired between you and Jeb, but I do know it's all in the past now, and you have a bright future ahead of you. It'll all work out for the best. I know it will."

McKenzie didn't believe that for one minute, but she kep
her thoughts to herself, watching as the doctor and Danie
strode toward them. Daniel stood at McKenzie's elbow whil
Dr. James stopped next to Rachel. He eyed both women.

"Why don't you go home? There's nothing more you ca
do tonight," he said. "I promise to call if his conditio
changes for the worse."

McKenzie's eyes were bright with unshed tears. "Thanks
Dr. Ed. Thanks for everything."

He patted her hand. "Shall I give you something to hel
you sleep?" he asked, taking in the ashen color of her ski
and her overanxious eyes.

"I'll see that she's taken care of," Daniel said, speakin
for the first time. "And you too, Mrs. Fowler."

Rachel smiled but shook her head. "That won't be ne
essary, Daniel, but thank you anyway. I have my car, and
plan to go straight home to bed."

McKenzie wrapped her arms tightly around her aun
"Good night, Auntie. I'll talk to you in the morning."

A short time later, stepping outside with Daniel besid
her, McKenzie felt as though she carried the weight of th
world on her slender shoulders.

Then, miraculously, the cold, sweet air touched her like
benediction, and the healing tears began to fall.

McKenzie could not shake her depression. For two day
she'd been at loose ends. She'd done nothing but shuttl
between the office and the hospital. Even though Jeb'
name had not been mentioned again, Rosie had begu
making plans for his homecoming. She had aired his roor
and stocked the freezer with his favorite foods. Even Ra
chel, in spite of her worry over Carson, had an extra bound
to her step.

McKenzie tried not to dwell on his eventual arriva
channeling her energies into her work. But even that faile

She couldn't concentrate. Thoughts of Jeb occupied her mind, and she hated herself for that. Was Rachel right? Would he come back? Or would he ignore her summons and continue to roam the globe? God help her, but those questions and others had nearly driven her crazy.

Now as she began clearing her desk for the day, she paused and leaned back in her chair, closing her eyes for a moment. It had been a long, tiring day. A cloud hung over everyone and everything. The editorial staff had met and then called a meeting assuring the employees that nothing would change. But they all knew better. Someone with Carson's vibrant personality and energy would be sorely missed.

Suddenly, she was roused out of her troubled thoughts by a rap on the door.

Sitting up, she called, "Come in," thinking it would probably be Daniel wanting her to go to dinner with him. She was surprised when John Riley came through the door.

"God, you look like death warmed over," he said bluntly.

McKenzie couldn't help but smile. "Thanks, John. You certainly have a way with words."

Her sarcasm was lost on him as he grinned and plopped down in the chair next to her desk. Then his grin disappeared. "How's the boss?"

"Not good, John."

"Is he paralyzed?"

"Partially."

"Damn, that's a shame. He's never been sick a day in his life, has he?"

"Not that I know of. That's what makes it so bad. But the doctor thinks that with time and physical therapy, he'll be all right."

"Well, I'll shove off and not bother you any longer," John said awkwardly, starting to get up.

"You're not bothering me. What's on your mind?" She pushed an errant strand of silky hair aside as she watched him closely.

He eased himself back into the chair. "Thought I'd let you know that I went to the funeral today."

She frowned. "Funeral?"

"You know. Elmer Thurman, the construction worker killed at Cedar Plaza."

"Sorry. I'd forgotten. What did you come up with?"

John shrugged. "Nothing much, except that Dillard was there, offering his mushy condolences. That fellow gives me the creeps."

"Maybe it's you who should talk to the widow."

John nodded, pinching his nose. "Dillard sure as hell wanted to know if I had."

"Mmmm, sounds interesting."

"How 'bout your going with me to see Mrs. Thurman tomorrow?"

"If there's no change in Carson, you've got a date."

John smiled. "See you then."

An hour later, the stars winking at her from the sky, McKenzie brought her car to a halt in the circular drive. Home. At last. The second she opened the door, she heard Rachel's laughter. As though in a daze, she made her way toward the den, pausing at the door.

It was then that she saw him.

He was standing next to the fireplace, his arm resting negligently against the mantel. "Hello, little sister," he drawled. "Long time, no see."

Chapter 2

Suddenly, unexpectedly, like the cry of fire in a crowded room, there he was. All McKenzie's vocal mechanisms froze, and she stood helpless for endless seconds staring at him.

Eight years. Had it been eight years since Jeb had stormed out of her life? Now that he was here, in the flesh, it seemed more like an eternity. Her heart skipped a beat or two as her eyes studied his face.

Physically he hadn't changed—at least, not much. He was perhaps a little thinner than she remembered. But had his smoky green eyes always had that steel edge to them? His complexion, reminding her of the finest of leather, left no doubt about the months he'd spent in warmer climates.

His hair was still as thick and tawny-colored as ever; only now it was streaked with silver at the temples. It was roughly cut, overlapping the collar of his long-sleeved flannel shirt. Dramatic cheekbones complemented a mouth that was long and hard with a faintly sensuous-looking lower lip.

The tight-fitting jeans showed off trim hips and long legs, while the powerful muscles of his upper arms and shoulders rippled with his every twist and turn. He looked as dangerous and lazily attractive as ever. Panic welled up in the back of her throat.

"Taking inventory?" he asked. The drawl was still intact, yet his tone coolly impersonal and mocking.

McKenzie felt a shiver go through her and prayed that her unsteady legs would carry her to the nearest chair.

Suddenly, Jeb nudged himself away from the heat of the blazing fire and moved pantherlike toward the middle of the room, intercepting her.

Still she couldn't seem to utter a comeback to his caustic comment, especially now that he had stopped at such close range. Although the muscles in her throat constricted, she failed to make a sound. She merely stood shaking, feeling her legs becoming weaker by the second. The chair seemed miles away.

"What's the matter, cat got your tongue?"

"Hello, Jeb," she said simply, refusing to rise to his bait. The leaping tongues of fire behind him cast him in a golden glow. McKenzie could see a muscle twitching convulsively at the corner of his mouth and the tiny lines fanning out from his eyes. Her heart twisted with pain.

"My, my, is that all we have to say after all this time?" Jeb's voice was redolent with sardonic amusement. "You mean I don't even get as much as a welcome-home kiss?"

McKenzie had to quell the sudden urge to slap his face. Why was he tormenting her this way? After all, she was the injured party, the one who was betrayed, not he. It was that betrayal that had left deep scars, scars that had never healed, leaving a pain that was still tender to the touch.

Unable to stand his hard, appraising stare any longer, McKenzie turned and made her way toward the warmth of the fire. Dread replaced the blood in her veins as she leaned over, her back to him, holding her hands as close to the dancing flames as she dared.

Suddenly, she caught a movement out of the corner of her eye. Rachel. With dismay, it dawned on her that she and Jeb were not alone. A deep red color flooded her cheeks. What on earth, she wondered, must Rachel be thinking of their exchange?

McKenzie shifted her eyes quickly to her aunt's face. When she saw the strained, disapproving look mirrored in Rachel's eyes as they darted between her and Jeb, McKenzie knew.

Rachel stood up to full height. "Why don't I make a pot of coffee and rustle up some food?"

"Oh, don't bother," McKenzie said quickly, panicking at the thought of being left alone with Jeb.

"It's no bother. I'll only be gone a minute." A silence fell over the room as Rachel got up and strode to the door. Once there, however, she paused and turned around. "I hope you two can reach a polite understanding while I'm gone," she said pointedly.

Once the door closed behind her, the silence deepened, became oppressive. The deep flush of her face still intact, McKenzie returned her attention to the fire, a mulish firmness to her lips. She'd be damned if she'd let him use her as a punching bag. It was evident from the moment she set foot in the room that he was aching for a fight. Well, this was one time he'd be disappointed.

"Ah, McKenzie," Jeb murmured lightly, "time has certainly been kind to you." He'd closed the distance between them once again, taking his favorite stance by the hearth, resting his arm on the mantel, his eyes roving casually over her body.

She had been a lovely child, but she was a stunning woman. Feature for feature, she approached perfection—vital, blue eyes set wide apart, high cheekbones and full lips.

A mane of stunning strawberry blond hair and high, firm breasts were the backdrop for a trim, long-limbed body. When she moved, she reminded him of a kitten going after cream.

McKenzie looked up at him for a moment and his eyes held hers. Then in a rush she said, "I'm sorry I can't say the same for you. You've changed." And not for the better, she wanted to add.

He half smiled in a mocking manner, as though reading her thoughts. "Well, I think dodging bullets on a daily basis would have a tendency to change one's outlook on life, don't you?"

"You didn't have to leave the country, or 'dodge bullets' as you say." Her tone had a trace of tartness. "It was your choice."

"Oh, really," he returned bitterly. "I agree I didn't have to leave the country, but if you'll remember, my old man all but pitched me out on my ass."

The impact of his anger left her breathless. She stared at him, trying to think of something to say to ease the tension. Things were getting out of hand, going from bad to worse. "Please . . . Jeb . . . don't," she finally stammered.

"'Please . . . Jeb . . . don't,'" he mimicked, his expression fierce. "Is that all you can say?"

McKenzie's eyes suddenly flashed anger as her finger nails dug into the soft palm of her hand. "Did you come back to see about your father or to torment me?"

She saw by the muscle pulsating in his cheek that her shot had hit home, but it brought her no satisfaction.

"Dammit, you know why I came home," he muttered savagely.

McKenzie threw him a withering glare, wishing she had the courage to leave the room, to tell him to go to hell. But she couldn't; she was afraid her legs wouldn't carry her as far as the door.

Determined then to make the best of a bad situation, she tried changing the subject. "Let's talk about Carson."

"Rachel filled me in on the details," he answered abruptly.

"You know, then, that if he gets well, it's going to be an uphill battle?"

"I'm still finding it hard to believe that he gave a death-bed cry for his prodigal son."

"Don't you dare say that again," she snapped, anger giving her strength to put distance between them. "He's not dying; he's just very sick."

For a split second, she thought his face softened, but it must have been her imagination. Once again, his face bore that same closed, harsh look. "Well, sick or not, he'll still rule the roost and expect everyone to ask how high when he says 'jump.'"

McKenzie's eyes narrowed. "You're despicable."

He snorted. "God, after all this time, you still haven't learned his true colors."

But I sure learned yours, and it nearly cost me my sanity. She gritted her teeth. "I don't intend to argue with you."

"Who's arguing? I'm merely stating the facts. You don't even breathe unless my father tells you to."

"That's absurd!" she exclaimed hotly.

"No, it isn't and you know it."

"Cool it, Jeb. I refuse to listen to any more of this."

"Oh, I guess that means I'm supposed to roll over and play dead?"

Closing her eyes, she counted to ten, praying for patience before once again changing the subject. "Are you planning to stay with Aunt Rachel?"

"Hadn't planned on it."

McKenzie struggled to keep her voice light. "Then where...?"

"Here."

Her face flamed. Rage strangled all utterance. "What d
you mean!" Her voice came out a scratchy whisper.

"Just exactly what I said. I'm going to stay here, in m
old room, right across the hall from you."

"Then I'll leave."

He shrugged. "Suit yourself."

"For God's sake, Jeb, what are you trying to do to us
You saw the disapproving look on Rachel's face a momen
ago. I don't want you making things worse than they al
ready are."

"Spare me the lecture." His tone was so harsh it sen
shivers down her spine.

Their gazes were locked for a brief moment, the tensio
in the room climbing to a screaming pitch.

"I don't have to take this from you, Jeb. I'm not seven
teen any longer. I'm all grown up now, in case you haven'
noticed."

"Oh, I've noticed, all right," he said slowly, suddenl
moving closer, stalking her, never taking his eyes off her
Just to look at her stirred one's imagination, he thought, he
hair swirling around her shoulders and her small, flushe
face. Her lower lip was caught characteristically between he
teeth, showing her agitation. The top buttons on her blous
were open, showing a hint of the delicate curve of her sof
breasts. His heart began to pound like a drum in his ears.

McKenzie couldn't stop staring at him, nor could sh
move, as a tremulous wave of longing racked her body. Hi
green eyes were alive and glittering with an emotion tha
brought the past to mind in vivid colors, all the delightfu
pleasures they had shared: the way he loved to nibble at he
skin, the touch of his hand on her bare breast, the feel of hi
tongue against her nipple . . .

Suddenly, McKenzie pivoted on her heel. "I think I'll g
help Rachel . . ."

Jeb's hand tightened painfully on her waist, giving her a sharp tug that threw her off balance. He caught her, forcing her against his hard body. "Not before I get my welcome-home kiss, surely?" he whispered menacingly.

"No!" McKenzie pushed furiously at his chest, but she was powerless against his strength.

His mouth swooped down on hers like a peregrine and he kissed her roughly, wanting to hurt her, as he'd been hurting all those years without her.

McKenzie's fists clenched against his chest, her every muscle stiff with outrage, struggling to fight the delicious warmth that was spreading through her body.

"There was a time," he muttered against her mouth, "when you used to beg for this."

McKenzie gasped. Rage and humiliation combined to give her the extra measure she needed to free herself. Panting and still rigid with fury, she hissed, "Stay away from me. Don't you dare touch me again!"

She had been sitting in bed crying for hours. Stealing a look at the clock, she saw that it was one o'clock. With a moan, she flopped back against the pillow and closed her eyes.

Even now, several hours later, she still couldn't believe what had taken place between them. Why had she let Jeb get to her, knock down her defenses as though she hadn't spent years erecting them?

After practically flying out of the room and slamming the door behind her, she had almost collided with Rachel, bearing a tray of goodies. Her aunt's "What on earth is going on?" had stopped her only momentarily. Her throat had been too full of tears to speak, so with only a savage shake of her head, she'd scooted past Rachel and bounded up the stairs to the haven of her room.

For a moment, she forced her thoughts away from the ugly scene downstairs and let her eyes roam around the room that had been her security since early childhood.

The high sculptured ceiling looked down on a square four-poster bed covered with a bedspread that matched the creamy silk curtains at the windows. There was a secretary, a comfortable chair, and a love seat with a small wicker and glass table in front of it. Against one wall stood a small entertainment center housing a stereo, television, and a generous assortment of books. It was a bright, airy room and she loved it.

When she had first come to the Langley mansion, she thought she had entered fairyland. Over the years that feeling had not changed.

Shortly after her birth, her father had died from a rare form of cancer, and when she was five years old, her mother had married Carson Langley. He was a widower with one son, Jeb, who was fifteen years old. But then another tragedy struck a year later. Her mother was killed in a car accident. By this time, Carson was well on his way to becoming a newspaper magnate, and he used both his work and his young stepdaughter to soak up his grief and pain.

From the beginning, McKenzie had liked her stepfather. Carson was nothing like the wicked stepfathers depicted in the fairy tales she had loved to read. He was tall and robust, with steel-gray hair and twinkling, but shrewd, blue eyes, and he won McKenzie's heart completely when he whispered that he had always wanted a little girl of his own.

But with Jeb, her relationship had been truly special. Jeb was unique. Jeb had taught her how to cope with her mother's untimely death, showed her how to laugh and play, taught her about life . . . and love.

When she turned seventeen, however, her life took a drastic change. She knew she loved Jeb, not as a stepbrother, but as a man, a man whom she wanted to touch.

She wanted to share the intimacies that a woman shares with a man. But one fateful summer day when her stepfather caught her in Jeb's embrace, she found out that it was not meant to be. She had been incredibly naive and trusting until then, believing that the fairy tales she had read in her books would come true, hers for the taking.

She eased her face into the pillow, desperately trying to stem the flow of tears. That was when she heard the noise. At first she couldn't make it out, but then she realized someone was tapping on her door. She froze. Jeb? Was it Jeb coming to finish what he'd started? With knees knocking in competition with her heart, McKenzie stumbled out of bed and made her way slowly toward the door.

When she pulled it back, her fear changed instantly to relief. The hall light cast a shadow on Rachel, detailing her pinched, concerned features.

"I ... I just wanted to check on you," Rachel whispered, nervously clutching her flannel robe.

McKenzie gave her a watery smile as she seized her outstretched hand. "I'm ... fine, or at least I will be. It ... it was such a shock seeing him, that's all," she finished lamely.

"Do you want to talk?"

McKenzie's hand tightened on her aunt's before releasing it. "Oh, Aunt Rachel, you're a dear, but this is something I have to work out for myself."

"I understand," Rachel said sweetly, "but if you need me, don't hesitate to call." She paused and drew an unsteady breath. "It upsets me to see two people I love dearly suffer."

Fresh, hot tears filled McKenzie's eyes. "Speaking...speaking of Jeb..." She hated herself for asking, but she couldn't help it; she had to know.

"He's gone," Rachel answered, taking pity on her. "Left right after you went to your room. He was behaving like a madman. I do wish you two—"

McKenzie held up her hand. "Please," she whispered, "not now, Aunt Rachel. I'll see you in the morning."

Instead of crawling back into bed, she wandered aimlessly to the window and stared into the moon-filled night. The long windows overlooked the back of the house, while below, the terrace opened onto the lawns and flower garden that for a short time had been her mother's pride and joy. Beyond, a high wooden fence and a pool were visible. The pool that Jeb had loved . . .

Jeb. Her mind was filled with him. Was it possible for a man to change so much in eight years? Was this the same man who had trembled with passion when he'd held her in his arms?

No. That man was gone. A cynical hardness laced with ruthlessness had overtaken those gentler traits, leaving a man who rarely smiled and whose emotions could change as quickly as his eyes, from the cool of emeralds to the hardness of agates.

Their relationship was doomed eight years ago, and nothing had changed. Anyway, she knew he had come back only because Rachel had begged him. As soon as Carson improved—she refused to think otherwise—then Jeb would be off again, to parts unknown. Just as her stepfather had warned her, he would never be able to handle responsibility or remain in one place for long.

If only she could accept Jeb for what he was.

"What now?" she whispered aloud, resting her head against the cool windowpane, trying to sift through her thoughts. "Oh, God, what now?"

She knew the answer. She would have to go on with her life as though Jeb had not stumbled back into it. She would have to forget that she had ever loved Jeb Langley, forget that at one time he had been her world. Forget that when he'd walked out, he'd left her life in shambles.

But more important, she would not allow him to disrupt her life. She was going to marry Daniel, and she was content, if not happy, with that decision. She had her stepfather and she had her job on the newspaper. She had enough.

So where was the danger? That question was also easy to answer. When she had plowed into Jeb, every nerve in her body had come alive. Even in anger, his touch still had the power to wring her inside out and bring back what she had fought so hard to forget.

She must treat him as a long lost brother and nothing else.

Could she do it?

Of course she could.

She had no choice.

It wouldn't be easy.

Nothing ever was.

"Would you care for wine, sir?"

Jeb looked sourly at the bar hostess. She was a cute little thing—all plump and cuddly looking, with one of the sexiest backsides he'd ever seen. Normally that would have piqued a response, but tonight he was in an exceptionally foul mood. To put it bluntly, he was coldly furious with himself.

"No," he grumbled. "Just bring me three fingers of Wild Turkey." Then he turned toward the window, seeing nothing but McKenzie. McKenzie. Her terrified face swam before his vision, nearly driving him mad. He had terrorized her for no reason. God, what had happened to him? Was he no better than the rebels and mercenaries he'd been living with for so long?

And where the hell was his drink? This was the third bar he'd been to since he'd torn out of the house, but unfortunately he was still stone sober. Finally the drink came and, ignoring her seductive smile, he murmured his thanks.

Maybe what he needed was a sweet, obedient wife, he thought, gulping down a major portion of his drink. Then, suddenly, he coughed, almost choking. Dammit; the last thing he needed was a wife. Irritation pricked him. Hell, he didn't want or need *anybody*. He liked being by himself just fine.

He stared glumly out at the darkness for a moment, then drained the glass and plopped it down on the table. After slamming down some money, he strode angrily out of the bar.

Fifteen minutes later, he was at the hospital, standing over his father's bed in the intensive care unit. But getting there had been no easy feat. He'd practically had to get down on his hands and knees before the redheaded nurse had granted him permission to see his father at this ungodly hour of the morning.

Now as he stood looking down at the sleeping figure, a pang of regret shot through him for what might have been.

Rachel had warned him, but he hadn't believed her. The old man did look god-awful. And gravely ill as well. *Of course he's sick, you ass! After all, that's why you came home, wasn't it?* Or was it? Stubbornly refusing to answer that question, he lowered himself heavily into the nearest chair as though all the strength had rushed from his body, leaving him weak and light-headed. He had felt this way off and on since the last time he'd gotten too close to the combat zones and had barely escaped being riddled with bullets.

Suddenly, a low moaning sound claimed his attention. He leaned closer to the bed and watched as his father's eyes fluttered for a moment, but never quite opened.

A deep sigh filtered through Jeb's body as he eased himself away from the bed. Where had he failed? Was it because he was too much like his mother? Or was it because when he'd come back from Nam, he'd refused to work on the paper, refused to become another of his father's puppets? One would think they would have found some common ground, but they hadn't.

After all, this was his father—the one who had sired him, blood of his blood. But that was the only damned thing Carson had ever done for him, Jeb told himself fiercely. Until McKenzie, that is. McKenzie, the ray of sunshine who had transformed his dismal world into magic. Before she had come to live with them, he had tried to be what his father had wanted him to be, but he'd found that to be impossible.

When he'd pull even the most innocent of pranks, his father would shout at him, "You're no good, son. Sorry...you're sorry...just like your mother." Those words and others just as demeaning had been seared into his brain as though branded there with a hot iron.

And when McKenzie became part of the family, Jeb had just ceased trying. While McKenzie became the apple of his father's eye, he became the hell-raiser his father had always thought him to be. Where there was trouble, there was Jeb.

He should have been jealous of McKenzie, but he wasn't. She was a charmer, and she had charmed her way into his love-starved heart with an arrogance and ease born of true nobility. She had become his shield against his father. She had become his world.

Only, he hadn't fully recognized this until the summer she turned seventeen, and he was a seasoned twenty-seven. He had taken her to Galveston that day, to the beach—against his father's will, of course. Carson objected to their spending so much time together, but because McKenzie wished it, he kept his silence.

It was while she was frolicking in the sand, racing with the wind like the free spirit she was, that he realized how much she meant to him. It hit him like a swift kick below the belt. For the longest time, the imaginary blow stunned him and he couldn't move. That was when she had danced up to him, a wide smile on her face, her lips a seductive lure, challenging him to a race.

He knew he loved her then. But instead of feeling proud of it, he hated himself. He'd drunk more booze, smoked more cigarettes and bedded more women in his twenty-odd years than most men did in a lifetime. He wasn't fit to touch a hair on her head.

He fought his feelings long and hard, but he finally succumbed, after he learned she felt the same about him. And then he taught her how to love. What they shared was hot, torrid and complete.

A month later, all hell broke loose. Unwillingly, his mind took him back to that time when nothing but pain had filled his life....

Jeb had come home one afternoon on an early summer day to find McKenzie flung across her bed, crying her heart out. He'd rushed into the room and, closing the door behind him, sat down on the bed and pulled her body, as limp as a rag doll's, into his arms. He didn't know whose heart was beating the loudest.

"God, McKenzie, what's wrong?" he demanded urgently.

Her hands clawed at his chest like the paws of a frightened kitten. "Oh, Jeb," she wailed, "Dad is going to make me go off to school, to Dallas, to SMU."

His heart almost stopped beating. "Do you want to go?" he asked quietly, holding his breath, waiting for her answer.

"You know I don't," she said, her large eyes brimming with tears.

"Well, did you tell him that?"

McKenzie sniffled, swiping at her tears, reminding him of a little lost girl. Suddenly a pang of guilt blitzed him. *A little girl is all she is, only you won't admit it. Let her go. She still has her whole life in front of her. For heaven's sakes, let her go!*

"I . . . I tried to reason with him, but he just wouldn't listen."

Jeb pushed his pain aside and raked gentle fingers through her tumbled curls. "Maybe . . . maybe you should do as he asked. I . . ." He couldn't go on; he knew he'd die if he did.

She reached out and cupped his chin in her unsteady hand. "Oh, Jeb, I don't know what to do. I love you and I love Dad. I feel so mixed up, so torn." Her lower lip began to quiver. "Please, just hold me and kiss me."

"Shhh," Jeb whispered, trying to stop the new onslaught of tears as he squeezed her fragile body against his. He wished he could attach her to his soul and never let her go.

Suddenly, McKenzie began pressing moist, sweet kisses over his face, his Adam's apple and the soft pelt of hair exposed at the base of his neck. "Love me," she pleaded.

"Oh, God, McKenzie, I can't." He groaned. "Not here, not like this."

Even when she placed her soft lips to his and his loins constricted painfully, he pulled his head away, growling, "I've got to get out of here."

"No!" She held him tighter. "Don't leave me. I'm so scared." Her body was pressing against him.

Jeb was lost.

He kissed her—long, drugging kisses. "Dear God, I want to make love to you." His breathing was erratic. "I should never have begun this. I knew I wouldn't want to stop."

His mouth was hungry and possessive, his tongue rowdy and hot as it stroked the delicate insides of her mouth, savoring her warm and sweetly scented breath. His blood pressure jumped sky high and his ears roared, while his hands roved her body, branding her as his own.

The door opened but neither heard it. They both froze when Jeb's father hissed coldly, "What the hell!" He glared at them from under bushy gray brows, the slanting sunlight glowing in his eyes. "You just can't leave her alone, can you?"

Jeb pushed McKenzie away from him and got carefully to his feet. "You're out of line, Dad," he said savagely.

Carson's face was purple with rage. "You're the one who's out of line. Get the hell out of here before I give you the thrashing you deserve. For chrissakes, Jeb, she's your sister!"

"Stepsister," he corrected. Though he still hadn't raised his voice, there was an icy edge to his tone.

"Jeb, please—" McKenzie begged, grasping his arm. He shook it off.

A tension-charged silence permeated the room.

Carson finally broke it. "She's going to Dallas, Jeb, and there's not one damned thing you can do about it."

Jeb's expression was black. "I think McKenzie's old enough to make that decision for herself, don't you?"

Before McKenzie could say a word, Carson spat, "Where's your decency, man? Why don't you stick to your whores and leave McKenzie alone? You're ruining her life; is that what you want?" He moved a step closer. "Good God, she's not a part of your sordid world. Let her be!"

Jeb stood rigid, the blood draining from his face. His lips were clamped so tight that white lines angled up to the sides of his nose.

McKenzie was sobbing openly now. Her eyes were darting to one man, then the other. "Please—don't do this! I can't stand it."

Ignoring her pleas, Carson ordered, "Get your clothes and get out. You're no longer welcome in this house."

"Stop it!" McKenzie screeched, scrambling off the bed, staring wild-eyed at her stepfather. "Surely you...you don't mean that."

Carson laughed mirthlessly. "Oh, I mean it, all right. You know what he's like, girl; he'll make your life miserable. Is that what you want, to be just another one of his women?"

Jeb's eyes cut into his father's. "You've gone too far this time, you possessive old fool."

Ignoring Jeb, he hammered on. "Think about it, girl."

Jeb's eyes swung around to McKenzie, softening for a moment. He had to ask. "You comin'?"

"McKenzie, don't you dare!" Carson was visibly shaking now.

She stood reed straight, pushing the tangled mass of hair aside, her face bathed in tears. Her eyes locked with Jeb's.

"Well," Jeb demanded, the simple word shooting through the air like a bullet.

McKenzie shook her head. "Don't," she begged. "Oh, God, don't make me choose..."

Jeb reeled, feeling as though he'd had a fist rammed in his face. Then he sneered mockingly. "Good luck and God bless. I hope you'll be happy with *Daddy*. You two deserve one another."

Then, with McKenzie's sobs following him down the stairs, he walked out the door, and he had not come back. Until now....

Jeb blinked several times to clear his head. With a muttered curse, he shifted his position in the uncomfortable chair, rooting his underside deeper into the stiff leather.

Rehashing the past had done nothing for his disposition except fill him with the urge to get stinking drunk. But that wouldn't solve his problem and he knew it.

Why had he all but attacked McKenzie tonight? he asked himself again. What had he been trying to prove? He was still no damned good for her; that hadn't changed. But then, what difference did it make, anyway? She no longer wanted him—if she ever had, he added cynically.

That still didn't excuse his coming on to her like a savage. When he'd decided to come back, he had planned in all sincerity, to treat her like a sister and think of her only as that.

Yet when McKenzie had walked through the door, her shoulders stiff and straight, smelling of fresh rain, wind and flowers, the earth had seemed to shift beneath his feet and the years fell away. She had breezed right into his heart as she had done so long ago.

Even the sound of her voice when she'd said "hello" had been a turn-on: husky, fragrant, elusive, everchanging. He'd stared at her, his brain refusing to respond to the thousands of impulses screaming at him all in the same second. McKenzie had gotten to him and there wasn't a damn thing he could do about it.

Jeb got out of the chair quickly now, angrily shoving his hands deep into his pockets, his eyes darting back to his father's face. Had he made another mistake in thinking he could make amends with the old man?

Since his return, his life had become more complicated than he thought possible. At first it had all seemed so simple; he'd only wanted to make peace with his father, find several hundred acres of land, settle down, maybe even write that book he'd always dreamed of.

He wanted that. And more, Much more. *He wanted McKenzie.* He saw no reason to deny it any longer. His breath hung suspended. Was it possible? Could he court her, woo her as he once had?

No. His father was still right. He was too old for her, too... sorry. But even the sorriest of people received second chances, didn't they?

Without thinking, he reached out and gently touched the side of his father's face and whispered, "All I ever wanted was for you to love me."

Later, as he walked out into the cold November darkness, hunched against the wind, yesterday's loneliness rose and seized him by the throat.

He wondered why he bothered to draw a breath.

Chapter 3

It was barely seven o'clock the next morning when McKenzie steered into the parking lot of the *Tribune* building. She had bounded out of bed at the crack of dawn, knowing she could not start out the day by facing Jeb. Without so much as a cup of coffee, she had showered, dressed and stepped quietly out of the house.

Later, at the hospital, she'd sipped her first cup of coffee while being told by the doctor that her stepfather was continuing to hold his own.

She had stayed with him for about twenty minutes. He'd been too groggy to talk to her, but he'd applied pressure to her fingers, letting her know that he was aware of her visit. At one point, she even thought he'd tried to smile. Her eyes were misted with tears when she'd leaned over and kissed him goodbye.

Now as she made her way to the front entrance, her heels clicking on the concrete, she smiled briefly at the security guard who often acted as the doorman. "Good morning,

Jonathan," she said. He had been with the *Tribune* ever since Carson started the first presses rolling. No matter how early she got to work, he was always there.

He responded with a wide grin of his own, calling attention to his two missing front teeth. "The top of the morning to you, Ms. Moore." Then his smile suddenly disappeared. "Sure was sorry to hear about Mr. Carson. How's he doin'?"

McKenzie paused. "About the same, I'm afraid."

"Don't seem fair." He scratched his head as he shook it. "Sure don't."

With a mumbled, "Thanks for asking," she headed toward the elevator, determined to force her mind back on track. She had work to do—and lots of it. Although her concern for her stepfather had not lessened, she felt he would want her to carry on with her work. After all, Carson loved his newspaper, and if he thought it was suffering as a result of his illness, it would impede his recovery.

The building was relatively quiet, but soon that would not be so. Somewhere between nine and ten, the working day would begin for the editorial and news staff, transforming it into a hubbub of activity.

In spite of the problems that were now complicating her life, something akin to excitement coursed through her. Work had always been her salvation; when everything else failed, she could count on that.

Today was no exception. She planned to jump in with both feet, leaving no time to think. This morning she was scheduled to meet with Daniel and other members of the editorial staff to see who would be in charge in her stepfather's absence. She hoped Daniel would be that someone. As managing editor, highly respected and trained by Carson himself, Daniel was the best and most logical one for the job.

Also, she intended to tell the staff what she'd learned from John Riley about the accident at the shopping center, and that she planned to involve the news and editorial departments in it. Most members were aware of Carson's passionate dislike of the mayor and would fully cooperate with her in the matter. No way would they risk bucking Carson's authority, she reassured herself. Even from the sickbed, he still ruled the *Tribune*.

When McKenzie stepped out of the elevator into the newsroom, she felt as though she had just come home. She guessed she never would tire of the smell or the sense of excitement that went hand in hand with newspaper work.

She paused a moment, taking in the room filled with desks, each one proudly displaying a bulky word processor that looked like a television. Soon the room would ignite with the click clack of keyboards.

Every area of the building was laid out in much the same way, depending on its function: classified, advertising, sports, and so on, with editors' desks nestled in corner offices. As a part-time editor, she had inherited one of those offices.

Suddenly, she noticed she wasn't the only early arrival. "Hey, Mike," she said to the boyish-looking man occupying one of the desks. His face was bowed as he read a tattered operating manual next to his word processor.

At the sound of her voice, he jerked his head up and smiled broadly. "Hiya, McKenzie. I thought I was the only idiot who came to work at this insane hour of the morning."

She laughed. "Well, it's nice to know you're not alone, right? What's that old saying; misery loves company?"

After several more pleasantries were exchanged, with Mike inquiring about Carson, McKenzie crossed the threshold into her office. After flooding the room with light, she plopped her briefcase down on her desk and snapped it open.

To the left, next to her machine, lay a copy of yesterday's paper. Distracted now, she reached over and began idly looking through it, beginning with a photograph next to the headline in bold print. After quickly thumbing to page three, she scanned the page until she found the article bearing her name. McKenzie Moore. She smiled at seeing her name in print. Even after all this time, it never failed to thrill her.

The piece was about a privately owned nursing home on the East side that was grossly mismanaged. In a tight, angry story, she'd captured the injustice of the mental and physical abuse being done to the elderly residents. She'd limited it to the facts—nothing more. Already the response had been tremendous, and the home had promised to make changes. But she intended to follow up, aware of the expression: Out of sight, out of mind.

"Is it safe to come in?"

McKenzie raised her head, then broke into a smile, watching Daniel breeze into the room.

"My, but don't you look sharp this morning," she exclaimed, coming from behind the desk so that she could get a better look at him. He was dressed in a blue pinstriped suit set off by a crisp white shirt and matching blue pin-dot tie. Standing tall and grinning like a Cheshire cat, he reminded her of the archetypal successful business executive.

Yet with all his polished, urbane good looks, he couldn't hold a candle to Jeb. Even at his slouchiest, Jeb could put most men to shame with his mop of tawny hair, probing green eyes and his sultry don't-give-a-damn attitude.

"McKenzie?"

Suddenly realizing the dangerous path her thoughts had taken, she responded to Daniel's voice with fuchsia-colored cheeks. "Wh-what?" she stammered.

He playfully waved his hand up and down in front of her face. "For a moment, I thought I'd lost you. You looked as though you were on another planet."

McKenzie, once more in command, shook her head. "Hardly that," she drawled, giving him a halfhearted smile. "Maybe a slight case of hardening of the arteries is more like it."

"Well, my darling, I seriously doubt that," he said, pulling her into his arms. "It seems like ages since we had any time alone together."

His kiss was artful if not ardent, she noticed. Casually breaking the embrace, McKenzie wondered where that thought had come from. The last thing she wanted from Daniel was emotion. What was wrong with her?

Afraid the answer to that question would be too easy to come by, she walked back to her desk and sat down, unconsciously smoothing away a tendril of hair that had slipped from the gold clip behind her ear.

Daniel frowned quizzically at her as though trying to find a reason for her sudden distraction. "Is Carson worse this morning?"

"No, actually, there's been little change, which at this point is encouraging."

His face registered relief, but she spoke again before he could make any comment. "Are you ready for the staff meeting?"

"Ready as I'll ever be," he admitted, sitting down on the edge of the desk and gazing at the mess strewn out across it. "What's all this?"

"My notes," she said, covering them with her hand. "Sorry. No one sees these until I've had a chance to organize them."

His eyes lit up. "Ah, on to something big, are we now?"

McKenzie was schooled in the art of showing no emotion. "Maybe, maybe not."

"Huh. I know better than that," he said. "Come on, level with me. Let me in on the scoop."

She smiled. "No can do. Anyway, you'll find out soon enough. I intend to spill everything to the staff in—" she looked at her watch "—exactly two hours."

Daniel snapped his fingers. "Which reminds me, I'd better get to my office and get prepared for my presentation." He paused, his face suddenly becoming tense. "I'm looking forward to taking over the reins while Carson's ill. I just hope the staff cooperates."

For a reason she couldn't quite define, the look on his face made her uneasy. "I'm sure they will," she replied. "As far as I'm concerned, you're a shoo-in for the job. After all, that's what Dad's been grooming you for all these years."

With an air of inflated confidence, he sauntered to the door and turned around. "I'll meet you back here after a while and we'll go up together."

Once alone, McKenzie shuffled through her notes and clipped the first page to the metal paper stand beside her word processor. But instead of pounding the keys as she had planned, she sat as stiff as a statue, staring at the blank monitor.

For some insane reason, that feeling of uneasiness she had felt a moment ago still lingered. It was as though it had her by the throat and wouldn't let go. She gave an aggravated sigh. Why couldn't she settle down?

After all, things were once again on the right track. Her stepfather was holding his own. The paper seemed to be running as smoothly as could be expected under the circumstances. And she was excited about checking into the lead on the Cedar Plaza Mall. So why this feeling of being suddenly off track?

Jeb was the culprit. Just thinking about him a second ago had thrown her system out of whack. Suddenly disgusted with herself, McKenzie got up and walked to the window. She stared at the view for a moment, then shook her head and went back to her desk.

The view had filled her vision, but it had done nothing for the hollowness deep inside her.

Jeb swore as another sharp pain darted through his head. "Serves you right, old boy," he mumbled, "for trying to drink up all the damn liquor in the bar."

After he'd left the hospital, he'd gone straight to another bar where he'd really tied one on. Yet, he still hadn't gotten as drunk as he'd hoped.

He shrugged, wincing against another onslaught of pain. Maybe he'd built up such a tolerance that he'd never be able to sink into a drunken oblivion again. Somehow that was not encouraging at all.

Forcing himself to move, he rolled over very gingerly to the side of the bed and reached for the phone. On the second ring, he fumbled impatiently for the crumpled pack of cigarettes on the bedside table. He'd promised himself no more cancer sticks, but since coming back to the States, he'd smoked one, then another, and last night two packs.

Then, just as he started to light the foul-tasting thing, a soft voice said, "Good morning, Seton Hospital."

"ICU, please," he said in a clipped voice.

A pause and then, "Yes, may I help you?"

"This is Jeb Langley. I'd like to inquire about my father, Carson Langley?"

"Of course, Mr. Langley. Actually, he's awake and we've just fed him breakfast. He's about the same, though, resting comfortably."

Jeb breathed somewhat easier. "Thank you, nurse. Thanks very much."

After placing the receiver back in the cradle, he glanced at the clock in annoyance and realized he didn't have time to waste.

Minutes later, having showered, Jeb tugged on his pants, stumbling in haste; he cursed aloud at the reason for his delay, especially as another sharp pain racked his skull. He slid his arms into his shirt and grabbed a sport coat; he was already down the stairs and halfway out the door before the shirt was buttoned.

Time still on his side, Jeb's long strides ate up the distance from the main entrance of the hospital to ICU. The sterile room was just the way he remembered from his pilgrimage there last evening. After pausing in the door, he made his way cautiously toward the bed.

His father's eyes were closed, and Jeb's heart sank. He had been hoping to talk to him. It had been a long time....

Suddenly Carson's eyes popped open as though he realized he was no longer alone. "Nurse?" he croaked, looking around, his eyes trying to focus.

Jeb's knee made contact with the bed. "No, Dad, it's me, Jeb."

Silence.

Carson's chin wobbled slightly. "Son. Is... it really you?" Tears sprang to his eyes as he sought to see Jeb's face clearly.

Jeb grasped his father's hand and sat down beside him. "I'm for real," he said, suddenly feeling a tightness in his throat.

"Oh, Son," Carson began, clawing at Jeb's arm, "there's so much I... want... to say. I..." Suddenly, his voice played out, exhaustion taking hold.

"Shhh, Dad. Take it easy," Jeb whispered, fighting off the tears.

"I'm...so sorry...for so much," Carson labored on, ignoring Jeb's warning.

"Me too, Dad."

"We...have to talk...the paper...I'm worried... Evans isn't ready."

"Shhh," Jeb cautioned again, concern deepening his voice as he wondered who the hell Evans was. "I'll see to things. Don't you fret, you hear."

Suddenly, Carson's body went limp and the tears rolled down his cheeks. "Thanks...Son," he whispered, closing his eyes.

Then Jeb did something he'd never done before in his entire life. He leaned over and kissed his father on the forehead.

This feeling of contentment still prevailed as, some twenty minutes later, he slipped through the rear door of the *Tribune* and crossed to the elevator.

He was a man with a mission—a mission he didn't intend to screw up.

McKenzie was tearing the perforated sheets from the printer, proud that she had finally managed to organize her notes and get them on the screen with time to spare, when the phone jangled in her ear. She almost jumped out of her skin at the jarring sound, so engrossed was she in the task at hand.

"Yes," she said shortly, holding the receiver against her shoulder while continuing to rip the edges off the pages.

"McKenzie, it's me, Rachel."

She stopped what she was doing. "Oh, hi, Aunt Rachel," she said. "I've been thinking about you, but just haven't gotten around to calling you. There hasn't been time. I—"

"That's all right, my dear," Rachel replied, stopping her flow of words. "No apology necessary. I can imagine what it's been like around there with Carson gone."

"Speaking of Dad, I stopped by the hospital early this morning and sat with him for a while."

"Well, I'm on my way there now, but I just wanted to make sure you were all right. After last night..." She left her sentence unfinished.

McKenzie's sigh was deep. "Please, Auntie, don't worry about me. I'm going to be just fine. I'm a survivor, remember? Anyway, it's Dad we need to be concerned about, not me."

Rachel's sigh echoed her own. "I know, and I should have been to check on him long before now, only—" She paused, then went on hastily, "Never mind. I'll..."

"Only what, Aunt Rachel?" McKenzie pressed.

"Well, if you must know, I stayed up until all hours waiting for Jeb, hoping we could talk, but I finally gave up. I'm...I'm not sure he ever came home."

A long silence followed.

McKenzie was gripping the phone so hard, she wouldn't have been surprised if it had snapped under the pressure. Every time *his* name was mentioned, it was as if a giant hand reached out and squeezed her heart.

She cleared her throat. "Aunt Rachel, I don't—"

"I know. You don't want to talk about Jeb."

Another silence.

While McKenzie was searching for something to say to ease the awkward moment, her eyes carelessly drifted toward the door.

Suddenly, she jerked upright as every nerve in her body froze. When at last she found her voice, her words came out in short, raspy spurts. "Auntie, listen, I've got to go now. I'll call you later, okay?"

Jeb was using the door of her office to bear the brunt of his weight, a smile turning the corners of his lips upward. "Gotta minute?" he drawled.

McKenzie swallowed, making an effort to moisten her throat so she could speak, but nothing could stop her pulse rate from escalating wildly. The unexpected sight of his big, brawny body, with that magnetic smile plastered across his lips, was almost more than she could handle.

Oh, dear Lord, was it going to be like this from now on? Was he going to continue to intrude in her life, dig into it, disturb it, *destroy* it?

Rubber-legged, she stood up. "What . . . what are you doing here?"

Jeb pushed himself away from the door and swaggered toward her desk, an unreadable expression on his face. "Can we talk?"

She eyed him with mistrust. "What could we possibly have to talk about?"

His grin was lopsided, and in spite of herself, there was a little catch in the area of her heart.

"Well, for starters, I'd like to apologize for my behavior last night. There was no excuse for it." He lit a cigarette, squinting at her through the smoke.

McKenzie looked stunned. Jeb Langley apologize? Unbelievable. Unheard of! There was a catch to it; there had to be. She sucked her lower lip back behind her front teeth and cocked her head appraisingly. "Why?"

He stared at her, openly admiring the rounded figure beneath the ivory silk blouse, the way the peach-colored wool suit molded to her slender hips.

McKenzie felt his gaze like a soft, insistent touch. Feeling the color seep from her face, she shifted her eyes, hating being off balance. "All . . . all right, apology accepted."

The tension in the air was acute.

Jeb took a step closer, still displaying a shadow of a smile. "I'd like to sit down; there's something I want to discuss with you."

Determined not to feed the panic building up inside her, McKenzie reached for the stack of papers in front of her and clutched them to her chest. "I'm...I'm sorry, but now's not a good time." Her eyes darted frantically beyond his shoulder to the door. "I have a meeting—"

"Good, that's what—"

"Excuse me," she interrupted breathlessly, a feeling of relief surging through her as she watched Daniel, with a grin on his face, walk through the door.

"Ready?" he asked, before stopping abruptly. "Sorry, didn't realize you were busy." His eyes narrowed curiously on Jeb, obviously waiting for an introduction. When none was forthcoming, he turned to McKenzie and added pointedly, "Have you forgotten our meeting?"

For the second time in a matter of minutes, McKenzie was at a loss for words. All the signs of panic were there: the fluttering in her chest, dry mouth, shaking hands.

"No...no, of course I haven't," she said, feeling as if the room, the sound of her droning voice, Jeb's steady gaze were all closing in on her.

Suddenly, as though he realized something was not quite right, Jeb took another step closer, concern tightening his features. "McKenzie?"

She shook herself mentally. "Jeb...Jeb Langley—" she barely recognized her own voice "—meet Daniel Evans, the managing editor of the *Tribune* and my...my fiancé."

A flinty silence greeted the introduction.

There was a sinking sensation in the pit of Jeb's stomach, as if he'd just hit a huge dip while riding a roller coaster. *Fool!* he chastised himself silently. *You should have known she wouldn't be free*. But why the hell hadn't he been told?

Struggling to keep his inner turmoil from spilling to the surface, he turned toward Daniel and shook the hand that was outstretched. "A pleasure, I'm sure," he drawled lightly.

But McKenzie wasn't fooled by his calm attitude. She had watched as his face underwent a mysterious hardening. She didn't know why, but he was angry, so angry he was barely holding himself in check.

Unconsciously, her hand reached out and clamped down on Jeb's arm. At this unexpected contact, his eyes swung around to meet hers, the muscles in his arms bunching beneath her touch. She dropped her hand as if she'd been stung, but dropping her gaze was not as easy.

For a moment they stared at one another, oblivious to everything and everyone around them.

"So this is the long-lost stepbrother, huh, McKenzie?" Daniel asked, his taunting voice shattering the moment like shards of glass.

Jeb glared at Daniel, his face rigid. "That's right, Evans. What's it to ya?"

McKenzie was white-lipped with anger. "Stop it, Jeb," she demanded. "I don't know what this is all about or why you came here, but it no longer matters now. You'll have to leave. I—we are due in the meeting room in five minutes."

Jeb crossed his arms and said easily, "Well, in that case I'll just tag along." The grooves around his mouth deepened to suggest a smile.

"Now see here, Langley," Daniel chimed in.

"Stuff it, Evans. I'm not talking to you."

McKenzie was clinging to her sanity by a mere thread. How dare Jeb do this to her? Again. How dare he strut in here looking like a god, his skin glowing, his hair glistening, exuding the smell of pine trees on a spring day....

"Jeb, for heaven's sakes, will you please just go?" McKenzie finally asked with forced politeness.

Jeb didn't budge an inch. He merely sagged nonchalantly against the wall, a mocking grin on his face. "All in due time, darlin'. All in due time."

Daniel would have said something then, if it hadn't been for McKenzie's sharp look in his direction. He clamped his lips together, a sour expression on his face. McKenzie knew he was furious, but it couldn't be helped. She couldn't risk an all-out confrontation between the two of them. Daniel was no match for Jeb, and knowing her stepbrother, he wouldn't just stop with words; he'd take more drastic action if the situation warranted it. She shivered in spite of the warmth of the room.

Jerking her mind back on track, she demanded crisply, "And just exactly what do you mean by that remark?" An icy stillness had descended over her, disguising the chaos and momentary terror inside her.

Completely ignoring Daniel as though he weren't there, Jeb slanted McKenzie a sidelong glance. "I'll gladly tell you," he said. "In simple terms, it means that I'm going to be in charge around here until my father returns."

McKenzie gasped. But then cold rage gave her the extra measure of strength she needed to stand up to him. "You're crazy!" she screeched, searching his face, but nothing yielded, nothing confessed.

Jeb's eyes burned into hers, and he thought again how lovely she was, especially now, with her flashing eyes reminding him of cool blue marbles, and her bottom lip quivering ever so slightly. He had to crush the urge to haul her into his arms and kiss her until she begged him to stop.

He took a step backward, out of harm's way, and said softly, "You'd better get used to having me around."

Suddenly, Daniel laughed. "You're out of your mind, Langley," he sneered. "Even if you were capable of taking over—" the contempt on his face saying he didn't believe for one minute he was "—the editorial board would never approve it. Just who the hell do you think you are, anyway?"

Jeb's eyes cut into Daniel like ice picks. "I know who I am, all right. But it seems to me you're the one who hasn't figured that out."

"Why, you bastard!"

"Don't you dare say another word, either of you!" McKenzie cried, glaring at both of them. "This is too absurd even to be discussed."

But was it? Of course it was, she quickly assured herself. How stupid of her even to entertain such a question. Yet, fear churned in the pit of her stomach, egged on by the thought of how dangerous it would be to her peace of mind to work with Jeb on a day-to-day basis. But even if Jeb were serious, the board would never go for it. That jolt of agony she'd felt suddenly diminished.

Tilting her chin, she looked into Jeb's face. "Daniel's right, you know. There's no way the board will ever approve of such a crazy suggestion—even if Daniel weren't already groomed and ready for the job," she added on a defiant note.

Jeb smiled, not the least bit perturbed. "Let's go find out, shall we?"

McKenzie still could not believe it. The decision to make Jeb acting publisher was mind-boggling. But the moment Jeb had waltzed into the stately paneled room, with its rich, deep carpet and intricately carved mahogany table, and presented his case to the staff, he had them eating out of his hand.

As a journalist, Jeb had earned himself quite a reputation. He was highly respected in his field, with his work having appeared in many of the major newspapers and magazines of the world. With Jeb, they saw a chance for new blood to extend the scope of the paper. The circulation had shrunk too much in the last few years, far too much.

With the exception of Daniel, they had voted to support him. To add to McKenzie's chagrin and frustration, there hadn't been much of a discussion—only she and Daniel had protested, but to no avail. Then Daniel, with a snarl in Jeb's direction, had stormed out of the room.

Now, as she was readying herself to present her findings on Cedar Plaza Mall to the board, she kept her eyes from straying in Jeb's direction. Why was he doing this? What did he hope to accomplish? There he was, sitting casually at the head of the table, confident in his ability to take charge. Suddenly, McKenzie felt as though something were stuck in her throat, choking her, forcing her to swallow.

Dwight Harper, the city editor, a dapper man with a bald head, broke the short, strained silence. "Ms. Moore, I understand you may be on to something concerning our illustrious mayor. Are you prepared to give us a quick rundown?"

Jeb watched as McKenzie grappled to maintain her control after the blow she'd been dealt. He'd have to hand it to her, she had guts. Too damned many guts for that pantywaist she was marrying, he told himself furiously.

At Dwight's simple request, McKenzie stood up, noticing how the light played across his bald head. It looked as smooth as a baby's bottom. She wanted to smile.

Then, clearing her throat, she became all business. "Ah, yes, I do," she confessed. "I have an idea we might be able to find fault in the construction phase of the Cedar Plaza Mall.''

Harper appeared doubtful. "I don't see how. I can't see Witherspoon involving himself in anything that would hamper his chances of getting elected governor."

"According to my source there's a good possibility that he's involved in building fraud."

Dwight's eyes narrowed. "That doesn't sound like something we want to touch."

"It doesn't matter what *we* want; it's what Carson wants that's important. And he wants Jackson Witherspoon." McKenzie was angry.

"It's all right with me; it's better than nothing." Dwight looked around the table, stopping at Jeb. "What do you think?"

Jeb rose slowly. "Gentlemen, please consider this meeting adjourned. I'd like to speak with McKenzie alone, if you don't mind," he said politely. "I'll bring you up to date later."

McKenzie seethed as she watched Dwight and the others file out of the room.

Shortly, McKenzie was facing her stepbrother alone across the table. If looks could kill, he would have been dead.

"Was this stunt merely a display of your newly acquired power?" she asked sarcastically, her mind in an uproar.

"Hardly," he snapped.

"Then why—?"

"Is this Witherspoon the one that my mother was running around with before she died?"

For a moment, she faltered, the odd note in his voice catching her off guard. "One and the same," she replied hesitantly, hating herself for the momentary softening she was feeling toward him. Even after all these years, he could not escape his mother's sins. Shaking her head to free herself of the urge to reach out and touch him, she lowered her eyes in self-reproach. "And Dad's been looking for a way to get back at him ever since. Now he finally has a chance."

"Just exactly what do you have on Witherspoon?"

Begrudgingly, McKenzie gave him a quick rundown on what she had learned from John Riley.

When she had finished, Jeb crossed to the window, where he paused and massaged the back of his neck. Then he pivoted. "I don't like it," he said.

McKenzie bristled. "Well, that's just too bad, because I intend to follow through with the investigation, hoping to prove that not only are the contractors crooked and involved in fraud up to their eyeballs, but also that the mayor's right along with them."

"Drop it, McKenzie! It's too sticky and much too dangerous."

McKenzie saw red. God, what arrogance! Imagine thinking he could tell her what to do and she'd just snap to it like a trained puppy. Was he ever in for a rude awakening!

"No, you drop it," she said, her voice dripping with sweet sarcasm. "You drop this act of pretending you can tell me what to do. I—"

"It's not even your fight, for chrissakes! It's my father's."

McKenzie bowed her shoulders. "That's beside the point. I know he would want me to do this, and I don't intend to let him down, no matter what you say."

"I wouldn't be sure of that," he said, his voice deceptively soft, as he closed the gap between them, his eyes raking over her, intimately, knowingly.

Although her heart skipped several beats, she held her ground. "Stop it, Jeb. I won't have you interfering in my life. I have Daniel—"

"Oh, God, spare me! He's not the man for you."

"That's not even open to discussion."

"It sure as hell should be."

"Well, it's not. But what *is* up for discussion is how you think you can just prance in here and take over the paper without your father's even knowing it, much less approving."

He smiled strangely. "Who says he doesn't approve?"

McKenzie blinked. "What!"

"You got it. I'm in charge."

"I...I don't believe you," McKenzie stammered, stunned.

"Well, it's a fact. I just came from the hospital."

"But...but why?" she stammered again, shock widening her eyes. "You've never...shown any interest in the paper before now."

He frowned impatiently. "Let's just say I changed my mind."

"Jeb, don't do this."

"I have to." The tone of his voice dropped an octave, and before she knew what was happening, he reached out and ran a finger down the side of her cheek.

The gentle touch hit her like an electric charge, and she jerked away, turning her head. "Jeb," she whispered unsteadily, "I'm warning you."

"No, I'm warning you. Stay away from Witherspoon."

There was a moment of silence as the atmosphere grew taut and tense and explosive. The two seemed almost on the edge of violence.

McKenzie shook her head. "I won't do it."

Jeb's breath rattled in his lungs. "Then we'll work on it together."

"No!" she cried. "Absolutely not."

"Yes. It's my way or no way."

They stood glaring at each other, neither prepared to back down.

Suddenly realizing she was trembling, McKenzie held her arms to her chest. What was she going to do? She couldn't let him take over her life again; the fires he had once stoked within her were a long way from being burned out. He posed a threat not only to her hard-won peace of mind but also to the secure world she had rebuilt from the rubble of the past. She had to stop it now.

"I'll fight you every step of the way."

His eyes sliced deeper into hers. "And you'll lose," he whispered. "Trust me, you'll lose."

Chapter 4

And lose she had.

Even now, only one week after Jeb's untimely return, McKenzie felt she was no longer in control. Although she tried to pretend that Jeb had not come roaring back into her life like a Texas tornado in the springtime, it was easier said than done. His commanding presence made that impossible, especially when he stuck to his promise of remaining in the house and digging in with both feet at the newspaper.

When he wasn't in Carson's private domain dealing with the headaches of running a city newspaper, he was breezing in and out of the various newsrooms, familiarizing himself with each department.

To McKenzie's surprise, the workers at the *Tribune* were extremely receptive to him and were backing him one hundred percent. But then Jeb, with his charismatic personality, could charm the birds from the trees if he wanted to. The only adverse gossip making the rounds was about Daniel's inability to accept and cope with the change.

Daniel made no effort to hide his dislike of Jeb, and when in each other's company, he made little effort to be civil. Jeb merely took this in stride and delighted in forcing Daniel to cooperate by keeping him abreast of what was happening. At best, it was an awkward situation, one that at times was almost explosive.

In dealing with McKenzie, he was equally diligent. There seemed to be no avoiding him. At the newspaper he constantly made excuses to waltz into her office or call her into his. Every time she turned around, he was tracking her every move, his eyes roving over her with lazy ownership. In spite of herself she responded, her heart pounding, stirring up a yearning so intense it made her sick to her stomach.

To make matters worse, she and Daniel were not getting along well; he continually badgered her to move out of the house until Carson returned home, but she refused to do so. At this point, she simply could not handle another change in her life. Anyway, when she went home in the evening, Jeb was rarely there.

That, too, was unsettling. Where was he until all hours of the night? With another woman? After all, he was a virile man with strong appetites, and he was not going to be without a woman for long.

Yet, she couldn't control the pounding of her heart when he was near or when he looked at her in that certain way, or when he seemed to take up all the air in the room with his tall, muscular body and refreshing scent.

Why was he treating her so possessively?

What did he want from her? An affair? Or revenge?

These questions circled in her brain, refusing to be ignored. But even more important, what did she want from him? She honestly didn't know. All McKenzie Moore knew was that she was skidding on a thin sheet of ice, and if she wasn't careful, the ice would crack and she would be sucked under again in a misery of her own making.

Unable to stand her thoughts another moment, Mc-Kenzie got up from the couch. Stifling a weary sigh, she left her cup of coffee untouched and went upstairs to her bedroom. Now that it was early evening it was a relief that she finally had time away from Jeb's burning eyes and all-consuming presence, she thought, as she hastily began to take off her clothes. Later this evening she and Daniel were going to the local Cancer Society's charity ball at the Hyatt Regency Hotel.

She had been looking forward to the annual event for a month. It was to be a buffet dinner and dance. The women would be in the finest jewels and beautifully dressed in the latest fashions. Austin's elite would be in attendance, including the mayor.

And knowing Witherspoon's inflated ego, there was bound to be action, especially when the press went after him. Her main objective was to garner more ammunition for her war against the mayor and his alleged connection with the shopping mall project. To date, she had run up against a brick wall. She and John Riley had not had a chance to visit the widow of the construction worker but, when they did, she hoped they would learn something of importance.

Jeb had been drilling her with questions about Cedar Plaza, warning her not to make a move without his knowledge, and meanwhile doing some snooping of his own. It had often crossed her mind that it would be fun to work with Jeb on a story. If only...

"Forget it, McKenzie!" she said aloud. "Bag it!" It's over. *I know it's better this way. One can never go back, and I wouldn't go back for a million dollars!*

After giving an unladylike snort, she made a beeline for the bathroom, where she jumped into the shower, remaining under the lukewarm spray just until she could adequately wash her body. After toweling herself dry, she doused herself with perfume and then slipped into a light robe.

It took only five minutes to refine her makeup. McKenzie kept it light, adding an iridescent powder over her eyelids and cheeks. A flick of her lipstick brush and she was finished. To lift her flagging spirits, she had taken a spur-of-the-moment shopping trip that afternoon, wanting something glamorous.

The dress, when she slipped it on, clung to her body, molding the rich curves and accentuating her slender waist. It was velvet, the color of dusty rose, with a narrow skirt and tiny puffed sleeves. The color brought out the gold highlights in her hair and made her blue eyes gleam like crystal. She swept her hair back from her face, letting it fall heavily to her shoulders, and after fastening an antique necklace of pink coral above the low-scooped neck, she was ready to go.

She donned a lynx coat, which had been a gift from her stepfather, and while she waited for Daniel, her thoughts unconsciously turned to Jeb. Would he approve of the way she looked? Then, disgusted with herself for her one-track mind, she ran down the stairs and was waiting when the doorbell pealed loudly.

It was Rosie's night off, so she opened the door herself. Daniel stood there, impeccably dressed in evening clothes.

"You look sensational," he said softly. "Why don't we skip the ball and sneak off by ourselves."

McKenzie stepped aside and smiled, wishing her pulse could race at Daniel's seductive tone, but it didn't. "Sorry," she answered lightly, "no can do. You know it's good for the paper's image for us to be seen."

They remained in the house just long enough for one quick drink. McKenzie was eager to be gone, fighting the letdown that was nibbling at her. Daniel could not replace Jeb and that was that.

God! McKenzie, do you realize what you were just thinking? He's really gotten to you, after all, with his intimate looks and accidental touches. But she wasn't going to give in. No, sir. She would fight him to the bitter end, and herself as well, if that's what it took.

By the time they arrived, the ballroom was alive with milling crowds. Before they found a table, McKenzie went into the ladies' room to check her makeup. Satisfied that her overall appearance was still intact, she watched throngs of the most elaborately clad women compete with one another in their magnificence.

McKenzie quickly applied a fresh coat of lip gloss before rejoining Daniel at the arched entrance to the massive ballroom. He was standing where he could see the lobby, a cigarette dangling from the corner of his mouth.

"If you're ready, let's go in. There's already a crowd here. We need to find a table before they're all taken."

"I'm starved. How about you?"

"I could eat, that's for sure," he said, instantly signaling a waiter bearing a tray of hors d'oeuvres.

McKenzie smiled her thanks as Daniel supplied her with a napkin and the choicest of tidbits before helping himself to the delicacies. "Delicious," she said, munching.

"Mmmmm. Once we get seated, I'll get us something to drink."

"Please, just a glass of wine for me."

Daniel arched an eyebrow. "Sure?"

"I'm sure. It's been a long day and I want to be fully alert when the bigwigs arrive, especially the mayor." Her face was animated. "Knowing how Witherspoon loves the limelight, I'm sure he'll answer questions, and I'm willing to bet something will be said about Cedar Plaza."

Daniel shook his head in disgust as he steered her across the floor to a table close to the dance floor. "Even though I hate to admit it," he began, holding out the chair for her, "this is one time I agree with Langley. I wish you'd forget this damned vendetta against the mayor. It can only lead—"

"Drop it, Daniel," she interrupted coolly. "Nothing you can say is going to change my mind, so don't even try." Her chin jutted defiantly.

Daniel made a face. "I don't know why I bother to try to reason with you, anyway. Ever since your stepbrother—" he sneered the word "—appeared on the scene, you're not the same person. You're as skittish as a cat." With a petulant twist to his lips, he stalked off to the bar.

McKenzie released a pent-up sigh of regret and turned so that she could scan the crowd. This was just one of the many small skirmishes she and Daniel had had of late, and she refused to let this one ruin her evening.

Many of the participants in this year's gala she recognized; some were longtime friends, others mere acquaintances. In years past, she had attended this function, and others just like it, on the arm of her stepfather. He was at his most charming when in the company of hundreds of people. Suddenly, she experienced a stinging sensation behind her eyelids. She still couldn't believe that Carson, who loved life so, was lying helpless....

"I'm sorry I was so short with you a moment ago."

Daniel's hot breath tickled her neck. She swung her head up and around and smiled absently. "That's all right. I'm sorry, too."

After placing her glass of wine in front of her, he sat down and began sipping on his martini, covering an awkward silence. After a moment he commented, "The buffet looks good, and right now it's not very crowded. How about heading that way?"

With a nod, McKenzie stood up and preceded him, weaving and dodging through the crowd. Finally, after being stopped numerous times and answering countless questions about Carson Langley, they reached the long table positioned against a back wall. No longer hungry, she took sparingly of the rich food. Daniel was much less inhibited. Laughing, she offered to help him carry his plate.

After the meal had been consumed, he went to the bar. When he returned, she grabbed hold of his arm, keeping him from sitting down. "Here comes the first of the bigwigs, the mayor. Let's move closer to the action."

Daniel covered her hand. "You're right. Here he comes."

As the mayor made his well-timed entrance, people began to push forward, flashbulbs going crazy.

McKenzie watched as the mayor mounted the band platform and, stamping his campaign-working grin across his lips, bowed to the audience. With his chest protruding, he gloried in the whistles and cheering that followed.

Even without the platform, he could have been seen. Witherspoon was a tall, large-boned man with an oversized waist to match his oversized mouth and ambition. Ruddy skin and a mop of wiry red hair lightened with gray enhanced his flashy good looks, making him appear younger than his sixty-odd years. He looked like a steel wool pad, McKenzie thought with a smile.

For the life of her, she could not see how any woman could have chosen him over Carson Langley. Jeb's mother must have been a fool.

Yet attached to his side was a small blond woman who reminded McKenzie of a painted china doll. Shelley Storm was her name, and from all accounts—both gossip and fact—she had him exactly where she wanted him and that was almost at the altar. Rumor also had it that she could spend more money in one day than most people could in a year. That was a very good reason why Witherspoon just might be primed to run a scam. Smiling, McKenzie hugged this thought and listened.

Jackson Witherspoon was in his element as he singled out a reporter who had a question.

"Sir, do you see Cedar Plaza Mall as your project, as well as your one-way ticket into the governor's mansion?"

McKenzie held her breath, waiting for his answer.

There was no hesitation. Witherspoon bulldozed straight to the point. "It's the best thing that's ever happened to the city of Austin." He bowed again to the unexpected applause, giving a clear view of his teeth in a smile that, McKenzie suspected, he believed irresistible.

"It's been a long time coming, especially with practically no help from the state. And yes, I'll take the credit, but only behind the taxpayers." He turned his head. "Next question."

McKenzie was seething, her breasts moving in time to the uneven tempo of her heart. "Did you hear that old bag of wind pat himself on the back?" she whispered tersely. "And even at that, he didn't answer the question."

"Shhh, calm down," Daniel said, his voice on the whiny side. "I won't allow him to dominate our evening. He's not worth it. Come on, let's go back to our table and dance awhile."

Daniel was right, she knew; so with a careless shrug, she strolled beside him, but all the while her mind was working furiously. Tomorrow, without fail, she needed to get together with John Riley and, if at all possible, go visit Elmer Thurman's widow.

They sat silently for a while, sipping their drinks and watching the dancers. One group was trying to do the Cotton-Eyed Joe, but they were laughing so hard they couldn't do anything right.

The band flowed into an old Simon and Garfunkel tune. "Shall we dance?" Daniel asked, breaking the silence.

She laughed. "I'm more than ready."

Daniel smiled his perfect smile and took her arm. The circled the floor and she felt as though her feet had wings. This had been such a hectic week; she had been so uptigh about her stepfather—and Jeb—that it felt good to relax to the music.

They sat down, but not for long. Again changing th tempo, the band struck up a Michael Jackson tune, and McKenzie grinned at Daniel. "Are you game?" she asked.

"Why not?" he said, dropping her hand. They made i through the entire dance and were laughing when Mc Kenzie's eyes strayed to the nearest entrance.

She saw a party of five enter the room and slowly mak its way toward a table near the back wall. One of the fiv was Jeb Langley.

Daniel frowned as McKenzie stiffened. "What's wrong?"

"Don't look now," she whispered, "but Jeb just walked in. He's with some old friends of his."

Daniel's lips clamped into a thin line. "Damn!" he spat "What's he doing here?"

"Good for the image, remember?" McKenzie said, feel ing the blood thunder against her temple.

"You don't have to remind me." His expression had grown fierce.

"Please...could we sit down?" she murmured, fighting off the urge to flee.

While they made their way to the table, McKenzie's mind was shorting out. She still couldn't believe that Jeb had showed up at this type of function. It certainly wasn't his cup of tea. But then Jeb never did anything without a rea son, and she didn't think for one minute he was doing so now. *But why had he decided to come tonight?*

Once they were comfortably seated, Daniel demanded sullenly, "How long do you think Langley intends to keep up this charade?"

She made a limp gesture with her hand. "Until Dad improves and kicks him out on his you-know-what."

He snorted. "Do you think that's likely to happen? After all, this is what Carson's always wanted."

McKenzie shook her head. "I . . . I don't know." And she didn't, especially in the light of Jeb's recent coup. But she saw no reason to tell Daniel this. In his present state of mind, he was better off not knowing.

Daniel downed the last of his drink and beckoned to the waiter for a refill. "Well, what I am sure about is the way he looks at you," he said suddenly, "as though he owns you." Ignoring the panicked expression that flickered across McKenzie's face, he hammered on. "One of these days, I'm going to punch his lights out."

"Don't be ridiculous, Daniel," she snapped, while making an effort to hide a smile. Not in her wildest imagination could she picture Daniel taking a swing at Jeb. In the first place Daniel, though well built, was no match for her stepbrother's whipcord strength. Jeb would quickly make mincemeat out of him and would welcome the chance to do so.

Daniel's eyes were glaring. "You can deny it till hell freezes over, but I still think he considers you his property. It's there for the entire world to see, damn him."

McKenzie flushed. "You have nothing to worry about," she murmured softly. "Absolutely nothing." If only that were the whole truth, she thought despairingly. It seemed as though she had been living her life in the fast lane since her stepfather's stroke and Jeb's unexpected return. She wanted to slow it down, get everything back in perspective, stop thinking about Jeb and his presence in her life.

Daniel's face hardened. "I just wish he'd stayed the hell away, that's all," he muttered, more to himself than to her.

McKenzie finished her wine and stood up. "Excuse me for a moment," she said. "I'm going to the ladies' room."

There was so much Daniel didn't know about her and Jeb. But some things were better left unsaid.

"Fine." Daniel rose abruptly. "Don't be long."

Once in the coolness of the foyer, McKenzie patted her hot cheeks with her hands as she wandered slowly along the carpeted corridor to the powder room. She was almost there when she saw Jeb.

He was using the wall as his customary prop, smoking a cigarette and talking to his old buddy, Malcolm Perry. In a black tuxedo, with a stark white shirt highlighting his bronzed skin, he radiated a raw attraction. He looked good enough to eat, every male inch of him. Just the sight of him made her shake on the inside like jelly.

Unerringly, she moved toward him, her approach causing Jeb to glance her way. Suddenly, she wondered how she had let him walk out of her life.

Now as his eyes met hers she came to a dead stop. Not a word was spoken. Her entire being, body and brain, seemed to have received a massive electric shock that, for a moment, deadened all her senses. They were immersed in a private world of their own making, just the two of them.

Taking his eyes away, Jeb straightened and dropped his cigarette to the floor and ground it out with his heel. His companion saw her too, though from the look on his face, he didn't recognize her.

"Jeb," she murmured, holding up her head, her eyes steady.

"McKenzie." He nodded, his eyes flickering, freezing her out. He turned to his companion, a man of about forty, with unruly brown hair, and a wide, friendly grin splayed across his broad face.

Before Jeb could say anything else, however, the man said appraisingly, "Times haven't changed a bit, my friend. You still have the uncanny ability of attracting all the best-looking women in town."

Jeb almost smiled. "McKenzie," he said, "this is an old buddy of mine, Malcolm Perry. Malcolm, this is my... This is McKenzie Moore."

"Hello," McKenzie said, looking at him closely while he pumped her hand vigorously.

"It's a real pleasure," he responded warmly.

"You don't remember me, do you?"

Malcolm's eyes narrowed, and for a moment he looked slightly disconcerted. "No...can't say that I do." He swung around to Jeb, a question mirrored on his face.

Jeb lifted acorn-colored brows. "It's McKenzie—" he stressed the name "—my stepsister."

Malcolm slammed the palm of his hand against his head. "Why, of course! It's little McKenzie all grown up." He paused thoughtfully. "How the hell...But I thought...I mean, how come you two never got together?"

Jeb did not say a word, but a muscle worked furiously in his jaw.

McKenzie felt her cheeks turn fire-engine red.

"Jesus!" Malcolm mumbled. "Talk about putting my big foot in my mouth, to say nothing of making an ass out of myself."

"We all make mistakes." Jeb replied shortly. "Just ask McKenzie."

The color of McKenzie's face went from red to white. She abhorred being discussed as though she weren't present, and worse, she hated the direction the conversation had taken. *Why won't he leave me alone? Why is he doing this to me?* Suddenly, she knew she had no choice but to put Jeb in his place before things got further out of hand.

"If you gentlemen will excuse me, I have to return to my table." Then she looked directly at Jeb, her eyes showing a defiant spark. "Daniel will be wondering what has happened to me."

"Nice to see you again, McKenzie," Malcolm said awk
wardly, tasting the tension in the air.

"Same here," she murmured, casting one final look a'
Jeb. Her parting shot had disturbed him, no doubt about it
He stood aloof, sporting a thin white line of tension aroun(
his mouth.

McKenzie forced herself to walk slowly across the floor
though she felt Jeb's eyes like hot pokers searing into he
back. What did he expect? she asked herself furiously. Ever
games had rules. Didn't they?

Jeb was miserable. Since returning to his table, he'(
gulped down two drinks, one right after the other. He hadn'
wanted to come to this damned lash-up to begin with, bu
when Rachel had told him McKenzie was coming, he'd beer
determined to make an appearance. Then when Malcolm
had called, hearing he was back in town, he'd taken Mal
colm up on his invitation to the charity function. But he'c
declined his friend's offer to get him a date. Now, he al
most wished he'd taken him up on that, too.

Seeing McKenzie with that damn Evans was enough tc
make him bite a nail in two. His hands itched to paste him.
He knew coming here was a mistake the minute he'd set foo
in the door and saw her with him. It was like having his
lungs suddenly punctured so that they collapsed, leaving
him insufficient air to breathe.

Suddenly, he was jolted out of his dark thoughts by a slap
on his arm. "Hey, Jeb," Malcolm was saying, "wake up
We're missing something." Jeb looked up with a start and
noticed a crowd of people around the dance floor.

Reluctantly, Jeb let himself be swept along. By the time
they reached the edge of the floor, all the other couples had
stopped dancing; everyone's eyes were glued to one lone

couple, fast dancing to the loud music. Evans and...
McKenzie.

He felt the muscles of his face grow taut, tug downward,
while he tried to combat the thumping of his heart and the
thickness in his throat. Sweet Jesus! She was doing a
damned good job of extracting her pound of flesh. Perspiration dampened the collar around his neck, and he stood
helpless against the hot, blinding jealousy that tore through
his gut.

After watching the exhibition for another minute, he'd
had enough, especially when McKenzie's tight little ass and
breasts—he'd bet his life she didn't have on a bra—moved
in perfect time to the rhythm, her dress a swirling cloud
around her. Biting his tongue to keep from cursing aloud,
he turned to Malcolm. "Look," he said tightly, "I think I'm
going to split. I've had enough. It's been a long day."

Malcolm swatted him on the shoulder, a knowing smile
on his lips. "Anything you say, old buddy. It's been great
seeing you."

"Same here. Make my apologies to the others, will ya?"

"Will do."

"I'll be in touch." With those words, Jeb turned and
struck out for the exit.

Once outside, Jeb climbed into his car and lit a cigarette
before starting the engine. Then he guided the sleek auto-
mobile out of downtown and onto the freeway toward the
house.

His hands had a death grip on the steering wheel as he felt
his jaw muscles become tense and his back teeth begin to
grind together.

Then it dawned on him what had been bothering him.
The tightness in his chest was gone. It had been replaced
with a lump of cold, black fury—fury at himself for having
the unmitigated gall to think he could win McKenzie back.

But dammit, she wanted him. He'd seen the burning flash of desire in her eyes. Or had he just imagined it, simply because he wanted it to be there?

Later, after he'd let himself into the dark, lonely house and crossed to the den, he reached for a bottle of whiskey and filled a glass.

It was going to be a helluva long night....

Chapter 5

It was well past midnight when Jackson Witherspoon climbed into his chauffeur-driven limousine beside his companion, Shelley Storm.

"Thank God, that's over," he said with a grimace, leaning his head back against the cushioned seat.

"Not half as glad as I am," Shelley giggled, moving closer to him, laying her hand on his thigh. "I've been waiting to get you to myself all day."

Witherspoon shot her a sidelong glance. "Hell, Shelley! It's been a long day and I'm tired."

Her bottom lip protruded. "Surely you're not too tired for a little tender loving care," she whined, her hand busy massaging his leg. "Anyway, I want to model my new spring wardrobe I charged to you today."

"Dammit, didn't I just buy you a new winter wardrobe?" He was sweating profusely now. "What the hell are you trying to do? Send me to the poorhouse?"

Shelley cuddled closer. "Oh, just wait till you see them," she cooed, her fingers concentrating on the zipper of his pants.

Witherspoon's comeback died a natural death in the back of his throat as her fingers found their mark and began their enticing arousal...

"Oh, yes, yes," he whispered, his own trembling fingers clawing at the buttons on her dress. In a moment her breasts had spilled into his groping hand.

It was all he could do to lean forward and tap on the glass. "Adam, turn around. We're going to Ms. Storm's apartment."

Hours later, back in his own condominium, he was climbing out of the shower and knotting a towel around him as the doorbell rang.

Letting go with a colorful oath, he stomped to the door and jerked it open. For a moment, he stared at the figure on the steps.

"Dammit, Dillard," he said through clenched teeth, "I was expecting to hear from you, but not at my house and *not* at this ungodly hour of the morning. It'd better be important," he added, moving aside for him to enter.

"I'm sorry, Mayor, but I thought you'd want this. It's late already." He held out a small, nondescript satchel.

"Thanks, Dillard," Witherspoon said, immediately unzipping the bag. He dipped his hands inside and came up with a fistful of hundred-dollar bills.

"There'll be more next month."

The mayor squinted up at him. "Good, I'll be expecting it."

"Well, I guess I'll be off then," Dillard said, shuffling his feet, suddenly feeling uncomfortable under the mayor's watchful eye. "How's it going?"

"So far so good."

"Anything else?"

Witherspoon tossed the bag onto the nearest chair. "Yes. Don't come here anymore."

Dillard gulped. "Yes, sir." He turned and started toward the door.

"And by the way, Dillard, I don't want anything else to go wrong. In plain English that means no more screwups. Do you get my drift?"

When Daniel shifted his car into park in front of the Langley mansion, McKenzie was almost asleep. The interior was warm, and the easy-listening music coming from the stereo was lulling; but even at that she was surprised she could relax.

She was still recovering from the shock of finding Jeb, along with the rest of the awed spectators, watching her and Daniel dance. She had looked on as his expression grew blacker by the second and his eyes dripped ice, and she had wanted the floor to open up and swallow her.

From that moment on, she had been wound as tight as a guitar string. Finally, Daniel had given up trying to please her, suggesting they call it an evening and head for home.

Now as she sat up straight, struggling to get her bearings, she felt hot tears press against her eyelids. She fought them back, though she longed to cry until her heart was content.

"McKenzie, are you awake?"

She twisted around as Daniel slid across the leather seat, stopping within touching distance of her. The moonlight, peeping though the glass, was a welcome intruder, McKenzie thought, as she heard the seductive undertone in his voice and saw the look in his narrowed eyes.

"Invite me in," he whispered, before she could utter a word. Then he leaned closer and placed his mouth against hers. She flinched inwardly, totally unable to answer the moist softness of his lips. It was as though her emotions were locked in an airtight bag, crippling her, making it impossible for her to feel, to respond.

After a moment Daniel pulled away, his mouth drawn in a taut line. "How much longer are you going to keep shutting me out? We're engaged to be married, for Pete's sake!"

The muted darkness hid her flush. "Daniel...not now."

A disgusted sigh filled the close confines of the car as he scooted back to his side. "All right, McKenzie, I'll let you off the hook...again. But beware, my patience is wearing damned thin."

"It's...it's been a tough week with Carson and my...and with Jeb—"

"I know, I know," Daniel cut in impatiently, "but I can't help how I feel." He paused. "Sometimes I wonder why you consented to marry me."

So do I. Then feeling a pang of guilt, McKenzie hurried to change the subject. "Thanks for taking me to the ball. I'll see you tomorrow."

After walking her to the door and pecking her on the cheek, Daniel was gone.

The house was quiet, eerily quiet. But then it was late, McKenzie reminded herself. She guessed Rosie had long ago gone to her room. Deciding she was too uptight to go straight to bed, she meandered down the hall into the den.

It was only moments after she had flung her purse and jacket down on the couch that it dawned on her there was a fire smoldering in the fireplace.

The heat and light from the sizzling logs made the large room warm and comfortable. And as if to prove it, Jeb was sprawled in a chair with his eyes closed, a bottle clutched in his hand.

McKenzie's stomach took a plunging dive as she stared down at him. She was close enough to track every detail of his face, beginning with the deep grooves around his mouth, the faint black shadow that darkened his jaw, and the long, thick eyelashes. His tawny hair was wild and tousled, as though he'd been threading his fingers through it.

He looked exhausted—and drunk.

Suddenly her body felt hollow, as if all the blood had drained from it, and her mind went ice-cold. Oh, God, she couldn't keep on going like this, letting him interrupt her life and tear at her future, leaving her nothing but pieces of dreams.

Clutching at straws to calm herself, she forced herself to look around the room. Evidence of his presence was everywhere. His coat was slung carelessly on the arm of a chair, while an ashtray at his elbow spilled over with ashes. A pack of cigarettes and a dirty glass sat next to the ashtray.

She looked down at him again, taking a step closer. His tie was askew, and he had folded back his cuffs. His shirt was partially unbuttoned, too, revealing the forest of brown fur on his chest. He looked absurdly young, and she had to squelch the compelling desire to touch him, to make him aware of her.

She knew that would be a fatal move. It would be like playing with a stick of dynamite, knowing it could blow up in her face at any moment. No, the best course of action for her was to go upstairs to her room and lock the door.

But by then it was too late.

As though sensing her presence, Jeb's eyes flew open, and before she could react, he stood up with surprising agility and was towering over her.

"So the princess has finally come home," he sneered.

McKenzie stiffened as the warm whiskey scent of his breath washed over her. "You're drunk, Jeb," she whispered, stepping back.

He matched her step for step. "I wished to hell I was drunk," he said violently.

"Back off, Jeb," she demanded, edging slowly toward the door, her legs weakening beneath her. "I don't intend for this to be a replay of the other night."

"I don't think you're in much of a position to be issuing orders, do you? Anyway, I'm not like your wimpy fiancé; I don't take orders."

"Jeb...don't," she pleaded, quickening her backward tread, quelling the desire to turn and run, knowing the effort would be futile.

His eyes never faltered, nor did his steps. "Naughty, naughty," he taunted. "You mean you don't want to stay and tell big brother all about your evening?"

McKenzie caught her breath as her shoulder brushed the paneled wall. She went limp, using it to brace her trembling body.

"What...what did you say?" she stammered, her eyes widening in shock.

"Ah, so now you want to play the innocent," he said nastily. "Surely you haven't forgotten how we used to tell each other everything."

There was an ugly underside to his tone, and for the first time she felt a twinge of fear. "You're insane!"

"That's right," he confessed, his upper lip curling. "I'm insane thinking about you with Evans."

McKenzie moved her head from side to side. "Please..." she cried, but there was no escape. His hands were plastered flat against the wall on either side of her, his strong arms holding her prisoner, making flight impossible.

Then suddenly a finger snaked out and made a hot trail down the side of her face, to her neck, and then to the exposed portion of her rounded breast. There he paused, his breath coming in ragged gasps.

"Does he touch you like this?" he rasped. Oh, God, just the thought of Evans with her, his hands cupping her breasts, his tongue—

"Damn you, Jeb," she whispered, making an effort to free herself, her hands pushing against his chest.

"No, my princess, you're not going anywhere," he said softly. "Not until you've answered big brother's question, that is." His face was granite-hard and again she felt a spurt of fear.

"Oh, God, why are you doing this to me? I..." The lump in her throat kept her from going any further.

"Because I have to." His words were choked. "I have to know."

Jeb let his hand drop from her breast. He took her hand and turned her palm into his lips, so that she trembled in his grasp. His eyes were half-closed now and drowsy, but she was sure he knew exactly what he was doing.

"Jeb," she protested, trying to break away again, knowing that if she didn't it would soon be too late. She had never been able to resist him, and now, with his hot breath sizzling her skin, she was feeling the treachery of her own body.

But he stilled her movement, sliding his hand possessively over her. Another whimper tore from her and her head fell back against the wall, like a flower on a broken stalk.

Sensing her acquiescence, Jeb placed his mouth where his finger had worked its magic, on her throat. He kissed the side of her neck, then her shoulder, his tongue painting a tiny circle there.

Then, bringing his mouth up to hers, he let his tongue paint circles over her lips. The action made her hungry, blinding her for a moment. Her eyes locked shut at the weight of his head on her breast, his cheek feeling scratchy. His mouth painted more circles around her distended nipples, thrusting against the fabric of her dress.

"No!" she cried. Her insides were shaking and her breath was catching in her chest, coming hard. She felt a fine sweat breaking out, a loss of strength in her legs, a pressure in her chest, a giddiness that meant her brain wasn't getting enough oxygen. It wasn't fair. Oh, God, it just wasn't fair.

"I want you," he groaned thickly, burying his face into her hair. "I can't help it. You're driving me crazy, do you know that?"

No! Don't let him lure you down this forbidden path. But McKenzie paid no heed to the cry of her conscience. He had the ability to make her forget herself, forget everything but him. It was only when she was away from him that she regained her objectivity. In his presence, all her promises to herself seemed to evaporate into the air like so much smoke.

"McKenzie, sweet, sweet, McKenzie," he murmured, their faces close. Totally lost now, McKenzie stared at him, devouring him, tears drenching her lashes.

Slowly, as though moving in a dream, she stood up on her toes and clamped a hand onto his shoulder for balance. McKenzie's defenses had crumbled; she had to feel his mouth against hers or die.

His lips melted into hers, drawing on her sweetness, and she heard herself make small, involuntary sounds she couldn't control.

"Oh, God...I can't take much more," he groaned, closing his eyes and resting his cheek against her temple. "Let me love you. Now. Here."

The weight of his muscled body against hers was a potent seducement, and she ached to give in to his pleadings. She wanted to let him do what he liked with her and to hell with the consequences.

But the past suddenly reared its ugly head and with it came the guilt, the deceit and the pain she had suffered at his hand. The moment was shattered.

"I can't," she wailed, taking advantage of his weakness and breaking his hold, flinging herself out of his arms.

Jeb did not, could not, move a muscle. He merely watched her as she straightened her dress and pushed her tangled curls aside.

But his dark expression spoke volumes. "What's wrong?" he demanded sharply. "Afraid you'll compare Evans to me and he'll come up lacking?"

McKenzie grabbed her stomach. Her face turned the color of chalk. "Why...why, you bastard! Just go away and leave me alone!"

"Goddammit, I can't." His face was savage. "I wish to hell I could."

Sobs tore loose from her throat.

Jeb looked at her for a long, aching moment, then hammered on, unwilling to let her go. "What are you trying to do to me...to us?"

"To *you*?" McKenzie's breasts rose and fell beneath the soft material of her gown.

"Yes, to me." He pushed his hand through his hair. "McKenzie, don't you know that the thought of you with another man—" He broke off.

Oh, God, she thought desperately, what was she going to do? "Jeb, we...we can never go back." Her voice was faint, far away.

"I don't believe that and neither do you."

"Believe it, Jeb. It's true." Her voice shook. "The price is just too high and I'm not willing to pay it. Not anymore."

Before he could reply, she turned and walked to the door. Pausing, she turned around just in time to see him sag against the wall and close his eyes. Then she left the room and went up the stairs without looking back.

Jeb stood there, feeling as if she'd left the imprint of her physical body on his. There were empty spots now where her warmth had been. The skin of his hands and throat felt faintly singed.

Finally managing to drag his abused body up and into his room, he sought relief in push-ups and a cold shower.

With a disgusted groan, McKenzie kicked the covers off her, sat up and looked at the clock. Another groan split the air when she saw that it was eight-thirty. She had overslept. But she was not surprised, after having spent a restless night trying to suppress the erotic yearnings that Jeb's touch had triggered within her.

It took her longer to dress than usual, and it was close to impossible to cover the dark circles under her eyes and the blotches on her face. She had cried until she could cry no more and now felt as limp as wilted celery. It was a struggle just to put on her salmon-colored wool gabardine suit and sweep her hair away from her face.

She was to meet Rachel at the hospital for a consultation with the doctors about her stepfather, and she was late. She snatched up her purse and briefcase and stepped into the hall, silently thankful that Jeb's door was closed, but the sound of the phone stalled her.

She dashed back into her room and picked it up. "Hello," she said.

"McKenzie, it's John. John Riley."

"Good morning," she said, relieved it wasn't the hospital.

He returned her greeting absently and then said, "Look, I had an appointment for us to visit Mrs. Thurman, but something more pressing has turned up. You think you could talk to her alone?"

McKenzie didn't hesitate, desperately needing something constructive to do today. "I don't see why not," she replied. "It'll have to be later, though. I have to meet with the doctors this morning."

He didn't bother to disguise the concern in his voice. "Oh, is Carson worse?"

"No. No," McKenzie quickly assured him. "The doctor just wants to bring us up to date."

"Good. Well, I'll call Mrs. Thurman and tell her to expect you sometime this afternoon."

"Thanks, John," she said, after he had given her the address. She put the receiver down and walked out of the room.

The remainder of the morning and the early part of the afternoon flew by. McKenzie arrived at the hospital to find Rachel waiting for her, but no Jeb. Relief coursed through her, even though she knew he had purposely stayed away because of her.

Carson, she was told, had suffered several light strokes since the crippling one that had sent him to the hospital two weeks ago. Yet, the team of doctors administering to him gave her and Rachel encouragement, stressing that he would eventually begin to show improvement.

But McKenzie wasn't so sure, and her heart was heavy as she pulled into the driveway of the Thurman home late that afternoon, suddenly despising the idea of questioning the woman about her husband's death. Her feet dragged as she got out of the car.

As McKenzie slowly approached the front door, a tall, bony young man slipped out of his dilapidated Volkswagen and crossed the street to a phone booth. With grimy hands, he dropped a coin into the slot.

"Mr. Rollins?"

"Yeah. Who is this?"

"It's Tim Blake. Don't you remember? You told me to watch the Thurman place."

"Anything to report?"

"A visitor has just showed up, some lady." He snickered. "Could be one of them reporters; she had a notebook."

"When she comes out, follow her and see where she goes and then report back to me."

Rollins sat back in his chair, a grim expression on his face. He'd have to call Dillard, and he wouldn't like this one bit.

Discontent hounded McKenzie well into the evening. She sat on the den floor in front of the fireplace, carefully reading through the page of notes she had taken during her conversation with Mrs. Thurman.

Now that the visit was behind her, she wished more than ever she hadn't gone. Louise Thurman had been much too distraught to talk to her, much less tell her anything of importance. To her knowledge, her husband had no enemies. He minded his own business and got along well with his bosses and fellow workers. In her mind, her husband's death was an accident, and McKenzie had not let on that she didn't believe that for a minute.

The only concrete information she had learned was the name of the man who had worked closely with her husband on the job. She had stored his name away for future use, feeling certain she would have to pay him a visit.

The house was again quiet and lonely. She hated it. She missed her stepfather more and more with each passing day. McKenzie tossed aside her notepad and reached for the cup of coffee by her side. She took a sip, only to make a face. Nothing worse than cold coffee.

Daniel had insisted on taking her out to dinner when she had dropped back by the office. She had consented, though only halfheartedly. They hadn't tarried long, thank goodness. Daniel had sensed her distraction, attributing it to her being tired. Which was partly true. Talking to Mrs. Thurman had drained her, and for all the good her visit had done, she might as well have stayed home.

She would just have to keep digging.

Sighing, McKenzie lowered her head to her knees, fighting off her mounting frustration. Was she so anxious to have a story for her stepfather that she was getting carried away?

No. That was not the problem and she knew it. Jeb continued to be the source of her discontent. Thoughts of him festered within her, threatening to erupt at any moment.

God help her. Even now she was weak and trembling on the inside, wondering where he was and who he was with. The thought of him touching another woman as he'd touched her conjured up untold agonies.

But it hadn't always been like this between her and Jeb. Far from it. There was a time—it seemed so long ago now—when she could think of Jeb with tenderness instead of mistrust, with excitement instead of regret, with passion instead of pain, but most of all with love instead of hate.

One of those unforgettable times of pure happiness was when Jeb first made love to her. The memory of that day burned brightly in her heart and her mind....

He had awakened her to womanhood exactly one month before her stepfather kicked him out of the house. They had been together all day at Jeb's house in the Hill Country. The house had been left to him by his mother, the only thing of hers he'd kept.

It was a honey of a house, with two bedrooms, bath, and three acres of land surrounding it.

The gorgeous summer day had been filled with magic, and they had spent most of the day fishing in the pond at the back of the house. And to Jeb's chagrin, she had caught three fish to his one.

"That's going to cost you," he drawled, a fierce twinkle in his eyes.

"I'm not worried," she quipped saucily, and darted ahead of him.

From behind, he reached out and flipped a ringlet of loos hair. "You're getting too big for your britches now tha you've turned seventeen."

She threw him a sidelong glance. "I've been big for a lon time." Her voice was not quite steady. "But you've neve noticed."

He returned her glance. His eyes narrowed, unreadabl against the sunlight. "Oh, I've noticed, all right," he sai huskily. "I've noticed."

For a breathless moment the air around them crackle with electricity as their eyes held. And held.

Suddenly, unable to cope with the giddy sensation dee within her, McKenzie said in a shrill voice, "Last one to th shower has to . . . to grill the steaks."

Then before Jeb could react, she took off running, he coltish legs flying through the grass, her laughter misting th air.

Her laughter was short-lived, as Jeb came striding up be side her, not even winded, sporting a wicked grin on hi face.

"That's not fair," she stormed a few minutes later, fall ing in the back door, gasping for air.

Jeb was all smiles. "All's fair in love and war," he re sponded, breezing past her, heading for his bedroom. "Oh by the way, I like my steak medium rare."

McKenzie was still pouting later when she stepped out o the shower and draped a towel sarong-fashion around he breasts, thankful to be rid of the fishy smell on her body.

She padded into the bedroom and closed the door be hind her. Drying her hair, she began to cross to the mirror only to freeze suddenly in her tracks when the door wa thrust open.

Jeb stood in the doorway as though he were made o stone, his mouth gaping open, his Adam's apple workin overtime.

McKenzie wet her lips. "I...I just got out of the shower," he whispered inanely.

"Jesus! I'm sorry." His voice was thick, and his eyes widened as they took in the sight of her scantily clad body. "I...thought you'd be dressed by now." He was clinging to the doorknob as though his life depended on it. She could see his knuckles turning whiter by the second.

Her mouth felt full of cotton as she returned his stare, taking in his bare chest, the ragged cutoff jeans that in no way could disguise his arousal.

In spite of herself, McKenzie's eyes dipped to that unknown part of his body. And remained.

"God, McKenzie." His voice was agonized and it stirred her as nothing else could. It was then that she realized the danger.

"Please...Jeb..." she whispered huskily, "you'd better go..."

He made no reply, but moved toward her, his eyes burning into hers as his finger curved out and flicked aside her towel. "McKenzie...." He waited an interminable length of time, staring at her, and then leaned slowly toward her, whispering the words, "You're breathtaking, more beautiful than I ever imagined. Oh, God, I want to touch all of you.... Your breasts...oh, God, they're so perfect, so sweet."

"No, Jeb," she said, suddenly frightened, aware that he had shed his pants and was naked, too.

"Baby, baby," he murmured. "Don't be frightened. I won't hurt you. I want to feel you against me, all of you.... And I want you to feel me...."

His words burnt on her skin, her mind, her nerves, sending a wild surge of sweet longing through her. Her heart escalated to a pagan pitch, matching the violence of her physical desire as it pounded in her head.

McKenzie was not conscious of having moved. It was as though she had arrived in his arms without having to do a thing. She was not aware of anything except the warmth of Jeb's throat next to her cheek, the scrape of his chin against her temple, his arms holding her painfully tight, and his fingers moving gently, incredibly gently, stroking the nape of her neck.

He raised his head, breathing heavily, and she saw his eyes. The shock of what she saw in them made her clutch at him as if afraid she would fall.

She forced herself to speak, her throat moving convulsively, the words emerging gravelly and barely audible. "You . . . you shouldn't be here."

The dark mask of his face tautened, and he closed his eyes briefly. "I know," he muttered hoarsely, "but please don't send me away. . . . Not now."

"Oh, Jeb," she whispered urgently, the boundaries melting. There was nothing to separate their bodies, not clothes, not even skin; they shared the same pulse and breathed the same breath.

"God knows I never meant to go this far," he groaned against her lips. "But from the very moment I realized you were no longer a child, I believed in the impossible."

"I know, I know," McKenzie said brokenly, lifting her face to his, the waning twilight highlighting her delicate beauty, showing him the warmth of her blue eyes, her vulnerable mouth. Her hair hung in damp, coiled strands around her shoulders, framing the fragile beauty of her youth.

"Oh, McKenzie, I love you," he said with a force that shook her.

Then his mouth came down, parting her lips, hungrily demanding a response, his hands crushing her against his body.

From that moment on, McKenzie was lost. There was not one part of her body that was left untouched by Jeb's tender hands and seeking mouth. He handled her as though afraid her flesh might tear, and by the time he moved into her, the pleasure far outweighed the pain.

Later, as Jeb still lay buried deep inside her with his head on her breast and his declaration of love fresh on her heart, she fell into an exhausted sleep, thinking she had never been happier and her future more promising.

But fate had called it otherwise. One month later, Jeb had walked out of her life and that had been the end.

The same old story. No survivors.

Suddenly, with a painful cry, McKenzie struggled up from the floor. With grim determination, she reached for the poker on the hearth and punched at the logs. Recalling that evening eight years ago hadn't accomplished a thing. It only made her long for something she could no longer have.

With a dejected hunch to her shoulders, she crossed to the window and looked out. The sky was dotted with stars; the moon, glowing gold, was guarding the earth.

But tonight nothing seemed real. It had all been distorted by her memories of Jeb and what might have been.

Chapter 6

Jeb stared at the top of his cluttered desk with disinterest. He had more work to do than he could possibly get done, yet he was in no mood to do it, especially at midnight on a cold, rainy night.

A couple of long strides carried him to the small bar in the corner of the room where he poured himself a cup of freshly brewed coffee. While sipping the soothing liquid, he peered through the window at the twinkling lights of the Austin skyline. He could see the fine mist of rain as it blanketed the buildings before saturating the concrete. The dismal weather exactly matched his feelings.

Yet, he was pleased with what he had accomplished in the short time he had been occupying his father's chair. The lessons Carson had so often tried to pound into his thick skull since he was knee high had come in handy many times during the last few weeks.

He could still recall his father's exact words: "Boy, it doesn't take a damned genius to run a newspaper; it only takes a person who has enough sense to ask what, when, where, and why and to be able to point out the soft spots in the news and suggest ways to fix them.''

Miraculously, those words had managed to lodge inside his brain and had helped him more than once during his career. This week had been no exception.

He'd been behind closed doors with the staff on and off all week—more on than off. The editors had presented their long-range plans for their departments, and he had spent the majority of his time listening and then saying, ''That sounds good, but what about this idea, and have you thought of this one instead?''

What was more astonishing was that he had accomplished this in spite of McKenzie's unsettling presence. She had attended two of the editorial sessions, each time acknowledging him with icy politeness. As far as home went— well, she'd done her damnedest to avoid him there, too.

She worked too hard, he thought, and slept too little. He knew he was responsible for the dark circles under her eyes and the tight expression on her face. Guilt, like a layer of dirt, suddenly adhered to his skin.

To make matters worse, he was worried that McKenzie was spending too much time on the mall project. In the last meeting, she'd reported the results of her visit with the deceased construction worker's wife. Because she'd had nothing of importance to tell them, he'd put out a few feelers on his own, calling in favors from days past. To date, he'd also come up empty-handed.

If there was a scandal involved with the project and the worker's death was no accident, the lid was being kept on tightly. Logic pointed out—he'd thought so all along—that McKenzie was making a mountain out of a molehill, that because of his father, she was looking for something where there was nothing. And this was one time he hoped he was right. If not, her life could be in danger.

Damn Carson for making her his hatchet man!

With a sudden sound of disgust, directed at himself, he slammed the coffee cup down on the bar and strode angrily back to the desk.

But there was no rest for the weary. Thoughts, like demons, continued to plague his tired mind. When at long last he'd decided to return to the States, he'd had no intention of becoming involved with McKenzie.

In his mind, their relationship was over. Finished. Buried in the ashes of the past.

Likewise, he'd had no intention of having anything to do with the *Tribune*. Foolishly, he had become involved with both. But now he knew why his father hadn't been worried about his taking over the paper. After all, McKenzie was marrying the man of Carson's choice—not hers, he'd bet his life on that. So there was no reason to think that he, himself, presented a problem. McKenzie's future was tied in a nice little package and no one, certainly not the prodigal son, could untie it.

As a result, Carson was free to appease his conscience and make peace with his son. Peace. Sure thing. He should have known there was a catch. Yet there was no way he was about to sit back and let Evans have her.

McKenzie had always been—and still was—his obsession.

During the next few days, McKenzie was successful in staying out of Jeb's way both at the office and at home. When she wasn't at the hospital, she kept her nose to the grindstone, trying to come up with something concrete on Cedar Plaza. She could not let it rest; it was as though, by pushing herself relentlessly, she could force something incriminating to surface.

And it was finally paying off.

At this moment, she was hard-pressed to contain her excitement. She had finally gotten the break she'd been waiting for, and it couldn't have come at a better time. She had about decided that she would have to give up her investigation because of lack of evidence; she had virtually reached a dead end.

But this morning when she'd walked into her office, the phone was ringing. It was Hal Melrose, the man Mrs. Thurman had spoken to her about; he had worked with her husband. Melrose had asked to meet her at an out-of-the-way restaurant.

Now, as McKenzie rushed inside the restaurant—really nothing more than a hamburger joint—she spotted a man she was certain was her contact and began weaving her way past the checked tables.

Just as she reached his table, the man stood up and held out his hand. "I'm Hal Melrose and you must be Ms. Moore."

McKenzie took his hand while studying him. He was short but muscular, almost to the point of appearing overweight. He had close-cropped black hair and wore glasses.

"It's a pleasure to meet you, Mr. Melrose," McKenzie said, sitting down in the chair across from him.

A silence followed as a waitress sidled up to their table and waited for their order.

"I'll have a cheeseburger all the way and coffee. How 'bout you, Ms. Moore?"

McKenzie shook her head. "Nothing for me, thanks."

Once they were alone, Melrose's eyes shifted uneasily. "I'm real glad you came. Louise Thurman said you were a nice lady."

McKenzie smiled her thanks, then said, "I wouldn't have missed coming for anything. I'm most eager to hear what you have to say."

Melrose leaned forward, placing his flannel-sleeved elbows on the table. "You won't tell nobody else about this, will ya?"

McKenzie didn't hesitate. "Not if you don't want me to."

"Well, I don't," he said hastily.

"Tell me, Mr. Melrose, exactly what do you do for Dillard Construction?"

"I'm a foreman," he announced proudly. "Worked my way up from the bottom."

"Then you're in a position to see invoices on materials and check deliveries."

"You got it, lady," he said bluntly, though not disrespectfully. "In fact, I checked in material yesterday that was missing this morning."

McKenzie's eyes widened. "You're sure it wasn't used, in the construction?"

"Huh! There's no way that much material could be used that quick. No ma'am, someone's got a moonlight supply company going and is making a mighty good profit on the side."

McKenzie refrained from commenting while the waitress set the coffee and cheeseburger down in front of Melrose. The silence stretched as he took a bite and chased it down with coffee.

"Anything else?" McKenzie pressed at last.

"You betcha. Not only are the materials being stolen right off the yard, but we're getting inferior materials as well. For instance, last week they delivered some concrete and the damn stuff was plumb bad. It'd never meet specifications in a million years. Why, it wouldn't support my wife—and she's a skinny thing like you—much less any type of structure."

McKenzie managed to stay cool in spite of her rising excitement. "Who do you think is behind all this?"

He shrugged. "It's got to be Dillard and his sidekick, Chet Rollins."

"What about your friend's death?" She hated to ask but she had to.

Melrose's eyes lowered. "It wasn't no accident. I'm here to tell you that that cable on the elevator lift was wore out and Dillard knew it, too. It still had a red tag on it from the last state inspection, and whoever loaded it knew it couldn't pull the load. What I can't figure out is why Thurman ever got on it." He shook his head. "When it fell, it crushed every bone in his body."

McKenzie flinched at his vivid description. "I'm sorry," she said inadequately.

He pursed his lips. "Me, too. Only thing I can figure is that Elmer saw something, or heard something, and they done away with him."

"If you felt so strongly about this, why didn't you go to the police?"

His eyes darted away, then back. "You know why—don't have no proof. But that don't keep me from being scared, real scared."

McKenzie stood up. "Well, we'll just have to see what we can do about getting that proof, Mr. Melrose. Where can I get in touch with you?"

"When I have something else to report, I'll call you," he said quickly, shoving back his chair and getting to his feet.

McKenzie extended her hand, shocked to find it was trembling. "Thank you, Mr. Melrose. And don't worry, I won't let you down."

McKenzie exited the restaurant with a heavy heart. Melrose was frightened, but for that matter so was she.

By the time McKenzie turned the ignition off and stepped out of the car in front of the Langley mansion, she had worked herself into a frenzy. The more she thought about what she had learned from Hal Melrose, the more frightened she became. But she knew she couldn't back off now. She was committed; she had given her word. And she wanted to see justice done for the people of Austin and the state. They deserved to know what was being done with their money.

Burying the feeling of unease, refusing to let it fuel her rapidly growing depression, McKenzie let herself into the house. Suddenly every nerve in her body became alert.

Cigarette smoke wafted up to her nose. Jeb's brand. Jeb was home.

Rather than the anger and resentment she feared was imminent, a giddy weakness washed over her. Then, just as suddenly, she jerked herself under control. She couldn't afford to lower her defenses now, not when she was lonely, desperately lonely, feeling as though she'd been tossed out to sea to battle the waves all by herself.

"McKenzie, is that you?" Jeb questioned, sauntering out of the den, a can of beer in his hand.

Her heart did a flip-flop as she took in his unexpected appearance. Even though his green eyes were sunk far back into his head and his mouth had a tired slant to it, he still looked better to her than any man on the face of this earth. Damn him! she thought dejectedly.

The gold turtlenecked sweater he wore was a perfect foil for his hair and eyes, and the tight-fitting jeans adhered to his muscled flanks like a second skin.

He looked big, utterly male, and almost too attractive to be real.

In her present state, the warmth and nearness of his body was almost her undoing. She blinked and prayed for a stop to the pressure building inside her.

Jeb ran a hand through his unruly hair as their eyes met and held. The tender concern she saw there, quite against her wishes, began to melt the inner fear and numbness.

Neither said a word; the moment was suddenly too charged for that.

Jeb was the reality that she had always clung to, always believed in. But that was the past. Now here he was in the flesh, and she had to stifle the crazy notion to fling herself into his arms and beg him to hold her, to promise her that everything was going to be all right.

"I've been waiting for you," he said softly, honestly, and his voice was filled with concern.

McKenzie's hand clutched her purse, trembling, reflecting the twist her insides had taken. Her eyes misted. She turned her back, fearing the rush of emotion and the dangerous path her thoughts had taken. She swished past him and headed for the fireplace, keeping her back to him.

He followed her. She heard the surprisingly gentle tread of his feet, the whisper of denim as he walked to the bar. Turning slightly, she watched as he set his can of beer down and reached for a glass, then filled it half full of white wine.

"This will make you feel better," he said simply.

Still she couldn't speak. It was as though her throat had a lock on it. Damn! She was behaving as if she didn't have good sense. Nodding her thanks, she took the glass from him and twisted back around to the fire, concentrating on the multicolored flames shooting up the chimney. Then lowering her eyes, she sipped her wine.

At length, she turned around to see Jeb leaning against the bar, watching her.

"Bad day, huh?" he said tentatively, afraid she would spook like a frightened doe and bolt from the room.

McKenzie tried to smile. "You could say that," she said lightly.

He didn't push, grateful just to be close to her. "Don't take this wrong—" the corners of his mouth twitched as he ambled toward her "—but you look as if you've been run over by a train."

This time she did smile, and he caught his breath at the stab of desire that shot through him at such an innocent gesture. He even tried to avert his gaze so she couldn't read his eyes—she'd always been a pro at that—but the temptation proved too much. His eyes surrendered, savoring the riot of honeyed curls that kissed her face, the slimness of her hips and waist, and the gentle swell of her breasts beneath the cashmere sweater.

"How can I be offended," she began a trifle huskily, "when I know you're right?"

A loaded silence fell between them.

"Have you eaten?" he inquired lazily when his eyes at last worked their way back up to her face.

Suddenly piqued by the hot surge of desire his appraisal had touched off in her, she averted his gaze while trying to stamp out the smell of him, made up of tobacco and man. It was an intoxicating combination.

"No . . . why?" she asked after a moment.

"Well, it's Rosie's night off, but I could heat up that pot of chili she left in the fridge and mix a salad. We'd have a meal that even Steak n' Ale couldn't rival."

He meant it to be a joke, of course, trying to lighten the mood, but somehow she couldn't bring herself to smile. Suddenly the implication of what he was suggesting made her mouth go bone dry. They were alone. . . .

McKenzie thought quickly. "I'm . . . not hungry." She knew her excuse was lame, but under the circumstances it was the best she could do.

"Oh, come on now," he chided with little-boy eagerness. "I've never known you to pass up Rosie's chili."

"Jeb . . ." She couldn't care less about food. Instead she had the urge to escape once again to the security of her room. Then she quickly ridiculed herself: *Chicken!*

He took a step closer, then stopped. His eyes were narrowed, dark and sensual. "You have to eat, don't you?"

"I . . . I suppose so," she stammered, wondering if that wheezing sound had come from her throat.

He cocked his head sideways. "If I promise to be on my best behavior, will that convince you?"

She looked up and met his gaze head on. Although his eyes were disturbingly intent and his voice on the hoarse side, there was something different about him. He seemed tense, uncertain, vulnerable. Yes, vulnerable. That was it. Could she trust him? No. Never again. But she could trust herself. Couldn't she?

Suddenly a twinkling, endearing glint appeared in his eyes. "Well, shall I whip out the old apron?"

"Oh, all right," she said, though not very graciously, trying to appear indifferent to the effective, but elusive scent of him, as it pounded her senses, adding to her light-headedness.

She heard him breathe; it was almost as though he'd been holding his breath.

"Good," he replied, reaching for her glass, though careful not to touch her. "Now, why don't you hop upstairs and slip into jeans—" he grinned "—or whatever you women do to get comfortable, and I'll slap the chili on the stove."

McKenzie gave him an odd look before taking a tentative step toward the door. She was right. He was behaving totally unlike the Jeb she had come to know these past weeks. Gone was the hard edge to his voice, his eyes, his manner in general. But why the sudden change in tactics? What did he hope to gain by it? For her own peace of mind, she'd just as soon things remain as they were.

Sensing her hesitation, Jeb prodded softly, "Go on."

Snapped out of her preoccupation, she nodded, and then made her way out of the room and scooted up the stairs.

Once in her room, McKenzie leaned heavily against the door and forced herself to take long, deep breaths. Was she out of her mind agreeing to spend an evening alone with him? When her heartbeat had subsided somewhat, she tore across the room, shedding her clothes as she went. Stripped down to her bra and panties, she jerked an ivory velour jumpsuit off the hanger and stepped into it.

Cool it, McKenzie! she berated herself. *Don't make something out of nothing.* After all, what could be the harm in having a simple dinner with him and then coming back to her room to bed? Just let it happen. It was what she needed; to slow down and let someone else take her over for a while. She shouldn't be forcing anything.

After running her fingers through her hair, giving it a semblance of order, she dashed down the stairs, the mouth-watering aroma of chili assailing her nostrils.

"Mmmm, that smells heavenly," she said, coming to an abrupt halt inside the kitchen door. Jeb was standing in front of the stove wielding a large spoon, a chef's apron tied around his waist.

He grinned sheepishly, reminding her of the Jeb of old, when he used to be her best friend, before... She shook her head, her hands suddenly becoming clammy.

The grin still intact, he quipped, "Well, what do you think?"

"About what?" she asked innocently.

He gave a mock sigh of exasperation. "My outfit, what else?"

A smile toyed with her lips, finally winning out. "Oh, it'll do in a pinch, I guess." God, what a ridiculous conversation they were having.

"Hey, what are you waiting for?" His eyes were soft as they took in the picture she made standing there. She was lovely, he thought irreverently. "Come on in and have a seat," he added.

"Do you want me to make a salad?" she asked, trying hard not to notice the lean, tensile grace of his hands as they stirred the food.

Their eyes met unintentionally. They stared at each other for a long aching moment as though they were the only real and separate beings in the world.

Drawing a ragged breath, Jeb was the first to look away. "Every... everything's all done," he said at last, pointing to the bowl on the cabinet, filled with lettuce and tomatoes. "And to whet your appetite even more, we have Rosie's strawberry cheesecake tucked away in the fridge."

McKenzie shook her head. "Beats me how you could always twist Rosie around your little finger."

He grinned at her easily, causing her heart to leap. When he smiled like that... "What can I say?"

She felt herself relax, answering his smile. "Well, when you get through patting yourself on the back, I'd like to eat."

"Ah, you do have a point," he said, his eyes twinkling, glad the pinched, worried look had slipped from her face.

Moving quickly, he whipped out a chair at the table for two in the breakfast nook, already set with place mats, dishes and crystal wine glasses.

McKenzie shot him an incredulous look. "Since when did you become so domestic?" she asked, then sat down in the chair he was holding for her.

"Hey, you'd be surprised at what I can do," he said, chuckling.

She squirmed in her chair as she felt the rush of his warm breath tickle the nape of her neck.

"Of course, I never get the chance," he went on. "You know Rosie would clobber me if I intruded on her domain."

She laughed, the musical sound intoxicating the air.

He caught his breath and had to force himself to concentrate on what she was saying. "Unfortunately, the same goes for me. But every once in a while, I'll sneak in here and throw together a cake or something sweet." She paused and took a sip of wine. "Sweets are still my weakness."

"I find that hard to believe," he said softly. "You're too thin."

They looked at each other for another long, shattering moment before both jerked away awkwardly.

"Here, try this," he said at length, setting a steaming bowl of chili in front of her.

She closed her eyes slowly and sniffed the tantalizing aroma. "Mmmm, it's been a long time since I've been blessed with Rosie's specialty."

"Me too," he said, pulling out a chair with his foot and sitting down in front of her, performing a balancing act with a bowl of chili in one hand and a package of crackers in the other.

There was a silence as he reached for the bottle of red wine and refilled her glass. Then lifting his, he held it out, a serious expression on his face.

"To my father and his successful recovery."

McKenzie ignored a sharp stinging sensation behind her eyes and smiled sweetly. "I'll drink to that."

They drank slowly, and he watched her over the rim of the glass. Something about him, this moment, made her think of magicians, of fairy tales, of enchanted places where lonely travelers stop for food and lodging, only to discover some hidden danger. She hid her shiver.

"And to you, lovely McKenzie," he added, clearing his throat of a sudden hoarseness.

The look in his eyes made her drink quickly, dip her eyes and concentrate on her food. Goose bumps were playing havoc with her skin as she lifted the spoon to her mouth.

Jeb, watching the conflicting emotions cross her face, cursed himself silently. *You fool! You made a promise; now keep it.* But God, it was hard, especially when he felt as though he were being powered by an unknown force as his gaze absorbed her breasts, so beautifully taunting against the clinging material.

He deliberately took a huge bite of chili, nearly scalding his throat in the process.

McKenzie, too, was fighting her own inward battle; the feeling of his eyes on her caused her nipples to spring to life, ache for his touch.

It was Jeb's muttered "Dammit that's hot!" that broke the spell. She raised startled eyes just in time to see his face turn blood-red as he reached for the glass of wine and gulped it down.

Her laughter burst like a brook released by the first thaw. "Serves you right, you know."

Then they both laughed.

After that, the conversation reverted to impersonal subjects. He entertained her with humorous stories from the many countries where he'd worked. She in turn answered questions about the *Tribune* in general.

As they talked, McKenzie was conscious of everything about him: the way the sweater hugged his broad shoulders, the strong line of his jaw as he made short work of the chili, and the way his long, sensitive fingers curled around the stem of the wine glass, reminding her vividly of the way those same fingers had found the secret delights of her body... *Dear God, McKenzie,* she warned, *don't do this to yourself. It can only lead to more pain and heartache.*

"How 'bout dessert?" he asked with a grin, after they had polished off the last of the wine.

"Oh, no, I couldn't—" she patted her stomach "—not now, anyway."

"Maybe later, then." He smiled. "But I know you'll drink some coffee."

"You're right, but why not let me fix it?"

"It's already made. You just waddle into the den and I'll follow shortly."

She had barely lowered herself onto the couch and tucked her feet under her when he came through the doorway with two cups of coffee in hand. After placing them on the glass table, he made a beeline for the hearth. There, he poked the smoldering logs until they were once again covered with leaping flames.

He sat down beside her. "Comfortable?" he asked, watching her closely.

She nodded, suddenly unable to speak, feeling the intensity of his eyes on her lips.

"Are you feeling better than you did when you came home?" he pressed gently.

"Yes, much . . . much better," she stammered, her voice annoyingly husky.

"Would you care to tell me what's bothering you?"

McKenzie became instantly alert, staring up at him, her eyes wide, unblinking, lips parted, the lazy mood completely shattered. "Why?"

Tuned in to her withdrawal, he chose his words carefully, sensing he was close to the danger zone. "I want to help," he said truthfully. "Is it Dad?"

"No."

"What is it then?"

She stood up, avoiding his eyes. "I don't need your help."

He got up and strode to the fireplace, then turned to face her. "I think you do."

"There's nothing to tell, really." She lied, hoping to stall him.

"Let me be the judge of that," he said easily, the tone of his voice smooth, unruffled.

McKenzie felt herself weakening. She wanted to tell him, to share her burden, yet by the same token she feared the repercussions.

"McKenzie."

She looked at him soberly, then reached for her coffee as though it were a lifeline. She didn't need his consent, only his support. Should she chance telling him? "If I tell you, it can go no further."

"You have my word," he said, sipping on his coffee, though his gaze never wandered from her face.

McKenzie stared down into the murky black liquid and swirled it around. "My contact is afraid his days are numbered."

Jeb spluttered into his coffee. "Dammit, McKenzie! I—"

"Don't you dare say 'I told you so.'"

Jeb grimaced. "Is it Witherspoon? Can you nail him?"

"Not yet. I've never doubted his guilt, but unfortunately my feelings won't stand up in a court of law."

Jeb scowled, his brow rutted and creased. "I don't like it."

"Well, neither do I, but if Thurman's death was no accident, and there is a cover-up, I ought to be able to make the connection fast enough."

Jeb gave a frustrated sigh. "Why the hell didn't your contact go to the police?"

"It's simple. He's scared, afraid he'll end up like his friend."

He hunched forward, slamming his empty cup down on the mantel. "Dammit, do you realize how dangerous this is?"

She tensed. "Of course I do, but as I've already told you, I'm committed."

"Bull!"

She turned her back on him.

This fueled his anger and he ranted on. "You don't even realize what you've done, do you? Well, let me tell you. You've just kicked over a rock and found a scorpion underneath. And scorpions kill."

McKenzie inhaled sharply, turning to meet the glowing coal of fury in his eyes. "Don't worry, I can handle it."

"Goddammit, no you can't!" he shouted with wild anger. "You're off this project as of right this minute. If you're so determined to see it through, then I'll do the investigating. I've already been rattling several cages, trying to turn up information."

Her cheeks were dotted with red, and her eyes were dark with suppressed fury. "You do what you please," she hissed, stifling the urge to strike him. "I don't care, but don't you dare try to stop me."

"Are you crazy!" he answered harshly. "This isn't a game; this is for real. You could end up getting hurt or maybe even killed."

"No, I won't."

"How the hell do you know?"

She refused to back down. "Well, that's just a chance I'll have to take."

The word broke from him with explosive force. "No!"

"Damn you," she seethed, "get out of my way and stay out of my life!"

Then, before McKenzie realized what was happening, Jeb had clamped his hands around her upper arms, and she knew that he was mad enough to strike her.

Instinctively, her head jerked back and she went limp, nerveless, as the pressure of his hands dug into her arms. A whimper rose from her throat as she gazed up at him, completely at his mercy.

As their eyes locked, a volatile tension rocked the room. Afterward, neither one could say when his or her boiling anger had turned into aching desire.

Emotion nearly strangled Jeb's words as he hauled her quivering body into his arms. "Oh, God," he whispered incoherently, "I'm sorry...so afraid something will happen to you...want you so much...dying on the inside."

A sob tore through her as mumbled yearnings pierced her heart. "Jeb...I..."

He stared down at her, his tormented eyes stemming her flow of words, while a deep tremor shook the length of his torso, the play of opposing forces tearing at him. He wanted to let go of the passion that drove him—for her sake—but he couldn't.

This time the whimper came from *him* as his lips bore down on hers. For a moment, McKenzie greedily returned the pressure of his lips.

His arms engulfed her. Their lips parted, their tongues explored. Jeb was possessed by a physical urgency so compelling and overpowering that it seemed to break into another realm of consciousness.

Groping for breath, he tore his lips from hers. "Oh, God, McKenzie, let me love you. I want you so..."

McKenzie was lost, lost in the touch, sight, smell of him, and it wasn't until Jeb shifted his arms and began to lift her that she froze, turning stiff as a board in his arms. "Please...no...let me go."

While struggling to draw air into his lungs and to keep his legs from buckling beneath him, Jeb ground out, "What the hell?"

McKenzie wrenched herself out of his arms, her face covered with tears, her hair in wild disarray.

"It's no good, Jeb," she cried.

"Damn you, don't play that sanctimonious game with me," he said, his eyes still laced with a mixture of passion and pain. "You want—yes, *want*—to feel me tightly embedded inside you just as much as I want to be there, only you're too hypocritical to admit it."

She was openly sobbing now. "No!" she screamed, placing her hands over her ears. "Haven't you already done enough to ruin my life?"

His eyes clung to hers for a long torturous moment, trying to understand what she meant. "Please, McKenzie," he pleaded, "tell me what I did to you that you didn't do to me. We both hurt one another, but—"

The wealth of pain burning in her eyes stopped him cold. Fear froze him as he waited for her to speak.

"After...after you went overseas, I...I lost your baby."

Chapter 7

Her words seemed to snap something inside him. His head buzzed with foreign sounds. He expected his body to explode. His mind told him to reject his thoughts, to empty itself of everything.

"And I almost died from complications," she added, her words crashing into his consciousness like clanging cymbals.

"Oh...oh, my God..." he stammered, sinking slowly onto the couch.

Her chin wobbled. "Now you know why...why I won't...can't give in to you."

"But why...?" he stammered.

"Why didn't I tell you?" she asked, completing his question. "If you'll think back to the night I came to you and practically begged you not to leave—well, I was going to tell you then, but..." She couldn't go on; the tears bubbled over her lower lids and slid down her cheeks toward her mouth.

Jeb continued to sit as though paralyzed, unable to find any spark of life inside.

Wordlessly, McKenzie dabbed at her tears with a shredded tissue.

Jeb turned his head, unable to watch. It was like seeing a gaping hole in himself, watching the blood flow freely, his life slipping away.

McKenzie could not look away from Jeb's colorless face. It was as though a magnet had drawn her eyes there and refused to let them wander, holding steadfast, forcing her to watch the pain sweep slowly across his face.

She had wanted to tell him about the baby. She had gone to him that night with the sole intention of doing just that, but she could not get the words past her lips. Even now, after all this time, she couldn't bear to think about the events that had taken place that day. She had kept them under lock and key, never to be rekindled or rehashed again.

But now, as she was held by the agony in Jeb's eyes, McKenzie could not stop her mind from backtracking to that time when the final blow had been dealt, shattering her heart into a million tiny pieces....

When Jeb had stormed out of the house after her stepfather's verbal thrashing, she thought she would never again draw a breath that was not riddled with pain.

For days, she had moped around the house, cried into the wee hours of the mornings and virtually stopped eating. Without Jeb nothing mattered anymore; she was confused and miserable, unable to stand the thought that her bright hopes and dreams had been severed so harshly, so completely.

McKenzie was inconsolable even though Carson tried every way he knew how to make her happy—except letting her have the one thing she wanted most, and that was Jeb.

Jeb's name was taboo in the house. Even Rachel was reluctant to talk about him, drilling into McKenzie the fact that she should think of Jeb only as a brother, that anything else between them was impossible.

Yet deep down, McKenzie clung to the hope that Jeb would come back, finding that he couldn't live without her. And if not, then she would go to him, to beg if necessary for his forgiveness and to tell him she loved him, would never stop loving him.

So when days passed without word from Jeb, she began making her plans, only to have them suddenly thwarted. She became ill, began having trouble with her stomach, unable to digest any kind of food. She hid the fact from her stepfather and Rachel, thinking it was nerves and exhaustion from not sleeping. But when it persisted, she sneaked off to a doctor and learned she was pregnant.

McKenzie couldn't believe it! Pregnant. With Jeb's child. The first and only time she'd made love with him and she'd gotten pregnant.

She was ecstatic and couldn't wait to tell Jeb, convinced that if anything would lure him back to her it would be that.

Keeping the secret to herself, she'd finally pinned Rachel down to Jeb's whereabouts. She learned he was staying at a friend's apartment, but only until he could get his papers processed to go overseas as a journalist.

With her heart clamoring in her chest, she went up to the door and knocked on it, praying she wasn't too late.

At his terse "It's open," McKenzie slowly twisted the knob and walked hesitantly inside. He sounded so grim—so totally furious at having been disturbed.

At first she didn't see him. She hovered uncertainly, the living room empty except for the dog, wagging his tail, lying on the floor by the fireplace. Then she saw his silhouette in the door to the bedroom.

"McKenzie?" he muttered harshly, sounding as though he couldn't believe his eyes. Then, after blinking several times, he added, "What the devil are you doing here?"

McKenzie took a step forward. "Yes, yes, it's me, Jeb," she began unevenly. "How...how are you?"

But his physical appearance gave her the answer. He looked awful—thinner than she remembered, the grooves around his mouth deeper, and his eyes sunk in deeper behind the long lashes. His tan was no longer in evidence, making him appear washed-out and weary.

Waving aside what he saw as a polite platitude, he snapped, "I asked what you were doing here? I don't remember issuing an invitation."

McKenzie stared at him helplessly. Even deep in their sockets, his eyes were sharp, and she knew he could sense her uncertainty. Taking another step forward, she said, "I...Jeb...I had to come."

"Why? Why now? What has caused this change of heart?"

McKenzie flinched against the hardness of his tone. "There's been no change of heart, Jeb. I was confused...but not anymore. I..." She paused to wet her lips. "I love you...."

His eyes became even colder. "Love," he sneered. "No, McKenzie, I think not. You don't know the meaning of that word—unless it pertains to my father."

Suddenly feeling as though she were suffocating, McKenzie cut in, "No! That's not true. I *do* love you." Her eyes were pleading in their intensity.

"Well, it's too late," he said flatly, his stance unrelenting. Ignoring her gasp, he went on bitterly. "Anyway, my father's right. I'm no damn good for you. I'm too old and, as my father is fond of saying, 'too sorry.' You..." He paused and cleared his throat. "You have your whole life ahead of you." This time he averted her gaze, his mouth drawn in a grim line. "You'll be better off with someone your own age."

"No! No! No!" she cried, her vision blurred with tears. "I don't want anyone else. I only want you."

Still not looking at her, he repeated, "It's too late. I'm leaving in a couple of hours for the Mideast."

McKenzie shook her head disbelievingly. "You...can't," she whispered. "I mean..." Words failed her, though her mind was screaming: *Tell him! Tell him about the baby.*

But the words would not come; she just stood there mute with her heart stuck in her throat.

Then Jeb was looming over her with beetled brows. "Stop feeling sorry for yourself," he spat roughly. "I have to go— it's my job, that's all. Anyway, it's none of your business."

McKenzie thrust her trembling hands in the pockets of her slacks. "And...and the things you said to me, the promises you made?" she managed to eke out with timidity.

Jeb sighed. "I think you'd better try to forget about what I said," he replied bitterly. "After all, you made the choice."

McKenzie stood as though frozen in a block of ice. Until this moment she had harbored hope that she could convince him she'd made a mistake, that she did indeed love her stepfather, but that she loved Jeb more.

Now, hearing him tell her to forget everything they had shared, including their lovemaking, was like having him thrust a knife between her ribs and twist the blade with slow precision.

She stared at him in horror, tears choking her, only to hear him say violently, "Don't look at me like that, McKenzie, for God's sakes! It's for your own good! You're wasting your time with me."

With a muffled oath, he pushed past her and entered the bedroom, slamming the door behind him.

Exactly two weeks later, she lost the baby. Had she been given a choice, she would have died, too. It was only through the love and patience of her family that she'd been able to get herself back together and make a new life for herself....

Now, in the chilly silence of the room, McKenzie turned to Jeb, wanting to hate him for hurting her, yet hating herself more for still caring. "Now you know," she whispered in final agony.

His features were ravaged. "Oh, God, if only you'd told me," he whispered in turn, blinking back the tears gathered on his eyelashes.

She felt his pain but could not comfort him. "And what would you have done differently?"

"I'd have died before I'd let you go," he said simply.

"Oh, no," she whispered aloud, but her heart was crying, *Why now? Why tell me this now? When it's too late!*

He moved a little closer to her, rolling his fingers into a tight fist, damning himself to hell. "Did...does my father know?"

McKenzie didn't hesitate. "No, he never knew I was pregnant. Only Aunt Rachel. We...we convinced the doctor not to tell him." A sob shook her slender frame. "What would have been the point?"

"I see."

No, you don't see! she wanted to scream. *If you did, you would see what you're doing to me and go away, so I won't be reminded of what I can never have.*

He stared at her, tears glazing his eyes.

She stared at him, fear dimming hers.

He longed to put his arms around her, absorb her pain.

She longed to let him, yet she was afraid.

Neither moved.

The clock ticked away the seconds.

Then Jeb spoke, his voice low and gravelly. "I won't bother you anymore. You have my word."

Their eyes continued to mesh.

Survivors, she thought. Ambulatory, but barely. And still grieving. When he left, she listened until his footsteps faded. Suddenly, she felt cold.

And empty.

For days Jeb was like a madman. Yet he kept his promise. When they encountered each other in passing, they behaved like polite strangers, though McKenzie haunted him relentlessly. Visions of her body withering in pain, rejecting his seed, almost sent him over the edge. He damned himself more times than he could count.

Today was no different. As he prowled the space in front of his desk, he demanded of himself again, how could he have been so stupid as to have let something like that happen? After all, it should have been his responsibility to see that she hadn't gotten pregnant.

He had no excuse except to say that when he'd charged into her room that day so long ago and seen her standing half naked, the sunlight warming her body, he'd lost his head.

And then when he'd sent her away, he had convinced himself it was for her own good, never mind that his insides were bleeding. He'd even begun to believe his father, that there were too many strikes against them. So he'd let her go, only to plunge them both into a deeper and more lasting hell.

If only he could turn back the clock. If only she weren't getting married. If only he could stop wanting her. If only...

Yet he knew the "if only's" were facts he was going to have to live with. Jeb stopped his pacing in front of the window and bowed his head against the sill, thoughts of McKenzie still swirling in his mind. He had finally accepted that she would always remain forbidden to him. And hand in hand with that assurance came another: there was nothing he could do that would relieve the aching pain in his groin.

Jeb suddenly jerked away from the window when he heard a knock on the door.

"Come in," he demanded tersely, shaking his head to clear it.

His intruder was John Riley, the reporter, wearing a frown.

"Sorry to intrude," he said, "but have you by any chance seen McKenzie?"

Jeb became instantly alert. "No. I assume she's out on assignment. Why?"

"I just wanted to find out if she knew there'd been another accident at Cedar Plaza."

"What happened this time?"

"Don't know the details, only what I heard over the scanner."

"And that was . . . ?"

John made a face. "Well, for starters, a steel beam fell and injured several of the construction hands."

Jeb was almost afraid to ask. "Any fatalities?"

"Don't think so, just some major injuries."

"My God!" Jeb exclaimed. "What next?"

John sighed heavily. "Who knows? But something—or more to the point, *someone*—is sure as hell rotten on that project."

Jeb's face tightened. "Do you know if McKenzie's contact was one of the men injured?"

Riley sighed again. "Sure don't, but it wouldn't surprise me any. I've definitely come to the conclusion those big boys mean business, and if it means playing dirty, then so what!" He paused and ambled to the door, then turned. "If you see McKenzie, you might give her the message."

"All right. And thanks," Jeb muttered grimly.

The moment he was alone, Jeb reached for the pack of cigarettes on his desk. After lighting one and inhaling deeply, he lowered himself into his chair, lines of worry wrinkling his forehead. *What if McKenzie was next on the list?*

Suddenly, the blood in his veins turned to ice water.

A short time later, Jeb let himself into the house that was held in the grip of the night's silence, its serenity a further assault. Jeb ascended the stairs and came to a dead stop in the doorway of his bedroom, staring at his lonely bed. Determined to block out the fact that McKenzie was just across the hall, he crossed the threshold, stripped his clothes from his body, and climbed into bed.

But sleep wouldn't come. He kept mulling over his conversation with John Riley. Unfortunately, it was looking as though McKenzie was right, and not only were they (at this point he wasn't sure who "they" were) involved in fraud, but murder as well.

Although he hadn't seen McKenzie to tell her about the latest accident, he knew her well enough to know she would see this investigation through to the bitter end, no matter what the danger. She had made that point quite clear.

But neither would she be the first reporter to have died because her nose was stuck where it wasn't wanted. Suddenly, he made up his mind. As soon as possible, he'd take McKenzie and go to the mall site and have a look around, let the contractor know that *he* was also involved and that if a hair on McKenzie's head was damaged, there would be hell to pay.

With that pledge uppermost in his mind, he drifted off to sleep.

Dawn was creeping over the horizon when something snatched him from his sleep. What? he asked himself, be-

fore one swift kick sent the covers flying, giving his clammy
body a breather.

He rolled over, realizing he'd been dreaming, and tried to
head off the queasy feeling building inside him. After taking several deep breaths, he forced his mind to backtrack,
hoping to dredge up his nightmare, but instead visions of
McKenzie danced in his head like so many sugar plums. Her
vivid blue eyes beckoned him, her soft sweet lips lured
him....

For what seemed an endless moment, he let his imagination triumph over his will, giving his fingers freedom to trace
those eyes, those lips, before moving to seek the hidden delights of her silken body. Ah, those breasts, with their dusty
pink nipples—how he kissed them, round and round and
round, moving onto her hips, across her belly, down her
thighs.

Suddenly, he thrashed across the bed, his body aroused,
searching, hoping, praying, only to find the bed empty—as
empty as his heart. His eyes flew open, and he panicked as
reality came down on him with smothering intensity.

What if he couldn't protect her? What if she were harmed
in some way?

Those uncertainties and more stung his mind, making
sleep impossible. With innate agility, he bounded out of the
bed and, not bothering to turn on the lamp, felt his way like
a blindman until he found a pair of gym shorts lying rumpled at the foot of the bed. After slipping them over his nakedness, he moved over the carpet, opened the door and
stepped across the hall to McKenzie's room.

Jeb twisted the knob slowly but surely and pushed the
door open. Peering inside, the hall light aiding his intru-
sion, he could see her head on the pillow, her hair shining
like pure gold. He moved quietly to the bed and stared down
into the face so determined to haunt him. Was she dreaming? Suddenly, he wished he were able to meld into her sleep,

o join her inside her dreams. Would they be more pleasant han his?

McKenzie whimpered softly and then moved, claiming his ttention once again. The sheet had slipped, leaving a reamy breast exposed. He bit back his frustration while weat oozed from every pore and his insides flamed to life. Oh, God, how he wanted her—no, how he loved her. That vas the core of his dilemma. Oh, God, he cried again, how ould he let her go?

You can't, his heart argued, though his head immedi- tely taunted, *Yes, you can,* and then pounded him with easons why she was not his to keep, and never would be.

Without warning, Jeb began to dissolve on the inside, naking it almost impossible to douse the fires of desire still aging within him. But fight he did, until he felt the pinch- ng sensation in his gut begin to abate. Then, while his motions were under control, he bent his head and placed is lips against her hair, inhaling its fragrant scent.

A deep sadness made his footsteps heavy as he turned and valked out of the room.

Blues had him by the throat and wouldn't let go.

Chapter 8

McKenzie worked herself at a grueling pace, thereby keeping thoughts of Jeb at bay.

The majority of her time was spent digging up information about Jackson Witherspoon. She checked into his family background, his political campaign and his finances. And his finances were the most incriminating thing of all; his mistress of long standing had bled him of cash with her penchant for jewels, furs and expensive clothing. McKenzie was delighted with the facts she had gathered, which strengthened her conviction that the mayor could very easily be involved in the fraud.

All that was left to do was to prove it.

This morning, however, she'd vowed not to think about her work. Instead, she'd opted to go for a drive, desperate to relieve the tension gnawing within her. She'd slipped into a pair of slacks and a sweater and hustled out the door, only to decide suddenly that she'd go by the hospital before beginning her day's outing.

To McKenzie's amazement, her stepfather had been awake, and they had managed to converse, though his words were still slurred and unclear at times. But each day showed an improvement and that was all that mattered. Just to have him home again would be nothing short of a miracle.

Now, as the car ticked off the miles on the highway, McKenzie began to relax, to unwind. She felt like an escaped prisoner.

It was a gorgeous Saturday morning, and even though it was late November, many of the trees were still exquisitely garbed in colors of red, orange and gold.

Setting the cruise control on fifty-five, she concentrated on her driving, feeling the dazzling sunlight streaming through the windshield to caress her face, her arms, lulling her into a peaceful mood.

But her contentment was short-lived. As the car continued to eat up the miles, thoughts of Jeb began to intrude.

During the past two days, she had seen very little of him, except in passing. And during those times, she made it a point not to meet his eyes, though she was certain he could hear the thumping of her heart.

If only his effect on her were not so powerful, so life-changing, she'd cried silently. If only she could stop caring.

Suddenly, she gripped the steering wheel until her fingers became numb. "That's your whole problem," she muttered aloud. "You care too damned much."

She drove slowly onward, taking the back roads through the Hill Country. Then, before she realized what she was doing, she had branched off on a country road that led to what used to be Jeb's house. Her tongue thickened and her stomach lurched as the memories swamped her.

Hesitating only a moment, she accelerated and slowly inched the car forward. Finally, she stopped and looked around her. Nothing had changed. The house appeared exactly the same as she remembered it.

Suddenly furious with herself for behaving so foolishly, McKenzie pressed her foot on the brake and was about to shift into reverse when she heard a door slam.

Her head shot up, only to have her heart drop to the bottom of her stomach. Jeb was standing on the porch, looking down the drive, a menacing scowl on his face.

She froze. Oh, God, what now? she asked herself, panic drumming through her.

Jeb's stride never wavered from the path as he headed straight for the car.

"Oh, no," McKenzie whimpered, the words splitting the silence. She tightened her fingers into a fist, damning herself again for her stupidity.

Tears stung her eyes as she swallowed the last remnant of her pride and prepared to face him. The music had been played; it was time to pay the piper, she thought without humor. But when she heard the crunch of footsteps draw near the car door, she found she could not. Her nerve had completely deserted her.

"McKenzie!" he exclaimed, jerking open the door, staring down at her. "What the devil are you doing here?"

McKenzie had to force herself to look at him. "Would you believe me," she quipped, desperately trying to lighten the situation, "if I said I was just out for a scenic drive?"

Jeb glared at her, his lashes unable to veil the coldness in his eyes. He seemed remote, detached.

Feeling as though she'd just run into a brick wall, McKenzie began haltingly, "If...you'll let go of the door, I'll be on my way."

"No need to be in a hurry now." Sarcasm colored his tone. "You might as well get out as long as you're here."

"Oh, no, I couldn't," McKenzie began, her face flushed crimson.

"McKenzie?"

Knowing she had lost the battle, if not the war, McKenzie shrugged and did not try to stop him from helping her out of the car. When she was out, they looked into each other's eyes, and a warm weakness invaded McKenzie's body. To be so close to Jeb was both exhilarating and overpowering.

The trek up the drive was carried out in silence. But it was all McKenzie could do just to put one foot before the other. Each time she thought of turning and making a mad dash for the car, she would glimpse the tense set of Jeb's jaw and decide she had no choice but to see this charade through to the last gasp. After all, she was the one at fault, not Jeb. Yet still it rankled . . .

She gazed around in surprise. The interior was the same, the muted greens and golds giving the room an air of sophisticated cheerfulness. A brass-edged mirror and a large brass plant stand dominated one wall, and beyond that, French doors opened out onto a patio.

A fireplace, crackling with logs and flanked by built-in bookshelves and a wood box, covered the remaining wall.

McKenzie sighed and crossed immediately to the French doors as though she were trying to outrun the oppressive silence that hung between them.

"I'll get you a cup of coffee," Jeb said at last, slicing effectively into the quietness.

"I'm . . . I'm sorry I intruded," she murmured, halting his movement toward the door.

"No big deal," he replied, his green eyes unfathomable. "Would you rather have hot chocolate instead of coffee? I have both."

"Coffee sounds good. Thanks."

"I'll be right back."

McKenzie sank down on the cushions of the couch when she could no longer hear his footsteps. She closed her eyes tightly, fighting the humiliation of having been caught with her hand in the cookie jar. She'd had no idea she would run into Jeb. A mirthless smile reshaped her lips. This house, this room, was crammed with memories. And Jeb, he looked so good, smelled so good—but oh, so withdrawn, so cold.

Yet for a moment back at the car, when his eyes had searched hers, she had felt as though she had been given a glimpse into paradise.

When she heard Jeb's heavy tread, McKenzie's eyes suddenly flung open and she swiped irritably at the silky strands of hair brushing her cheek. She knew she was far from looking her best. But then she hadn't planned on seeing Jeb, either.

"You look just fine," he muttered before plunking down a tray bearing coffee and a plate of sweet rolls.

McKenzie's hand paused in midair at his unexpected comment. Disconcerted, she placed it in her lap and linked it with her other hand, then watched as he sat down beside her and poured her a cup of coffee. McKenzie willed her hand not to shake as she reached for it.

"Thanks," she managed to say as the cup changed hands, but she was conscious only of the gentle brush of his fingers. In response, her muscles tightened, like thousands of fine wires drawing taut.

"Sorry," Jeb said, his mouth twisting painfully, her reaction not lost on him.

"That's . . . all right." McKenzie's words were barely audible.

Jeb watched her take a sip of coffee, then looked away, his jaw fixed rigidly, his face taut.

"Tell me," McKenzie said, unable to stand the silence another second. "Why didn't you sell the house?"

Jeb stood up and extracted a cigarette from the packet on the table. He lit it, inhaling deeply, then allowed the smoke to drift out slowly through his lips.

"Just didn't," he said shortly.

She looked at him curiously and asked again, "Why?"

"Do I need a reason?" His face was cool, expressionless.

"No...no, I don't guess you do," she stammered, suddenly feeling that she had plunged into water over her head. What did it matter if he hadn't sold the house? After all, it was none of her business.

"Let me put it this way," he said abruptly. "It's an investment."

"Oh," she murmured meekly, killing any idea she might have had that he'd held on to it because of the memories, memories filled with laughter...and love.

Suddenly, McKenzie drew her lips between her teeth, stifling the urge to cry.

Seeing her expression, Jeb swore and turned his head, the tension in the room building to a screaming pitch.

The seconds ticked away as McKenzie was held spellbound, watching the sunlight dancing across his hair, reminding her of glistening tinsel. She had never seen him look better. His jeans were faded and worn, and the sweatshirt he wore had seen better days. But to her, Jeb was the epitome of the dangerous, predatory male. And she ached to reach out and touch him, beginning with the wisp of hair that caressed his forehead.

Suddenly McKenzie knew she had to leave, to get away from him. This was all so crazy anyway. Seeing him like this...

"I'd better go," she whispered, making an effort to get up.

As though Jeb sensed what she was about to do, he reached out and grabbed her arm. "No," he said thickly, "don't go." Her coming here unexpectedly was like a blessing from heaven, and he was not about to waste it.

McKenzie raised startled eyes to his, helpless against the dark passion she saw mirrored there.

"Don't go...please," he said, his hand moving from her arm to her face.

Instant panic. "Jeb...?"

"Shhh..." he pleaded, hating himself for breaking his promise but no longer able to help it. With his heart threatening to burst through his chest, he began smoothing her hair away from her face, then moved closer to trace the fullness of her lips with a passionate finger. "Tell me what you want and that's what I'll do," he added hoarsely.

What I want. How can I say what I want when it's been years since I knew what I wanted or what was good for me?

His fingers continued their assault on her lips. Blindly, she clutched at him, her heart pounding. Twenty-five years old, without control, and feeling like a very small child in a dark room. A moan escaped from her lips.

"What's wrong? Am I hurting you?"

Yes, but not the way you mean, she moaned silently. She needed this man. She needed his calming words and his caressing hands. She needed his comfort and his warmth and his gentleness. She needed his strong, lean body and protective arms. She longed for the feel, the taste of his lips.

But could she bury her guilt, ignore her responsibilities for a moment in his arms? She trembled against the tug-of-war going on inside her. *What am I doing?* Her mind demanded "go!" while her heart screamed "stay!"

"McKenzie..." His voice was vulnerable, beckoning, seducing....

She felt her resistance evaporate like dew on a rose petal, knowing that when she left this heavenly place, the real world would come crashing down on her head. But until that time nothing must interfere with the magic that surrounded them.

Then, knowing she shouldn't, knowing it was wrong, she captured his soothing fingers and pressed her lips to them in soft passion.

Jeb's insides gave a twist as he felt her warm lips nuzzling his hand, his expression darkening with the desire she had aroused with that one innocent touch.

"Oh, McKenzie, McKenzie," he groaned against the petal softness of her mouth. But even now, as he held her trembling body close to his, he still couldn't believe she was here, in his house, in his arms. *Why had she come?* Afraid to speculate, to hope, his hold on her tightened, his tongue probing, exploring....

He had thought it was over between them, that he'd never hold her in his arms again, feel her breasts crushed against his chest, feel the parted sweetness of her lips, or smell the scent of her skin, which had always reminded him of apple blossoms and still did.

He wanted to pray, to beg God not to let this be a dream but a real part of his life. Yet, he was afraid to have this begin, afraid it might end, leaving him shattered.

As his tongue sparred with hers, McKenzie felt herself sliding down into a well of feeling where nothing mattered, only that Jeb go on making love to her. She was caught in a sensual web of her own making.

"Oh, darling," he whispered huskily, drawing his mouth away from hers, his fingers kneading a breast. "You're so precious to me."

She experienced a moment of pure, somehow tortured anticipation as his mouth descended on hers once again, tongue meeting hers, sending a shaft of pleasure straight through the center of her body. She sighed with a shudder and closed her arms around him, ready to abandon all thoughts, all action, ready to become part of him.

McKenzie pulled back and raised her eyes to his. "Make love to me," she whispered. "Now."

Fearing her plea was a figment of his imagination, Jeb hurriedly untangled himself from her clinging arms and slid off the couch.

"Jeb?" she questioned, her voice a shaky whisper, not understanding his sudden withdrawal.

Jeb's hand moved to frame her face, his eyes still glazed with passion. "I think we'll be more comfortable in bed."

"Yes," she murmured feverishly, locking her arms around his neck as he shifted his hands to lift her effortlessly in his arms. He carried her into the bedroom and placed her on the bed.

"I'll only be a moment," he promised, turning to the fireplace where he stoked the dying embers into leaping flames that threw out an enveloping warmth.

Then slowly, leisurely, his eyes caressed her, and he began to shed his clothes. When at last he was standing before her in naked splendor, the sunlight paying homage to his lean hardness, she thought her heart would explode.

"You're as beautiful as I remember," she whispered as he stretched his long frame out beside her.

"And I'm all yours," he murmured, reaching for her sweater and easing it from her slender shoulders with passionate impatience. Her bra came next, releasing its burden into Jeb's hands. Her nipples flowered beneath his teasing tongue, and she moaned while he all but ripped the remaining clothes from her body.

Then skin against skin. Nothing in between.

McKenzie's blood seemed to have stopped circulating as his mouth began to explore her body.

"Soft," Jeb murmured, his mouth on her stomach. "More perfect than my dreams."

Her knees relaxed, thighs parted slightly, and she lifted a little closer to him as he showered her stomach and hips with tiny kisses.

With a groan, McKenzie closed her arms around him as his mouth came back to hers and his fingers stroked her inner thigh, higher. She opened more and held her breath. His fingers slipped into her, caressing.

Her heartbeat was without bounds; he was so gentle, so easy, tenderly taking her into another world of erotic pleasure.

"Oh, God," he uttered, "you're so tight ..." he paused, a shudder rattling through him. "Have you ... I mean ... is this ...?" His eyes, delving into hers, were glazed with both hope and pain.

Not pretending to misunderstand him, McKenzie whispered, "Yes. There's been no one ... since you. Daniel's never touched ..."

Suddenly, there was a silence and all he could hear was the song in his own heart.

Then Jeb went a little crazy, feeling almost drugged. There was not one place on her body that was left untouched by his mouth and tongue. His lips ravaged hers. When they parted, McKenzie was breathlessly smiling, giddy and feeling drunk. He kissed her throat, her shoulders, her ears, then moved to her breasts.

McKenzie's hands roamed over him, too, something primitive driving her to rediscover his body. Everywhere she touched, she could feel the muscles gather and clench beneath his skin.

"Oh, God, McKenzie," Jeb murmured, "you don't know how often I've dreamed of this."

"Me, too," she said boldly, reaching down and touching him, glorying in the hard swell against her hand.

He gasped. "Oh, please ... I can't wait much longer."

"Oh, Jeb ... now!"

Needing no second command, Jeb tenderly parted her knees and settled over her, very carefully, entering the soft folds of her womanhood.

"Am . . . am I hurting you?" he groaned, resting, considering the sensations.

"No...please don't stop," McKenzie groaned, settling her hands on his hips as he moved slightly, the motion recording itself everywhere inside her. His knees tight against her hips, he bent to kiss her, his body thrusting.

She heard his breathing change, felt it in the heaving of his chest against hers. He gasped, and she accelerated the fevered pitching of her hips, rapidly approaching a satisfaction that promised to be cataclysmic.

"Oh, yes, yes," Jeb moaned, matching her stroke for stroke.

McKenzie went rigid, her lips just touching his, her eyes clamped shut, suspended in pleasure, the breath leaving her lungs in a long, low groan.

Love. She fought against it, her eyelids suddenly feeling heavy. But it was already too late, she knew. The trap was closing. . . .

McKenzie hated having to move, but her body, exposed to the air, was cold. Was that what had awakened her? she wondered, willing her eyes to open, to focus.

Her confusion mounted until Jeb's vision filled her eyes. Her eyes widened in shocked dismay as the events of the day washed over her.

Jeb, bare to the waist, was sitting up beside her in bed smoking a cigarette. And sitting between them was the irrational sense of fear.

McKenzie's gaze dipped to the glass of Coke on the table beside the bed. She couldn't speak. The fear had locked her insides. She shivered.

That's when Jeb turned to her. Their eyes met and he searched her face, a slow, sweet smile opening his lips, while he ignored the stab of apprehension coiling in his belly. Oh, God, was she sorry? Was she regretting their magic coupling?

Her gold-fringed eyes seemed to take up her whole face as she gazed at him. He felt her shiver, though unsure whether from cold or remorse, and his smile deepened as he bent down and drew the blanket over her naked limbs.

"Jeb..." she began, feeling her heart relax and her fear recede in response to his beguiling smile, remembering what they had shared. It had not been a dream; it had been earth-shakingly real. How could something so beautiful be so wrong?

"Good afternoon," Jeb drawled, noticing the color dotting both cheeks, relieved that she no longer looked ready to bolt from his side.

"Same to you," she said sweetly.

"Want some Coke?"

McKenzie laughed at his inane question. He was so close now she could almost taste his warm breath.

"After today," Jeb said deeply, "my life will never be the same, you know. When I was nestled inside you, I felt a part of you."

His intimately spoken words made her tremble. "Oh, Jeb," she cried, "if only—"

"No!" he demanded, slicing a finger across her lips. "Don't say another word. Not today. No apologies. No recriminations. The rest of the day and night is ours. Let's make the most of it. Deal?"

She remained silent, while deep within her each component of her nature was at war with the others. Her heart won. "Deal." The whispered word caressed his ears as she snuggled under the cover, closer to him. She could feel the hair on his leg as she pressed against him.

"You won't be sorry," Jeb said, the feel of her against him sending a shaft of fire straight to his manhood. "Just consider yourself my captive," he added with a teasing note.

Caught up in the enchantment of the moment, McKenzie answered his smile, knowing that tomorrow would come and with it regret, recriminations, fright and certainly guilt and shame. But for now—there was only Jeb.

McKenzie capitulated sweetly. "But only if you feed me."

"Your wish is my command." Jeb laughed, springing from the bed, oblivious to his nakedness, and slipped into a pair of shorts draped across the nearest chair. "What would the madam like?" He made a sweeping bow, looking totally absurd and endearing.

McKenzie stalled. "Mmmm, let's see. How about an egg, hash browns and two pieces of toast?"

"Damn, woman!" Jeb exclaimed. "I'm not sure I can afford to feed you." His eyes twinkled, enjoying the picture she made propped up against the pillow, the top of a creamy breast exposed to his lascivious gaze.

"Well," McKenzie whispered saucily, "what's it to be? After all, my hearty appetite is all your fault."

Jeb gulped. God, she was even flirting with him. "Then I...I guess I'll have to get to it," he stammered, barely able to tear his eyes away from a rose-tipped nipple.

McKenzie blushed, and when she spoke there was an odd little cadence in her voice. "Wait, and I'll help."

A rather long time later, their plates heaped with hot food, they sat across from each other, McKenzie looking lost in Jeb's terry-cloth robe, Jeb clad in nothing but his jogging shorts.

They ate quietly for a moment, soaking up the cozy silence that enveloped them. Then suddenly McKenzie seemed to have drifted far away, her face becoming shadowed.

Jeb pushed the panic button. His voice shook. "McKenzie, what are you thinking about?" But he knew. Oh, God, he knew.

McKenzie's features suddenly cleared, but her voice held a waver. "Actually, I was thinking about work, about that second accident that took place at Cedar Plaza."

In spite of the grimness of her thoughts, Jeb experienced a stab of relief. "I gather, then, you spoke to John Riley?"

She nodded. "He told me he also spoke to you."

Jeb nodded, waiting for her to continue. He watched her closely, hating to discuss her work, resenting anything that took her away from him. But at least, he thought, she was willing to confide in him. That in itself was a miracle.

McKenzie toyed with the remaining food on her plate. "Thank God my contact wasn't hurt."

Jeb slid his chair back from the table and reached for the coffee pot. "Was he there at the time?"

"I'm not sure. I haven't heard from him, and that worries me. But John got me the list of the injured and my man wasn't on it." Her face turned bleak. "Damn, I feel so frustrated, like I'm trying to work with my hands tied behind my back. I'm getting nowhere."

"Where do you go from here?" Jeb asked, reaching out across the table and massaging her hand. It was stone cold.

"Just keep on digging until I come up with something concrete to hang the mayor and whoever else is responsible."

Jeb's gaze was steadily on her. "Even though you may be placing yourself in danger?"

"Even though I may be placing myself in danger."

He expelled a harsh sigh, removing his hand. "I want to go on record that I'm still against your pursuing this, but since I know you're determined, I want your promise that I can work with you."

McKenzie didn't flinch this time. "All right."

"Good." Jeb smiled like a cat that had just finished lapping up a bowl of cream.

Leaning back in his chair, he said, "Okay, suppose yo fill me in on the details."

"Well, for starters," McKenzie said, warming to his interest, "my contact thinks they're substituting inferior-grad materials for those specified in the building contract. I addition, when they unload the materials only half tha amount remains on the job site. The other half is sold an the cash pocketed. And more than likely, Elmer Thurma could have testified to that fact and was killed because o what he knew."

"It's all supposition, no proof."

"You have any ideas?" McKenzie asked, raising her cof fee to her lips.

"What about your contact? Can't he get you somethin concrete?"

"I sure hope so. If he could just get me forms signed b Witherspoon or a taped conversation linking him with Di lard."

Jeb held back a smile. "You don't want much, do you?

"Well, I can always hope, can't I?" McKenzie asked getting up and padding to the sink with their plates. Tha task completed, she turned around, only to find herse suddenly mesmerized by the way the hair on Jeb's chest gav his tanned body a healthy glow. She watched, transfixed, a he ambled toward her, empty cup in hand.

Jeb caught her staring. "What next?" he asked with a effort.

McKenzie hesitated. "Visit the building site and hop fully run into Dillard. I've never met the man face-to-face.

"Care to have company?"

Silence.

"If . . . if you want to."

"Ah, princess," he said shakily, "don't you know by now I'd go to the ends of the earth just to be with you?"

"Oh, Jeb," she whispered in a broken voice, "what are we going to do?"

Quickly closing the distance between them, Jeb swept her into his arms, burying his hands in her curls, nestling her face in the crook of his neck. "I know what I'd like to do," he murmured huskily.

McKenzie raised tear-stained eyes to his face, a question mirrored in them.

"I want to make love to you again," Jeb whispered. "Make you mine..." He couldn't go on; his voice seemed to close on him.

With a soft moan, McKenzie burrowed closer against him. "I thought you'd never ask," she said, her warm breath scorching his skin.

For the second time that day, she was lifted up into his arms, carried into the bedroom, and placed atop the now rumpled sheets. Jeb was silent except for his eyes—they spoke volumes—as he quickly disposed of his shorts before lowering his long frame down beside her.

For the longest of moments, Jeb was content just to cradle her in his arms, losing himself in the feel, the smell, the touch of her.

Then he shifted slightly so that he was able to look down into her eyes, the light from the crackling flames allowing him free perusal of her.

"Everything's going to be all right, I promise," Jeb said with a smile, flicking the end of her nose playfully, determined to remove the sadness and fear from her eyes.

Suddenly, McKenzie answered his smile and brought her hand lovingly to his cheek. "I know," she said tremulously, feeling his hands roam the entire length of her body.

"Do you know your nipples are perfect?" His fingers
were shaping first one and then the other into burgeoning
pebbles.

"They...are?"

"They're full and pink and very tempting...if you know
what I mean." He grinned into her face.

"Oh, Jeb..." she sighed.

"Is that all you can say?" he muttered.

Suddenly, McKenzie's tongue darted out and traced his
lips with its hot moistness. Instantly, she felt his ardent response against her stomach.

"Kiss me...please."

"Oh, yes. All over."

And he did. Every moment of their passion-filled day was
relived until far into the night. McKenzie knew with each
precious moment spent in his arms that if she never saw Jeb
again, she would be able to live on these memories for the
rest of her life.

For now she had to be content with that.

And she was.

It was the following evening when Jeb followed Mc-
Kenzie back to the Langley mansion, both of them dazed
and replete from the marathon days of lovemaking.

The moment Jeb helped McKenzie out of her car, she
noticed that almost every light in the house was burning
brightly.

"Jeb...?" She clutched at his shirt.

"Shhh," he cautioned, slamming the car door shut and
urging her up the walk. "Let's don't borrow trouble."

It was in that moment that the front door swung back on
its hinges and the figure of a woman stood in the lighted
doorway.

McKenzie came to a sudden standstill, fear knotting her
stomach.

"Oh, thank God, thank God you're home," Rosie cried, her voice loud and piercing in the still night air.

McKenzie stood as though wedged in cement, shaking inside.

"It's Mr. Carson!" Rosie added. "He's . . . he's had another stroke."

Chapter 9

McKenzie was beginning to loathe hospitals. For three days now she had remained a virtual prisoner inside the barren walls. But thank God, her stepfather was beginning to rally again; the second stroke, though a definite setback, was not as damaging as first thought. The doctors were encouraging. Again they stressed it would take time, but, with love and patience, he would pull through this one, too. Well, the love she had in abundance, but the patience was another matter altogether.

She longed to see him up and about, able to come barreling through the door of the *Tribune*, his voice booming loud and clear, watching with a smile as everyone rushed to do his bidding. Ah, for those uncomplicated days! She feared they were gone forever.

When Rosie had met her and Jeb at the door and delivered her bombshell, McKenzie had wanted to curl up and die. The remainder of the night had been one of the longest and most painful of her life.

All the way to the hospital, with Jeb driving like a man possessed, guilt had punctuated every breath she took, every word she uttered. Added to that guilt was a feeling of self-loathing that threatened to make her physically ill.

She had let her dreams get in the way of her sound judgment. And for what? A few stolen hours in the arms of a man who had once before destroyed her life and who was capable of doing so again, who had no intention of offering her anything permanent.

Jeb had tried to reason with her, but his words had fallen on deaf ears.

"McKenzie," he'd pleaded, taking his eyes off the road and staring at her tense, pale features. "Don't shut me out."

In spite of her effort to maintain control, her voice quivered and the tears spilled over her eyelids. "Please...Jeb... not now."

"We need to talk." Again his tone was pleading.

"No." She was adamant. "What we did was wrong."

"Dammit," he said tersely, "don't you dare say that. Nothing that wonderful could be wrong and you know it."

"You're wasting your time," she said bluntly.

He stifled a curse. "I won't let you shut me out."

"I don't need you, Jeb," she lied, turning away, staring into the night, the street lights the only relief from the inky blackness.

He'd bitten back a further retort, though his face remained like a thundercloud ready to burst as he swung the car into the hospital parking lot. They raced inside to confront an anxious Rachel.

All three had waited far into the morning, McKenzie pacing the floor, Jeb chain-smoking, his eyes never leaving McKenzie for long, and Rachel sitting, her eyes brimming with tears.

Finally the doctor came in to give them an updated report on Carson's condition. He'd stabilized, he told them, and was again out of danger.

Later, when they arrived at the house, McKenzie had gone straight to bed, ignoring the hard, closed expression on Jeb's face. But she'd found no solace in being alone. Instead, she'd been haunted by thoughts of Daniel.

How would she ever face him? she asked herself. And her stepfather? What of him? Those unanswered questions had gnawed at her brain throughout the night, and there had been no rest for the weary.

Now, as she sat beside her stepfather's bed watching the steady rhythm of his heart, on the monitor, she longed for Jeb, longed to feel his protective arms around her. Oh, how she wanted and needed him, even when she knew it was wrong; she was unable to exorcise him from her heart and mind.

"McKenzie."

The softly spoken mention of her name drew her out of the deep trance and back to reality. She whirled as her aunt came tiptoeing across the room.

"How is he?" Rachel asked, placing a hand on McKenzie's shoulders, preventing her from getting out of the chair.

"About the same," McKenzie replied dejectedly.

Rachel squeezed her shoulder before reaching for another chair and pulling it close to McKenzie's. "I came to relieve you," she whispered.

"No." McKenzie shook her head. "I don't want to go. I keep thinking he's going to open his eyes, and I want to be here when he does."

Rachel's expression bore concern as well as sympathy. "Honey, you're wearing yourself out staying here day and night. You've lost weight, the circles under your eyes are no longer blue, they're black, and—"

"You've made your point, Auntie," McKenzie cut in, massaging the back of her neck. She knew Rachel was right, but she was still unable to leave her stepfather; guilt was playing havoc with her insides.

"Well, what are you going to do about it, then?" Rachel's tone was firm but gentle.

"I know I should rest, but I just feel if I'm here, he'll know it and maybe that will help." McKenzie shrugged. "Sounds crazy, I know."

"Of course it's not crazy," Rachel responded softly. "But you know Carson wouldn't want you making yourself sick."

McKenzie sighed. "I know you're right, but—"

"No, 'buts' about it," Rachel said sternly. "I want you to get away from this hospital for the rest of the day. Go shopping. Go to the office. Go home. I don't care what you do just as long as you're not sitting here brooding."

McKenzie smiled. "Oh, Aunt Rachel, what would I do without you?"

Rachel beamed for a moment. "Well, I certainly hope you don't have to find out anytime soon. After all, someone has to be around to keep you in line."

The smile disappeared from McKenzie's lips. "I'm afraid that's an impossible task," she said, thinking about the mess she'd made of her life in just a few short weeks.

Rachel didn't miss the shadow that slipped over McKenzie's face or the darkening of her expression. "Don't forget that when you get ready to talk," she said sweetly, "I'm ready to listen." When McKenzie remained silent, she went on, "I'm aware that...that you've been seeing Jeb—" she paused as though searching for the right words "—and that it's tearing you apart on the inside."

McKenzie's lip quivered slightly. "You're...right, but it's something...I can't talk about right now." A lone tear seeped from her eye and trickled down her cheek. "Maybe when Dad's better, I'll be able to get my act together."

Rachel leaned over and kissed McKenzie on the cheek. "I know I'm a nosy old busybody, but I can't stand to see you suffer. Or Jeb either, for that matter. And the last few days, he's been like a bear with a sore paw."

McKenzie kept her silence, images of Jeb's stormy eyes and grim mouth flashing in front of her. Would this nightmare ever end?

After a moment, Rachel spoke again. "Now go on, get out of here. I'll call you tonight."

Seeing the determined expression on her aunt's face, McKenzie dragged herself wearily to her feet. "All right, you win," she said. "I do have a thousand things to do at the office, but promise you'll call if there's any change here."

"I promise," Rachel said, getting up and following McKenzie to the door. "Oh, by the way, have you forgotten that day after tomorrow is Thanksgiving?"

McKenzie's mouth dropped. "As a matter of fact, I had. But then I'm not surprised. My mind has been nothing but mush lately."

"Well, anyway, it doesn't matter, because I told Rosie to get a turkey and all the trimmings. I think it'll do us good to get together and have dinner. Even though he can't be with us, I think Carson would want that, too."

With Rachel's last statement, any objections McKenzie might have voiced died in her throat. How could she tell her aunt that she couldn't bear to be in the same room with Jeb and not touch him?

Instead, McKenzie leaned over and gave Rachel a brief hug and said, "Whatever you think best." Then she turned and began making her way down the hall at a brisk pace.

Her mind was a million miles away as she crossed into the main lobby, thinking about how she should spend the rest of the day—whether to work or try to soothe Daniel's ruffled feathers, when a low-pitched voice said, "You going to a fire?"

The pace of McKenzie's heart quickened in response to the voice. She stopped suddenly and looked up. Jeb's tall frame stood in her path. Unconsciously, she adjusted her jacket tighter against her as if feeling the chill of a non-existent wind.

Jeb's green eyes studied her, his expression acknowledging that he was aware of just how difficult these past few days had been for her. Compassion, and another expression equally potent, shone from his eyes as he closed the narrow gap between them. He stopped just short of touching her, jamming his hands into the pockets of his pants instead.

"How's Dad?" he asked.

"He's . . . he's stable. Not much change."

McKenzie heard his sigh of relief while his eyes continued to hold hers. "That's good news," he said, his voice deep and sensual.

McKenzie suddenly felt light-headed. She had barely laid eyes on him since they had returned from the Hill Country. As before, she knew Jeb had purposely stayed away from the hospital for fear of running into her. It was obvious from his haggard look that he was faring no better than she. May God forgive her, but she wanted him to hold her . . . to love her.

"How long's it been since you've had a decent meal?" he asked, breaking into her fragmented thoughts.

His gentle tone was almost McKenzie's undoing; she fought for control. "I'm not sure," she admitted weakly. To her surprise, she spoke the truth. Her eyes shifted to the clock on the wall; the hands said one o'clock. She hadn't eaten, but she'd had numerous cups of coffee. Could that be the main cause of her trembles?

"Hmmph!" Jeb snorted. "You're coming with me and I'm not letting you out of my sight until you've eaten a solid, well-balanced meal."

Without giving her a chance to argue, he nudged her lightly on the arm and steered her out the door into the afternoon sunlight.

The inside of the car seemed too small, and Jeb was intensely aware of her nearness. Out of the corner of his eye he could see the curve of her thigh and the swell of her breasts. His hands itched to reach out and touch her, to feel the softness of her skin. He exhaled slowly.

"Where are we going?" She turned to face him, her eyes slipping to his lips, lingering there. The sound of her breathing matched his own. Suddenly, she was in his arms, and he was pressing her close as though he'd never let her go.

His lips found hers. They were soft and warm and clinging. He could barely contain himself, yearning to forget everything and drive her to the nearest motel to while away the afternoon making love to her, nestled deep inside her. God! He had to get control of himself, forget about the pressure ripping his gut to pieces, and just be thankful that she was in his arms.

Jeb shifted so he could more fully receive the impact of her breasts and flat stomach nestled against him. Feeling like a starving man, he let his fingers wander over her face, trace the outline of her mouth, investigate the fullness of her lower lip. His tongue pried, utterly aroused by the heat of her mouth; her fingers wound securely in his hair and he could feel his insides coiling like a giant spring.

McKenzie, too, was having difficulty clinging to reality. The last thing she'd planned when she had docilely preceded him out of the hospital was for him to touch her, to end up in his arms right here in broad daylight for the whole world to see. But for the life of her, she couldn't seem to break his embrace.

As though it had a mind of its own, her tongue met and equalled each rousing stroke of his, and she felt herself being pulled down into a vortex of sensuous, aching need.

Then, just as quickly as it had begun, it was over.

A tapping sound on the window sent them scurrying to their respective sides of the car.

Gasping for air, Jeb whipped around to the window.

"Sorry, sir," the man said, an embarrassed edge to his tone, but—"

Jeb held his hand, halting his speech. "We were just leaving," he said, realizing on closer observation that the stranger was a security guard.

The guard shifted his eyes to McKenzie and then back to Jeb, an admiring twinkle in his eyes. "Be seein' ya," he drawled before turning and lumbering off in the direction of the main building.

Battling the uncomfortable silence, Jeb turned to look at McKenzie, fearful of what he would find there. Though her face was as white as tissue paper, she met his eyes head on. They stared at each other and then burst out laughing.

In that moment, Jeb had never loved her more.

"Thanks for lunch," McKenzie said an hour later after stepping out of the elegant restaurant into the damp November wind. Once more comfortably seated in Jeb's car, she shivered slightly, still feeling the biting chill of the wind. It looked as if they were going to have a cold crisp Thanksgiving after all, she mused. In Texas one never knew. The old saying, If you don't like the weather in Texas today, just wait until tomorrow and it will change, certainly had merit.

She let her head fall back against the raised cushion while she waited for Jeb to come around the car and climb in behind the wheel.

At Jeb's recommendation, she had consumed a salad and barbecued shrimp. For an appetizer, they had shared a plate of thinly sliced onion rings fried light and crisp. The food had been delicious, and under Jeb's watchful eye and with his constant encouragement—"Just one bite and I promise I won't bug you anymore"—she had eaten much more than she had thought possible.

But throughout the meal, McKenzie had been aware of the tension crackling in the air. Uppermost in her mind had been the soul-searching kiss they had exchanged. Even as she'd listened to Jeb talk about the national economy and his business predictions, she hadn't been able to erase that kiss from her mind.

Now, as he slammed the car door behind him, McKenzie felt again that old magical pull. Turning away abruptly, she held herself very still, as though by doing so, the disturbing feeling inside her would disappear and with it this all-consuming passion she felt for Jeb.

"Where to? Your wish is my command," he joked lightly to break the uneasy tension.

McKenzie made the pretense of straightening the hem of her skirt, reluctant to face him. "I . . . really should go back to the hospital—"

"No, you should not," Jeb said emphatically.

"You didn't let me finish," she countered mildly. "I was going to add that I would go to the office instead."

"How 'bout instead we drive to Cedar Plaza and take a look around?" He fished in his pocket for a cigarette. After lighting it, he went on. "Who knows? Maybe we'll run into Dillard and can put him on the spot with a few questions."

McKenzie swallowed against the heat rising up the back of her throat. Even though she was in favor of visiting the mall site, she knew it would be dangerous to be alone with Jeb a second longer than she had to. She had indulged herself enough as it was.

"I'd like... to," she finally stammered, "but I'm afraid I'll miss Rachel if she calls me," she added lamely, her gaze completely averted now.

"McKenzie," he ordered softly, "look at me."

Responding, as though she were a puppet on a string, she brought her face around to his.

"I thought we had called a truce, that we had agreed to work together," he chastised gently.

McKenzie wet her lips nervously. "We had..."

"Well then, let's do it," Jeb said, forestalling another excuse. "Let's make the best of a bad situation and go from there and see what happens. Okay?"

McKenzie remained mute, unsure of what to say. Was it actually possible to work together? When she had agreed to his help on the investigation, she hadn't expected it to ever really come about. Now, she was being put on the spot, and she didn't know what to do about it.

"McKenzie, I'm not going to hurt you, ever again," Jeb promised huskily, wanting to ease the desperate look in her eyes.

Even now, as his eyes cross-examined her, she could feel the current pulling her toward him, his soothing words moving her deeply. What was the point in fighting? she asked herself, defeat wilting her resistance. She was only half a person without him, no good to anyone, certainly not to herself. So why keep dishing out the punishment?

Jeb didn't move a muscle, knowing the decision had to be hers.

Suddenly, McKenzie whirled to face him, sought his eyes, a beautiful smile parting her lips. Jeb's heart leaped with joy as her silent surrender reached out to him, their eyes sparking in mutual need.

Reverently, Jeb leaned over and placed his lips against the quivering sweetness of hers, savoring the moment like a miser does a penny.

Then with an inward groan, he raised his head and said in a raspy voice, "I think we'd better take care of business."

A thick silence hovered as Jeb skillfully directed the car toward their destination. McKenzie sat stoically, concentrating on calming her racing heart, conscious of an underlying sense of excitement with each breath she took, while in her mind echoed the quote, "Fools rush in where angels fear to tread."

Twenty minutes later Jeb braked the car against a chain-link fence that bordered the construction site of Cedar Plaza Mall.

"Is this your first time here?" McKenzie asked, looking straight ahead, her eyes closely monitoring the activities inside the fenced area, hoping to catch a glimpse of Hal Melrose. Men in hard hats were milling about everywhere, and huge pieces of machinery were noisily at work. But in spite of the busy atmosphere, very little of the building had actually been completed.

"Yes, it is," Jeb finally answered, his eyes also locked on the scene before him.

McKenzie faced him. "Well, what do you think?"

Jeb answered with another question, his eyes finding hers. "How long have they been working on this?" he asked.

"Several months for sure."

"That's what I figured."

"Are you thinking what I'm thinking?"

"Sure as hell am," Jeb drawled. "I'm no builder and don't pretend to be, but I'm positive that this building should be a lot further along than it is now."

"My sentiments exactly," McKenzie agreed readily. "I drove by here several times last week, and if there's any progress being made, it's at a snail's pace. And they sure can't blame it on the weather."

"Let's go have a look around," Jeb suggested, his hand on the door handle. "I'm banking on running into Dillard. I'd like nothing better than to see you put him in the proverbial hot seat."

McKenzie laughed, the musical sound causing Jeb's heart to flutter in response. God, but it was going to be a long afternoon.

As they made their way across the graveled area, McKenzie noticed that several of the men stopped what they were doing and stared at her and Jeb with open curiosity.

As Jeb placed his hand on the gate, a big bear of a man stepped forward, his stance hostile as he blocked the way. "That's as far as you go, mister," he declared. "No one's allowed in here."

Simultaneously, McKenzie and Jeb whipped out their press badges, flashing them in front of the man's face.

If anything, he became more hostile, his eyes narrowing until they were tiny slits in his round, beefy face. "We don't allow no newspaper people around here," he said gruffly.

"Are you in charge here?" Jeb asked, not in the least bit intimidated by the stranger's surly manner.

"No, I ain't, but—"

"Then go get your boss," Jeb ordered bluntly.

"Now, you listen here, fellow. I told you—"

"Anders, what seems to be the problem?"

They all three swung around in the direction of the unfamiliar voice, and watched as a short, stocky man in khaki pants and shirt came toward them.

"Ah, Mr. Rollins, no problem," Anders sneered. "I can handle it. These here people are from the newspaper, wanting to snoop around."

The man named Rollins, his round cherub face matching his short, stocky build, eyed his subordinate. "It's all right, Anders. You go back to work. I'll take over."

"Whatever you say," Anders mumbled, making it know that he would much rather stick around for the action.

"The name's Chet Rollins," he said, unlocking the gat and motioning for McKenzie and Jeb to come through "I'm Mr. Dillard's assistant," he added boastfully, a though he wanted to let it be known that he wasn't just an other flunky.

Their introductions were followed by a short but uncom fortable silence while Rollins eyed them closely, cautio tempering his expression. "What can I do for you?"

Jeb spoke first. "Well, for starters we thought we'd loo around, maybe visit your boss and ask him a few ques tions."

"What makes you think Mr. Dillard would be here?" Although his voice reeked with suspicion, it had lost non of its forced cordiality.

"No reason, exactly," Jeb replied. "Just thought we' take a chance."

Rollins shifted his weight from one foot to the othen "Well, it just so happens you're in luck. Jeff stopped by little while ago and is still in the office. If you'll wait righ here, I'll get him."

Once he was out of hearing distance, McKenzie looked u at Jeb. "I get the impression he's running scared."

"Exactly." Jeb's eyes flashed. "This is getting more in teresting by the minute."

Before McKenzie could reply, the door of the neares metal building swung open and out came a tall, lanky ma with dark hair and full red lips. A long, ugly scar ran dow the side of one cheek.

Two steps brought him within touching distance o McKenzie and Jeb. After polite introductions were agai exchanged, Jeff Dillard looked to McKenzie and asked "Just exactly what can I do for you?"

Out of the corner of her eye, McKenzie saw Jeb move closer to her. "I'm gathering information for a story on the center, Mr. Dillard," she answered. "Any pertinent information you can give will be appreciated."

Dillard seemed to relax. "Sounds good to me. This project means a lot to this part of Austin—and to the entire city, as far as that goes. This section was an eyesore until we began building the center. As head of Dillard Construction, I'd be right proud to give you and Mr. Langley a grand tour and answer any questions you might have."

McKenzie suppressed the urge to look at Jeb, positive he was thinking the same thing she was—that Jeff Dillard was going out of his way to be nice. Why?

"What's the targeted completion date?" McKenzie asked, feeling Jeb's hand under her elbow, guiding her around a piece of equipment lying on the ground. She flashed him a grateful smile before focusing again on Dillard.

"Well," he hedged, removing his hard hat and scratching his head, "several more months, I expect. We've had problems getting the material on time." He paused and laughed, though it never reached his eyes. "You know how that goes. Can't depend on other folks. But hopefully it'll be ready by early spring."

"When you say you can't depend on the other folks, are you referring to fraud, Mr. Dillard?" McKenzie asked bluntly.

If Dillard was taken aback, he failed to show it; his voice was as even and cool as McKenzie's. "Explain exactly what you mean by fraud." His lips thinned slightly when he stressed that word.

"What she means," Jeb chimed in casually, "is that it's a known fact that on projects such as this, contractors sometimes rip off materials, to sell them on the side for huge profits. As a result, the buildings never get finished."

"Well, I can assure you, both of you," Dillard said coldly, "that nothing like that is going on here. Our problem doesn't stem from mismanagement, only inferior help."

I just bet it does, McKenzie thought, feeling Jeb's presence beside her, the wind tantalizing her nostrils with the elusive smell of his cologne. She had to force herself to concentrate on what she was doing.

Taking a different approach, McKenzie inquired, "How will the store owners be able to keep their costs down so they can sell their merchandise at a discount? After all, that's the purpose of the center, isn't it, to give the people of this area a first-class shopping mall, but offer goods at bargain basement prices? From the looks of these diagrams, the grounds and building are going to be quite plush."

They had stopped in front of a glassed-in case housing large-scale drawings of the mall, showing both interior and exterior designs.

"No problem, Ms. Moore," Dillard answered, apparently recovered from Jeb's biting accusation. "The city fathers want the outside decor to be no different from the other shopping centers in our fair city, so they're assuming the additional cost—"

"You mean the taxpayers, don't you?" McKenzie interrupted.

"If you like," Dillard retorted, then went on. "But as in any other center, the store owners will be responsible for their own decorations. If they choose to cut the costs that way, then it's their prerogative."

Another silence followed as McKenzie made a pretense of taking notes, while Jeb casually smoked a cigarette.

Then slowly they began to meander through the shell of the building, McKenzie using the time to scan the premises for Hal Melrose. When she was convinced he was not working, her sense of unease increased.

At length McKenzie focused her attention on Dillard. 'Have there been any more accidents on the job lately?'' she asked, scoring with deadly accuracy.

Dark color swept up to Dillard's hairline, and for a moment his steps faltered. "Before you go any further, Ms. Moore," he said, his eyes sparking dangerously, "I want to set the record straight. The accidents were exactly that and nothing more. And I personally resent your insinuating otherwise."

Jeb took a final puff of his cigarette and, after flicking it to the floor, ground it out with the toe of his shoe. "Don't take it personally, Dillard," he said, holding a moderate tone to his voice with difficulty. He longed to smash his fist into the lying bastard's face. "Ms. Moore is here to cull the rumors from the facts. Unfortunately, to get at the truth we sometimes have to ask questions that aren't popular. No offense intended."

A little of the hostility disappeared from Dillard's face. 'Well, you can't blame me for protecting my backside. I feel like what we're doing is worthwhile and I don't take too kindly to folks thinking otherwise."

McKenzie maintained her silence with an effort, wanting to shout the caustic comment burning her tongue. God! the gall of that man, acting as though he had just been given sainthood.

As though Jeb read her mind, he suddenly stuck out his hand. "Thanks for the tour and the interview, Dillard. We know how busy you are, so we won't take up any more of your time."

Dillard returned the handshake, his eyes once again turning wary as they dwelled on McKenzie. "I hope you see your way clear to giving us a good write-up," he said. "And feel free to come back and visit anytime."

A short time later, when McKenzie and Jeb were in the car, they looked at each other.

"Dillard's lying through his teeth," McKenzie said, he eyes showing her agitation. "And I'm going to prove it."

"I agree, but as I told you before, this could get real sticky before it's finished. Both Dillard and his beefy side kick Rollins give me the creeps. And I'm willing to bet tha slime ball Dillard picked up the phone to the mayor the sec ond we were out of sight."

"No doubt about it," McKenzie said. "Only, they don' know how tough I can be; I'll fight them to the bitte end."

That's what I'm afraid of, Jeb thought, his insides tak ing a brutal twist as he guided the car onto the street.

He just hoped to hell he could protect her....

Jeb wasn't far from wrong. Jeff Dillard did indeed picl up the phone to call the mayor, but not before sending fo Rollins.

When the foreman entered the makeshift office, Dil lard's eyes were snapping like firecrackers. "Those two ar a pain in the ass," he hissed, an unmistakable hint of vio lence in his voice.

"You just say the word, boss, and they're both dea(meat," Rollins drawled, an eager light popping into hi otherwise dull eyes.

Dillard slammed his hand against the desk, the sounc bouncing off the wall of the building like exploding dyna mite.

Rollins flinched. But Dillard didn't seem to notice as h launched into a tirade. "Not yet, dammit. We're too clos(to having enough money to cut out, to live the rest of ou lives like kings. I'm not about to let little twirps like tha Moore lady and lover-boy Langley put a kink in my plans. No, siree. I'll let you squash 'em like a bug when the time comes."

"Like I said, boss, just say the word. Even though I don't cotton to hurtin' no woman, I'll take real pleasure in takin' out Langley." Rollins's eyes were cruelly slanted.

Dillard suddenly looked a tad uneasy. "I wouldn't go underestimating the enemy if I were you. When I found out he was snooping around, asking questions of certain people, I did a little checking on my own. Found out he can be a mean sonofabitch himself."

A vicious laugh shook Rollins's entire frame. "Not when he's got a bullet buried in his gut."

"You know, don't you," Dillard said, lifting the receiver to his ear and punching out a number with the end of a pencil, "that Langley's mother was with the mayor the night she died. What I'm trying to say is that both the old man and the son—especially the old man—have an axe to grind."

"I sure as hell don't want to be no fall guy for the mayor," Rollins replied nastily.

Dillard held up his hand for silence as he turned his mouth into the receiver. "Dillard here," he said in a clipped voice. "Let me speak to the mayor."

After a moment of silence, he spoke again. "We got trouble, Witherspoon, and it comes in twos."

The days raced by, ushering Thanksgiving in and out like a whirlwind, though McKenzie would remember it as a special day for the rest of her life. As promised, Rachel and Rosie prepared a sumptuous meal, and the day was spent eating and drinking, and offering thanks that, while Carson could not be with them, at least he was improving.

Jeb went out of his way to be his most charming self, much to Rachel's delight and McKenzie's trepidation, causing her to question the sanity of their so-called truce.

Ever since their visit to the construction site, McKenzie and Jeb had steered their efforts jointly toward building their case against the mayor. The only time McKenzie was

not under Jeb's watchful eye was when she was with Dan
iel. But those times were rare; she used her work and Carson's second stroke as excuses for cutting short Daniel's
dinner invitations.

The real reason, however, was the gnawing sense of guilt
she felt for wanting one man while she was with another. Yet
Daniel seemed to have done an about-face in his attitude,
choosing to accept the time she spent with Jeb and not ha-
rassing her about it. What was he up to? More to the point,
what was she going to do about her relationship with Daniel?

To ease her aching conscience, she worked long hours on
the Cedar Plaza article, although she still didn't have
enough evidence to allow her to go to press. She had been in
touch with her contact in the construction company, Hal
Melrose, but to date he still hadn't been able to come up
with any tangible proof.

So with each day she spent in Jeb's company, the personal stakes climbed higher. Her feelings for him became
inescapable as she inhaled the scent of him, watched his
fingers coiling around his coffee cup, lost herself in the color
of his eyes. Every accidental touch caused her to tremble
with the need to feel his mouth and hands on her body.

It was an impossible situation both physically and emo-
tionally. Why had fate suddenly decided to pit her against
such overwhelming odds? she wondered despairingly.

Now, as she prepared to go into the office, even though
it was Saturday, she felt as though her head might simply
split from the swelling pressure on her brain.

A sigh rivaled the silence in her bedroom as she crossed
to the window and stared outside. Christmas. Signs of the
most celebrated season of the year were in evidence everywhere: in the air, in the streets, in the houses—everywhere,
that is, except in her heart.

It was as though the secure foundations of her life had quivered and fallen. Where would it all end?

She sensed she was not alone before she actually confirmed it. Feeling goose bumps tickle her skin, she whipped around, her eyes clashing instantly with Jeb's.

He was standing in her doorway, a smile lifting the corners of his mouth. "Don't you think it's about time we got a Christmas tree?"

Chapter 10

McKenzie felt as though she'd just been tossed out of a window. After mentally picking herself up, she stared at him, wild-eyed.

He looked fresh, ready to start the day, devastatingly attractive in his favorite garb, jeans and T-shirt with a windbreaker slung over his shoulder. Her breath sagged curiously in her lungs at his unexpected invitation.

"Well," Jeb said softly.

"Well...what?" she stammered, stalling for time, trying to gather her wits into some semblance of order. Oh, God, she wanted to go with him, but dared not. To do so would merely prolong the agony, further break her heart into smaller pieces.

"A Christmas tree." His smile, though gentle, was mocking, as if he could read her thoughts. "Surely you planned on having one."

McKenzie swallowed with difficulty, reaching up and lifting her heavy curls from under the collar of her dress.

"I . . . I guess so," she stammered again, suddenly feeling foolish. "Actually, Christmas this year kind of snuck up on me."

Jeb laughed, the heady sound making her stomach knot with yearning. "I can understand that," he replied sincerely. "All you've been doing is working and worrying about my father. But with only ten days till Christmas, I refuse to let you off the hook. And anyway, it's a perfect day to hunt for a tree."

McKenzie's voice held regret. "I really do need to work."

"Hogwash!"

She laughed spontaneously, feeling herself weakening. "Well, now that you put it that way . . ."

"Then you'll go?" His tone was odd.

Dare she? Dare she grab the moment and run with it? After all, what he was suggesting was really quite harmless. She could handle it, couldn't she? Her hesitation was brief. "Just try to get away without me," she said breathlessly. "Whoever heard of Christmas without a tree?"

The surge that went through Jeb made him feel as though he'd just received a new lease on life. "Hurry and change your clothes," he said with difficulty. "I'll wait downstairs."

Once alone, McKenzie discarded her dress and panty hose in a frenzy. She tried to keep her mind blank, not wanting any unpleasant thoughts to dampen her excitement. It was foolish of her to be doing this, she warned herself. Spending the day with Jeb was not the answer to her problem. *He was the problem.* She should do other things, find other ways to weary her body and mind.

Refusing to heed these warnings, McKenzie slipped on a pair of jeans and a heavy sweater, opting to forgo a coat, unwilling to be hampered while she selected a tree.

Her cheeks were splotched with red as she raced down the stairs with a little-girl eagerness and found him waiting impatiently for her by the front door, an answering eagerness mirrored in his eyes.

Suddenly, she didn't regret her decision. Tomorrow would be soon enough to question the sanity of today.

"How 'bout trying the nurseries first?" Jeb suggested moments later as he nosed the car onto the highway, toward the outskirts of the city. Then, after a moment, he turned and found her watching him. Her eyes were soft and warm, reminding him of robins' eggs.

The silence that followed was filled with a suffocating tension.

"That's fine with me," she murmured at last, indistinctly, forcing herself to concentrate on their destination rather than on the way his eyes smoldered with desire, the way his hands curled around the steering wheel, the way the silver hair edged the top of his ear, or the way his jeans cupped the powerful muscles in his leg that was within touching distance.

Jeb cleared his throat, but his voice came out raspy, unclear. "If we don't have any luck in town, we'll head for the country and chop down our own tree."

McKenzie smiled her consent as she turned toward the window. The day couldn't have been more perfect. Christmas was definitely in the air. It was cold and cloudy, looking as though it could snow at the drop of a hat, which would be a rarity this time of year in central Texas.

Yet one could hope, McKenzie told herself. She would like nothing better than to see the tender white crystals cascade from the heavens, making this day even more perfect. She knew she was dreaming, but she couldn't seem to erase the fantasy of the fresh pure snow covering up all her problems, her heartaches. Starting with a clean slate . . . she and Jeb . . . everything perfect.

"Tired?" Jeb asked, breaking her train of thought.

She flashed him an impish smile. "Actually, I was wishing it would snow."

Jeb chuckled, taking in the fetching picture she made, her hair its usual wild profusion of curls, her lips moist and rich in color. And the heady scent of her perfume—it suddenly replaced the air in his lungs. He ached to touch her. "Maybe if we hold our mouths right, it'll do just that," he said instead.

McKenzie laughed. "How about if I twitch my nose like Elizabeth Montgomery used to on *Bewitched*?" she asked, playing along with his outlandish suggestion, enjoying this moment of rare camaraderie to the hilt.

"I'll go along with that," Jeb said gently, "especially if it'll keep that smile on your face. Besides, I'm determined to get you the prettiest tree this side of heaven," he added with a deep laugh.

McKenzie was held spellbound by the way the line beside his mouth shifted as he spoke. It made her tingle deliciously, dangerously. "I'll hold you to that," she said at length.

Another silence prevailed as Jeb maneuvered the car along a side street not far from one of Austin's largest and most popular nurseries. From this distance, she could see a roped-off area crammed full of trees in all sizes and shapes, and colors.

Although McKenzie felt her excitement mounting, she made no effort to curb it. It was a treat to slow down, to relax, to take a chance. She hid a smile. She would just enjoy the outing, allow the morning to happen, she promised herself, as moments later they ambled toward the large stock of Christmas trees.

"I've never seen so much activity in one place," she said, soaking up the sights and sounds around her. People were wandering around, garbed in bright-colored coats and scarves, making oohs and aahs over this tree or that one,

and "The Twelve Days of Christmas" was literally screaming over the loudspeaker boxes positioned at intervals
around the grounds.

From the banks of trees stacked against the stand, the
sharp, pungent odor of needles wafted to her nostrils,
bringing the pain of nostalgia. This would be the first
Christmas she could remember without her stepfather.

Jeb's eyes were warm as they peered down at her. "See
one that strikes your fancy?"

McKenzie tilted her chin. "Mmmm, that one—" she
pointed at a huge fir "—looks like it might do." She was
unshakable in her bias where Christmas trees were concerned. The idea of coating trees with artificial paints filled
her with horror.

The tree would have to be green. Custom, and the dimensions of the den with its high-beamed ceiling, decreed
that it should be a certain shape and size, that it should re-
semble as closely as possible the ones from preceding years.

"Good as done," Jeb said with a smile, one long stride
taking him to the tree. Snaking out a hand, he stood it upright for her scrutiny.

McKenzie cocked her head to the left, then to the right.
"Won't do. Too tall."

Patiently, Jeb dropped that one and chose another, moving now within touching distance of her. "How does this
one suit you?" he asked, his voice containing a husky
tremor as their eyes met and locked.

Suddenly, it was as though they were alone, existing on a
planet of their own.

Although Jeb continued to hold the tree, McKenzie
merely shook her head, hardly aware of its dimensions,
aware of nothing but Jeb's closeness. It seemed to her there
was something terribly unfair in their being so near and yet
forbidden to touch, to hold, to give warmth to each other.
She knew he was making an all-out effort to keep his prom-

ise, to leave her be, not to push himself on her, honestly believing that was what she wanted. Oh, God, if only that were so.

In her mind, she had pictured it as being so simple to say a word or make a gesture that would destroy the barrier between them like brittle glass. Everything would be solved quickly and easily if she could only cry out to him, hold out her arms, instead of standing with hands at her sides, mumbling about the tree, pretending to care how it looked.

Then suddenly the moment was shattered.

"Can I give you folks a helping hand?" a booming voice broke the silence, causing them to swing their heads toward the sound.

Fleetingly, McKenzie thought she heard Jeb swear as he made a gallant effort to compose himself.

Jeb feigned a smile, when all he wanted to do was sweep McKenzie up in his arms and take her home and make love to her far into the night. But he knew that was impossible. He had given his word and he was trying damn hard to stick to it. But God, being with her and not being able to touch her was pure torture.

"Some mighty fine live specimens there," the man pointed out before Jeb could reply.

"We're just helping ourselves," Jeb finally managed, once again in complete control. "If that's all right," he added sarcastically.

The man's round belly shook as he laughed, bringing a smile to McKenzie's lips. She thought he looked just like a miniature Santa Claus. "Go right ahead. Just holler when you find one the little lady likes." He winked. "I know how it is, pleasin' the women folk." Throwing them a toothless grin, he wandered off toward another group of lookers.

McKenzie laughed out loud. "I hate to admit it, but he's right," she said, glad things were calm once more, although a certain air of expectancy still hung between them. "I'll never make up my mind," she added helplessly.

"No need to panic, little lady," Jeb mocked with a drawl, flashing her his most rakish grin. "We have the rest of the day to find that perfect tree."

They went to four nurseries before McKenzie found the ideal tree: a ten-foot blue spruce. It was indeed a thing of beauty, and she could hardly wait until they got home so she could decorate it.

The day was one that dreams were made of, truly magical. As they dashed from one nursery to the other, McKenzie saw a side of Jeb that she had thought was long dead. He told jokes, smiled easily and often. She found herself listening more than talking, watching him, delighting in just being with him. *Take the moment and run with it,* her heart cried, and she listened, not being greedy, just simply enjoying the stolen moments of enchantment.

Home now, with twilight further darkening the overcast sky, McKenzie watched as Jeb crawled out from under the tree, having just secured the stand; he stood, a look of triumph on his tanned features.

"Well, princess, what's the verdict?"

McKenzie clapped her hands enthusiastically. "Oh, Jeb, it's just perfect."

His smile was indulgent as he thought again how much she did remind him of a princess. While he had climbed into the attic and rummaged around until he located the boxes of lights and other decorations, she had gone upstairs and changed into a red velvet caftan. Her hair was swept up on top of her head in wild profusion, leaving her creamy neck bare, calling attention to the pulse beating at the base of her throat like the flutter of a hummingbird. How the hell he was going to keep his hands off her was beyond him.

During the days they had been working together on the Cedar Plaza investigation, he had been plagued with a constant ache in his loins, unable to block out thoughts of her delectable body—so close, yet so far.

Today had been sweet torture.

"I know you're ready to start decorating, but I'm famished," he said, forcing his eyes away from her. "Why don't I see what Rosie left on the stove to eat while you go through those boxes of junk and get organized?"

"Those 'boxes of junk,' as you called them, can wait," she assured him quickly. "I'll take care of the kitchen duties." She smiled. "That's the least I can do after watching you wrestle with the tree."

He manufactured his best grin. "Nope, I insist on assuming the KP duties. If Rosie doesn't have anything that whets our appetite, I'll rustle up the meanest bacon-and-tomato sandwich you've ever tasted."

She veered her eyes to his. "Well, what are you waiting for? You don't hear me arguing, do you?"

His laughter was still caressing her ears some minutes later as McKenzie crawled around on her knees sorting out the strands of twinkling lights, comforted by his banging around in the kitchen.

By the time she was finished, Jeb had the bacon frying to a crisp, dark brown and the tomatoes sliced. She watched him put the sandwiches together and she made fresh coffee. She carried the mugs into the den, and they sat on the floor, Indian-fashion, in front of the fireplace, while the flames danced cheerfully.

"Mmmm. This tastes heavenly," McKenzie said.

"I told you, when it comes to being chief cook and bottle washer, I'm a pro." He looked up at the tree. "You outdid yourself in choosing the tree. It's about the best-looking one we've ever had."

McKenzie's eyes tracked his. "If not the best then close to it," she mused, remembering Christmases past, when they were young and it was truly a special day.

"Too bad we can't turn back the clock," Jeb responded softly as though he had read her mind.

McKenzie smiled and jumped up, shaking off the somber mood that threatened to dampen their spirits. She refused to let anything mar this perfect day. "Let's get this show on the road, shall we?" she demanded huskily, yanking a string of lights and thrusting the opposite end toward him.

Jeb watched her with a smoldering gaze that suddenly turned her bones to liquid. "Lights first?" he asked inanely.

"Lights first," she repeated, turning her back on his heart-stopping charisma.

In record time they had the entire tree strung with hundreds of twinkling lights.

Then McKenzie moved the small ladder Jeb had brought from the attic and hastily climbed it. When she had positioned herself on the top rung, she gazed down at Jeb and held out her hand. "If you'll pass me the ornaments, we'll be off and running."

Jeb smiled, his eyes suddenly even with her delectable bottom. He swallowed against the surging heat building from within and quickly went to do as she asked. With unsteady hands, he grabbed a glossy red apple and lifted it to her.

"Thanks," she murmured, carefully avoiding both his eyes and his fingers, knowing that one spark would set off an explosion that neither was prepared to handle.

"Hey, you'd best be careful," Jeb cautioned gently, his words effectively splitting the silence. "You're reaching too high. If you'll get down, I'll do that." He stepped back and eyed her handiwork. McKenzie had worked herself half way around the tree, bringing it to life. "It's looking great," he added. "After I put a few more ornaments toward the top, we'll be finished."

"Hand me that satin dove, please," McKenzie responded, holding out her hand. "I can see the perfect place for it. Then I'll get down and let you have it."

After securing it in her hand, she stretched, her arm angling high above her head.

Then it happened. Without warning.

Jeb's frantic shout, "Watch out!" gurgled in his throat as both McKenzie and the tree began to topple toward him.

"Jeb!" McKenzie screamed, desperately groping to regain her balance. But it was fruitless; the damage had been done. She teetered only a second on the edge of the ladder, losing her balance completely.

Panic froze her vocal cords and rendered her helpless.

All she was able to do was clutch at the branches, the sharp needles digging into her hands, while she felt herself falling.

Jeb acted quickly. His cry of alarm was lost as he suddenly bore the brunt of McKenzie's weight, her body crashing into his, the impact momentarily knocking the wind from his lungs, the heavy tree slapping them both to the carpet and crashing on top of them.

For perhaps a second, Jeb couldn't move, couldn't speak. But thank God he could feel, feel McKenzie's inert body lying beside his, her heart pounding like a sledgehammer against his ear. Oh, God, was she hurt?

Panic-stricken but determined, Jeb slashed his way through the branches until he managed to squeeze his hands under her back. With superhuman effort, he inched his way out from under the tree, dragging her with him, ignoring the sharp, stinging prick of the needles as they buried in his back.

Suddenly, Jeb noticed he was in front of the fireplace, the orange flames offering him light.

He looked down at her and demanded urgently, "McKenzie, say something!" His hands probed her body, searching for broken bones.

McKenzie's eyes were squeezed tightly together, a tear just managing to slip from under her lashes to slide down her cheek. "Jeb," she whispered pathetically.

"Oh, God, McKenzie, are you all right?" he asked with gut-wrenching apprehension.

Her eyes opened slowly. "I...I think so...just stunned," she stammered, conscious of his hands on her body.

Every nerve in Jeb began to twitch with relief and he laughed, gathering her in his arms like a bouquet of wild flowers, exquisitely fragrant and fragile. "I shudder to think what would have happened if I hadn't been standing there."

An answering smile forced her lips open. "Well, for one thing, I'd have busted my buns, or worse."

"Or worse," he said, his grin still intact.

Suddenly, she roused herself enough to peer over Jeb's shoulder. Her eyes widened and her mouth gaped open as she assessed the damage. The huge tree was sprawled across the floor, ornaments scattered to the four corners of the room. Things were in a shambles.

"Oh, no," McKenzie groaned, falling back against the carpet.

Jeb's eyes twinkled with suppressed laughter. "Made a mess, didn't ya?" he drawled, his hand resting comfortably across her stomach.

"It's really not funny, you know," McKenzie began stiffly, only to realize suddenly how close he was, the position of his hand, the warmth of his voice....

Jeb's grin blossomed. "It's all according to how one looks at it," he said huskily, a finger delving into her navel. "Now that I know you weren't hurt..."

A fervent desire erupted in McKenzie with a force that sent her senses reeling. "Well, you'll...have to admit that when I do something, I do it right." Her words came out in a breathy gust.

"That you do," Jeb whispered thickly, unconsciously leaning closer. "That you do."

The tip of her tongue suddenly darted between her lips. "Wanna help me clean it up?"

Jeb's voice was rich with amusement—and something else. "In a minute."

"Promise?"

"Cross my heart."

"And hope to die?"

"Never, if it means leaving you," he said hoarsely.

An abrupt tension swept away all humor. The stark desire on his face made her mouth go dry.

"Jeb?"

"Oh, God, McKenzie," he murmured like a crazed man. "My sweet, sweet McKenzie." His mouth hovered above hers, his eyes questioning.

McKenzie felt a sudden stirring in her stomach, thinking, *I'm at his mercy.* Then he brought his mouth to hers, his tongue hot as it parted her lips.

There was no brief exploration this time, but a languorous probing, circling, then darting. Her body made small writhing motions as his hands pressed into her shoulders almost roughly, and then, softening his touch, he pushed aside the folds of her caftan, baring her breasts.

McKenzie arched her back from the carpet to offer the smoothness of her breasts to him, full, rounded and nibbed roseate circles. She gasped as his lips closed over one, then the other, and he heard the half-cry that followed, a sound of delicious delight.

"I adore you, McKenzie," he rasped, his tongue working magic.

"Oh, Jeb," she cried brokenly, clutching at him wildly.

Suddenly they went crazy. Clothes were discarded with heated haste. The floor in front of the fire became their bed. His arms crushed her against him, then pushed her away. Only to smash together again, on target, as one.

Then nothing but sweet-sipping caresses, lips warm and potent, brimming with unselfish fondness and consideration.

Their bodies surged again, clinging, thrusting, violently demanding, soaring so high until they thought they would disintegrate and the fragments scatter among the stars.

He was insatiable.

She was a temptress.

He wooed her.

She bedeviled him.

He directed.

She possessed.

They surrendered.

Only when the fire no longer provided them with warmth did they find their way to bed and back into each other's arms.

"I'll never get enough of you," he said.

"I'm glad."

"You're mine," he boasted.

She lowered her hand.

"I can't take much of that," he said after a while.

"I hope not," she whispered, stroking, squeezing, teasing.

"I'm still too old for you," he ground out.

"Never," she whispered, filling her hand with his.

"We must sleep."

"Later," she challenged.

"Ah, yes . . . later."

And they did. Much later.

The night came to an end all too soon. As dawn spun its colors of gold and orange through the sky, they lay wrapped together, each drawing warmth from the other.

After their lovemaking the night before, they had slept like newborn babies, sated, exhausted, until they had both awakened, thrown on robes and, giggling like children, scampered downstairs to clean up the mess.

While Jeb righted the tree, McKenzie had made cups of hot chocolate with floating marshmallows and whipped cream. Later they had drifted back upstairs, arms entwined, leaving the tree standing tall and proud, dressed to perfection, once again ablaze with dozens of brightly colored lights.

Now, lying beside him in the light of dawn, watching the steady rise and fall of his chest, she refused to think about the future, realizing that nothing had been settled, merely experienced. Her obligations and problems were still glaringly real, but at the moment nothing was important except Jeb and what they had shared.

Tomorrow held the promise of wonderful things to come. And because of that she could face today.

McKenzie was standing by the side of the bed. She had just slipped into her robe when she looked up and saw Jeb standing in the doorway with a tray in his hand.

He tipped his head to one side. "Good morning, sleepyhead," he murmured.

The low, husky tone of his voice feathered down McKenzie's spine and left her breathless. "Is . . . is it late?"

His lips twitched. "It's after nine o'clock."

A hand flew to her cheek. "Oh, no, I should've been at work long ago."

"Well, since I'm the boss," he drawled, advancing further into the room, his jeans slung low on his hips, "I guess it's all right if you're late, considering you didn't get much sleep last night." He unloaded the tray onto the nearest table.

McKenzie flushed at his reference to their hours of lovemaking. She reached out and latched onto the cup of coffee he handed her, hoping to mask her sudden confusion.

"McKenzie?" His eyes were searching hers with disturbing intensity, loving her, wanting her. "We have to talk. We can't keep on going like this indefinitely."

She looked away. "I . . . I know," she whispered, loath to break the spell of magic that hovered over them. And even though she loved him, had never stopped loving him, trust still came hard. And there was her stepfather. And Daniel . . .

Gut instinct warned Jeb to take it easy, that now was not the time to put their relationship under a microscope. He saw the play of conflicting emotions flicker across her face, and though he longed to reach out to her, he did not, sensing that to push her would be tantamount to losing her.

"Jeb, I . . ." she began, only to have her sentence die on her lips.

"It's all right," he cut in gently, placing a finger across her lips. "Later. We'll talk later. Anyway, I have something else in mind. Something equally important."

McKenzie felt slightly intoxicated as she looked up at him. "Oh?"

"Oh, is right," Jeb whispered, his mouth descending on the fresh sweetness of hers as his masculine body contoured against her own. Red-hot hunger united them. McKenzie prayed this moment would never end, yearned to tuck Jeb inside her heart and run away.

It was several hours later before they made it to work.

Days later McKenzie was still basking in the memories of her and Jeb's magical day and night together. Every time she thought about the Christmas-tree episode, a smile fanned ter lips. But then the smile would just as quickly disappear; she knew the inevitable was fast approaching. Jeb was determined to have that talk and was not going to let her off the hook much longer. His patience, she knew, was on a short fuse and could explode at any moment.

McKenzie's mind was centered on that one thought when the jarring sound of the phone penetrated her sense. She flinched, then lifted the receiver and said, "Hello."

"Ms. Moore, this is Hal Melrose." His voice was low, raspy. "We have to talk."

Relief at hearing his voice almost made her giddy. "Thank God you called. I've been so worried."

"Can you come now? I've got something really important."

"Just tell me where."

"There's a truck stop at Hwy 106. Meet me there in, say, thirty minutes."

She could hear the fear in his voice.

"I'll be there," she promised, noticing as she hung up that her hands were clammy.

McKenzie glanced down at her watch and saw that she had at least twenty minutes to kill before she had to leave. What could Melrose have to tell her that held such urgency? She hoped it was the break she needed to blow the lid off the mall scandal.

The newspaper article she had written was the first brazen act she'd taken against the mayor and Cedar Plaza, and though Jeb hadn't been keen on it, he hadn't stopped her.

McKenzie's eyes fell to the article still sitting prominently in the middle of her desk. The bold, black print leaped out at her: WHAT'S HAPPENING TO YOUR TAX DOLLARS? The article described the plans for the shopping mall and its supposed contribution to the city, but then went on to detail the delays, the politics involved, and the "accidents," one of which had taken a man's life.

When she had taken the copy into Jeb's office, he'd played the devil's advocate....

"I want to run this as soon as possible," she'd said, handing the copy to him, purposely avoiding his eyes.

After scanning the page, Jeb leaned back in his chair. "It's still all conjecture, nothing substantial."

"I know," she began, "but—"

"No 'buts,'" Jeb interrupted. "Proof. We need proof. All I see here is supposition." His eyes were hard. "As you've already said, we need either the mayor's or the contractor's voice on tape or their signatures on something. We sure as hell don't want to be sued for libel. Heaven forbid. What would the old man say?"

"But the fatal accident..."

"The police ruled it just that—an accident."

"My source..."

"Name him. Ask him to come forward and spill his guts."

McKenzie was furious, but she managed to keep her cool, knowing that Jeb was right. There was too much at stake and she couldn't afford any wrong moves. "All right, I get the point. I'll change it, tone it down, use it as a weapon to shake them up."

"I like that. In other words, let Witherspoon and Dillard know that we're on to them for sure, that we're nipping at their heels."

"That's right. Force them into making a mistake."

"And a follow-up. Are you planning one?"

"Several, in fact. From one article to the next, they'll never know what to expect."

They looked at each other for a moment, aching to be in each other's arms.

Jeb was the first to look away. "I approve. Go with it. I just hope we haven't bitten off more than we can chew."

That had been two days ago, and since then she had made it a point to stay out of his way, spending the majority of her time working on the follow-up article, or at the hospital with her stepfather, or shopping. It was hard for her to believe that Christmas was just a few days away, even though every time she walked into the house and looked at the tree, she was reminded of it.

But now McKenzie had a more pressing problem to attend to. She had to meet Melrose.

She stood up and reached for her purse, only to realize she was no longer alone. She looked up with a start. Jeb stood in the door, watching her, looking unusually attractive in a brown pin-striped suit, his expression dark and unreadable.

"Goin' somewhere?"

There was another disturbing silence as she tried to subdue the butterflies in her stomach. "Yes...as a matter of fact I am."

"Important?"

"I hope so."

"Want company?"

No hesitation. "I'd love it," she said, trying to sound normal.

He pushed himself away from the doorjamb. "Lead the way."

The truck stop appeared deserted when they arrived, except for one fairly new pickup truck and an old battered Ford.

For the most part, the drive had been carried out in silence, except for when she had briefed him. A taut thread seemed to run between them, raising the strain of her nerves almost to the braking point. She was constantly aware of him. Yet Jeb made no attempt to touch her, almost as though by keeping his distance he was punishing her, forcing her to talk to him, to make a decision.

"Do you think it'll make any difference if you're no alone?" Jeb asked as he came around and opened the doo for her.

"Well, now that you mention it, maybe I'd better go in b myself. He sounded awfully skittish."

"I'll give you twenty minutes and then I'm coming in."

"All right," she agreed.

Jeb leaned against the car and watched as she made he way toward the door, wondering how he had kept from touching her for five days. Rebellion flared his manhood a his eyes devoured her long, shapely legs, trim hips, th round, firm buttocks.

Her body never failed to grip him. And though he knev every luscious curve of that body and each of its intimat secrets, he yearned to know more. But he didn't just wan her body; he wanted the total woman: her sharp mind, he laughter, her sincerity and her dedication.

He honestly didn't know how much more time he coul give her....

Exactly fifteen minutes later, McKenzie appeared wear ing a cautious but excited expression.

Jeb kept a rein on his tongue until they were both in th car and on the road.

"Well, don't keep me in suspense," he said, drawin; deeply on a cigarette.

McKenzie's voice trembled with excitement. "You'll neve believe this," she cried, "but I have the goods, the proo you've been demanding." She opened her purse and whipped out a sealed envelope. "In here is a tape recordin; of a conversation between Witherspoon and Dillard. Jus wait till you hear it!"

Jeb slowed the car almost to a crawl and threw her an in credulous look. "How the hell did your man pull it off?"

McKenzie hugged the envelope to her chest. "By plant ing this little gizmo in Dillard's office." Her expressio suddenly became serious. "But he's scared, really scared," she emphasized. "His bags are packed and he's going to stay with his brother out of town until Dillard is either arrested or forced to close down or both. Of course, that goes for the mayor, too." She slapped her knee and laughed for the sheer joy of it. "But we've got him now. Right where we want him!"

Jeb was so engrossed in what McKenzie was saying that he failed to notice the car creeping alongside him.

When he did, it was too late.

Metal met metal in a loud, resounding crunch.

"Jeb!" McKenzie screeched, before being slung against the door, the breath knocked out of her.

Jeb was trying his best to maintain control of the car, his hands gripping the steering wheel for dear life.

"Hold on!" he shouted. "This crazy idiot is trying to run us off the road!"

But McKenzie was too panic-stricken to move. All she could do was watch in horror as the car kept on bashing into the side of theirs. Then suddenly her eyes locked on the face staring at her. "Oh, my God, Jeb!" she gasped. "It's...Chet Rollins."

"Dammit to hell!" Jeb cursed as he tried to outmaneuver his assailant, but it was useless. They were blocked in with nowhere to go.

Again metal on metal.

Jeb hung on, his face ashen, stinging rivulets of sweat running down his face.

Then suddenly the Cadillac lurched, spun faster...faster.

"Jeb, what—" McKenzie cried before instant fear paralyzed her.

The car went skidding down an embankment.

And directly in front of its path was a tall tree.

Jeb stomped on the brake, but it was too late.

The last thing he remembered was McKenzie's bloodcurdling scream and the final crunch of metal before a lightning pain cracked through his skull and everything went black.

Chapter 11

The room was quiet. Too quiet. McKenzie peered for what she knew must be the hundredth time at Jeb's still form stretched out on his bed. He was sleeping like a baby, the swelling above his eyes gone down considerably.

Using a soggy tissue, she swiped at the tears streaming down her cheeks. It was funny, she thought without humor, that she could still cry. She would have sworn she had no more tears left.

"Oh, Jeb, will you ever forgive me?" she whispered aloud, staring out the window. The clouds were hanging low and heavy on this December evening just days shy of Christmas, threatening rain.

She paused again in her tormenting thoughts to blot the tears from her face, begging herself not to think, not to replay the accident again in her mind like a bad old movie. But her mind refused to slow down, to stop dwelling on the events of that day. They kept rolling across her mind's eye with a vengeance.

At first she hadn't been able to move, waiting for some type of gut-wrenching pain to hit her. With lips that were chalk white, her tiny shoulders hunched up, her upper body folded in on itself like a question mark, her breathing came in rapid pants. Her throat tightened. Clammy sweat broke out in pinpoints all over her body. For seconds she remained stunned, horrified and nauseated. She thought she would throw up or pass out, maybe both. Eventually, she sagged against the door and inhaled slowly, deeply, willing tensed muscles to relax.

Jeb! Oh, God, Jeb. That was when she whipped around and saw the blood. Jeb's inert figure was slouched against the steering wheel, blood trickling down the side of his face.

She had never known such fear as she felt in that moment. Her heart stopped. Her world collapsed. She thought he was dead.

Then, frantically, she unbuckled her seat belt, her heart lodged somewhere in her throat, and bounded across the seat. She gently lowered Jeb's head back against the cushion.

"Jeb, Jeb!" she sobbed, feeling for a pulse at the side of his neck, making sure he was still alive.

Had she heard a moan from his thin, ashen lips, or had she imagined it?

"Jeb, Jeb!" McKenzie repeated. "Oh, God, can you hear me?"

The blood suddenly began dripping faster, more profusely, and with a soft, whimpering sound torn from her throat, she leaned down and searched the floorboard until she found her purse. She jerked it open, and dumped its contents onto the seat, then began searching for something to stanch the sticky flow of blood.

It was then that she heard the shrill sound of the sirens. Sobbing so heavily that she could barely see, McKenzie shoved the door open and scrambled out of the car. But the second her feet touched the ground, she plummeted to her knees, rocks and debris digging into her flesh.

"Oh, God, please," McKenzie cried, struggling to stand up once again on her jellied legs, oblivious to her own pain. Nothing mattered except Jeb. Her every thought, her every ounce of energy, her every breath was for Jeb and Jeb alone.

By the time she climbed the embankment and before she could raise her arms to signal, the ambulance and police car had skidded off the road and onto the shoulder.

The paramedics dashed by McKenzie, ignoring her frantic cry, "Please...hurry...help him!" and headed for Jeb. While Jeb was being attended to, the policeman took her statement, in which she fingered Chet Rollins as the man sitting on the passenger side.

Determined to ride with Jeb in the ambulance, McKenzie dashed back to the car and, grabbing her purse, she stuffed the contents back into it, including the tape Melrose had given her. She knew that it was the key to making them pay for what they had done to Jeb and what they had tried to do to her.

At the hospital she was told that Jeb was suffering from a concussion, in addition to the gash over his eye. When he regained consciousness a while later, she was sitting by his bed.

His eyelids fluttered several times before they finally opened.

McKenzie moved closer to the bed and peered into his colorless face, blinking back the tears.

"Princess," he whispered, lifting a hand and groping for hers, "is that you?"

"I'm here," she said, bending low and placing her mouth next to his ear, concern and worry pinching her face.

Jeb moistened his dry, cracked lips. "What the hell happened?" He groaned, his eyes closing for a second, then flying open in a panic as though afraid she had disappeared.

McKenzie put more pressure on his hand. "You mean you don't remember?" she asked, trying to control the panic surging through her. Had he lost his memory?

"Vaguely," Jeb said, his voice a raspy whisper. "Someone tried to make us a statistic, didn't they?" Then his eyes suddenly turned frantic. "Oh, God, what about you? Were you hurt?" he demanded on a wheezing note.

"No, not even a scratch," McKenzie soothed, raising his hand to her cheek and holding it there. "But don't try to talk anymore. Not now. Just rest."

Suddenly, Jeb winced as a sharp pain zinged through his skull. "God, my head."

"Please, Jeb," McKenzie begged, lowering his hand but refusing to turn it loose, feeling her heart turn over as his fingers clung to hers. "Don't move. You're suffering from a concussion and a cut over your right eye."

"When can I go home?" he demanded, reminding her of a petulant child.

"Probably tomorrow, but don't worry about that now. Just try to rest."

His eyes sought hers. "Will you stay with me?"

"A blast of dynamite couldn't pry me away," she whispered huskily, no longer bothering to hold back the tears...

Standing now at the window of his bedroom at home, she turned once again toward Jeb. She shivered suddenly, trying to break her train of thought. She brushed up and down her left arm with her right hand, as though to instill warmth in her bones, but it was useless. It wasn't that the room was chilly; quite the contrary, the central heat was blazing. It was she. She had been frozen on the inside since she had seen the blood on Jeb's face. She would remember that moment forever. Even now, it reached out and laid an icy finger on her heart.

She blamed herself. If she hadn't been determined to pursue the investigation into the mayor and his cronies, this would not have happened. They, Rollins and another man whom she hadn't been able to identify—a hired hit man, the police had guessed—were after her, and because Jeb was with her, he had gotten hurt.

An all-points bulletin had been issued on Rollins and Dillard, who had also disappeared, but as yet they had not been apprehended. McKenzie was holding on to her ace in the hole: the tape-recorded conversation between Jackson Witherspoon and Dillard. And she intended to lower the boom on them just as soon as Jeb was up and around and could be in on the kill.

Even though the mayor would most likely escape criminal prosecution, there was no way he would be able to keep his job. A tainted public official, especially where attempted murder was a factor, would not be tolerated by the public he served. Of that she was sure.

After rubbing the weary muscles in the back of her neck, McKenzie lobbed her head against the windowpane and closed her eyes.

If anything had happened to Jeb, she knew she wouldn't have wanted to keep on living....

Jeb couldn't quite open his eyes, thinking he was still in the hospital and hating the suffocating feeling within him that this knowledge brought. As he forced his eyes open, he expected to see the bare walls of the hospital threatening to close in on him. He had an aversion to hospitals. They brought back painful memories of Vietnam, El Salvador and other places and times he'd just as soon forget. A great sense of relief charged through him when he recognized his own room.

He moved his head sideways, testing for pain, and was again pleasantly surprised to find he was practically pain free.

Suddenly feeling braver, he twisted his head farther to the right and that was when he saw her. His heart almost swelled out of his chest as he peered at her forlorn figure silhouetted against the window. Oh, God, just the thought of her being in that car when it smashed into the tree made him sick.

What a mess they had gotten themselves into! But he intended to rectify that as soon as he could. Nobody was going to get away with even the *thought* of harming a hair on McKenzie's head—or with marking him for an early grave, either. When he got his hands on those sonofabitches, he'd take them apart limb from limb.

His eyes greedily feasted on her, taking pleasure in just looking at her, imprinting on his mind the image of her loveliness as the lamplight beside her cast her in an ethereal glow. Her hair was a fiery halo around her smooth, unblemished face; her skin was more lustrous than the most polished marble. She was dressed in what looked to be a silk lounging outfit, the color of salmon.

She had remained faithfully by his side the days he'd been in the hospital. Never once had he opened his eyes and not found her there with that white, tense look marring her perfect features.

He had longed to tell her then, as he did now, that he loved her, that he wanted nothing more out of life than to prove this to her. But admitting that he loved her would be no easy task. He was not without his own insecurities.

After all, hadn't she thrown his love back in his face once before, almost robbing him of his manhood? Would she do it again? Because of that embedded fear, the words wouldn't come. Too, he knew that she was still fighting her own private battles: the engagement to a man she didn't love, his father and his hold over her.

He abhorred the fact that Carson's thirst for revenge had almost cost McKenzie her life. And for what? An old debt that could never be settled no matter how hard his father tried. Witherspoon hadn't been the only man his mother had been with. It was just unlucky for Witherspoon that she happened to have been with him when she suffered a cerebral hemorrhage and died. But the scandal had done something to Carson, twisting something inside him, and he was never the same. Such a waste. Such a goddamned waste.

But none of this mattered now, he thought, as a deep, harsh breath rattled through him. Nothing mattered now except this hungry, excruciating need for McKenzie.

McKenzie paused in the massaging of the weary muscles at the base of her neck. She could feel his eyes on her, deeply, intently.

A heavy excitement percolated through her as she returned his steady gaze, her wide eyes revealing her innermost emotions.

"Come here," he whispered, raising himself upright and then back against the thick pillows, holding out his arms.

With a mewing sound, McKenzie closed the distance between them and, sinking down on the bed beside him, wafted into his arms like a floating feather, fragile, sweet-smelling, clinging, and pressed her cheek against his.

"Oh, Jeb, I'm sorry, so sorry," she sobbed.

He cradled her in his arms. "Shhh. Don't cry," he pleaded. "You'll make yourself sick. Anyway, it's not your fault," he added, conscious of nothing at all except the woman he held in his arms with such fierce, awesome love. With her presence, he had found the missing piece that filled the gaping hole in his life. And he knew he could never let her go.

"Oh, Jeb," she whispered, "I was so afraid you were dead." She clung to him with every ounce of strength she could muster. To her, he felt bigger than life, and she reveled in this heady closeness. Then, after a moment, she pulled back. "Will . . . you forgive me?"

"My darling, my darling," he crooned, flicking the tears from her cheeks with the tip of his fingers. "I don't blame you. My God, how can you even think that? I'm just glad it was me that got hurt instead of you. If they had hurt a hair on your head, I couldn't have handled it." His eyes took on an icy glare. "Those bastards will be lucky if the fellows in uniform get them before I do."

"Jeb, no, please," she began. "Promise me you won't take the law into your own hands."

"Hey, hey, no more tears now, you hear." He smiled. "I'll behave, I promise. Now let me see a smile. Come on," he coaxed, reaching out a finger and toying with her lips.

Playfully she bit his finger. She was relieved that he didn't plan to go off half-cocked after Dillard and Rollins. For he was still far from a well man. The blow on his head had been a nasty one, and he still looked completely washed out, bedraggled.

"You're not smiling."

A grin suddenly reshaped her lips. "How's that?"

"I guess it'll do in a pinch," he drawled.

"Well, it'll just have to, because right now I'm going downstairs to get you something to eat. Rosie has a big pot of homemade chicken soup simmering on the stove. Sounds good, doesn't it?"

"You bet it does," he said. "Damn, I'm famished. But then I can't imagine why." He grimaced. "That garbage they serve you in the hospital would gag a maggot." He reached out and tucked a loose tendril of hair behind her ear.

McKenzie laughed, while a fluttering sensation gripped her heart at the intimate contact.

"Ah, that's better. And when you come back, I want to see that same sparkle in your eyes." He scrutinized her closely and then added, "I'm fine, really I am." Then he grinned again. "A slight concussion and three stitches ain't nothing for a tough guy like me. This old body has been through a helluva lot more than that."

Without a word, McKenzie got up and crossed to the door, where she turned and flashed him a radiant smile. "I won't be long."

He blew her a kiss.

Suddenly, a giddy feeling of pure joy replaced the weakness inside her, driving adrenaline through her veins. It was in that moment she knew that she did indeed love him, had never stopped loving him, and would go to her grave loving him. She was barely able to close the door behind her before she collapsed against the door, the weak trembles overtaking her.

She loved him! Just to admit that to herself was a major feat. Now she wanted to shout it to the world. The only thing that kept her from doing so was her stepfather. His lingering illness and his likely disapproval were the sobering forces that couldn't be dispelled even in the wake of her newfound happiness.

Yet hope burned brightly, hope that she would have a home and a family with Jeb. It would work out. It had to.

The thudding sound of the front door closing jarred her out of her trance. With her heart hammering, she charged down the stairs, fueled by her accepted love for Jeb and her promise to feed him.

When McKenzie made her way into the kitchen, she was surprised to find both Rosie and Aunt Rachel there. By this hour Rosie had usually retired to her small apartment, and

Rachel, she'd guessed, was usually at the hospital with her stepfather.

McKenzie smiled at Rosie and then hugged her aunt. Yanking out a chair from the table, she sat down.

"Is Jeb feeling better?" Rachel inquired, a frown creasing her forehead.

"Yes, much better," McKenzie said with a heartfelt sigh. Then, twisting around to Rosie, she added with a smile, "And he's starving. I came down for a bowl of your scrumptious soup. Would you fix a tray please, and I'll carry it back up to him?"

Rosie nodded, her chin quivering. "Whatever that boy wants, he gets."

Rachel just looked at McKenzie and smiled before saying, "If he's hungry, that's certainly a sign he's on the mend."

"How's Dad?" McKenzie asked, feeling a spurt of guilt because she hadn't been able to spend much time with Carson, content to let Rachel take up the slack.

"Improving every day. He asked about you yesterday, and Jeb today."

She smiled her relief. "That *is* good news. Now that Jeb is out of the woods, I'll be able to spend more time with Carson."

Rachel's eyes suddenly clouded. "Are you sure that you and Jeb aren't in any more danger? I don't know all the details, but I can't help but worry."

McKenzie's gaze softened. "I don't want you worrying, Auntie. The law is after Dillard and Rollins. They've disappeared—my guess is Mexico—but I have complete confidence they'll track them down and arrest them. And Witherspoon—well, he's just as good as gone. When I get through crucifying him in the paper, he'll have no choice but to resign."

"I certainly hope so," Rachel said, though her tone still carried a hint of unease. "I had no idea that you were involved in anything so dangerous." She shook her head. "I'm surprised that you allowed things to go this far, to get out of hand. Carson wouldn't have wanted—"

"I know," McKenzie interrupted quickly. "But when I got the chance to go after Witherspoon, I jumped at it. Of course, I hadn't counted on Dad being out of commission, unable to help me. And then when...when Jeb..." Her voice faltered for a moment. "When Jeb became involved, and the accident—"

It was Rachel's turn to interrupt. "I'm going to tell you what you told me, and that was not to worry. Jeb's going to be just fine. And maybe then if we keep our fingers crossed, we'll have both our menfolk on the mend and our family back together." Her eyes were suddenly misty as they bored into McKenzie's.

She knows, McKenzie thought with a pang. She knows I love Jeb. Oh, God, am I wearing it like a beacon for the world to see? Probably so. But she didn't care, she told herself defiantly. She was too wrapped up in the golden dreams of a future with Jeb to care.

"I guess I'd better head for home," Rachel said.

"Don't you want to see Jeb first?" McKenzie asked, standing up at the same time as Rachel.

"No, not this evening. I'm bushed. Give him my love and tell him I'll see him tomorrow." After kissing McKenzie on the cheek and bidding Rosie a quick goodbye, she made her way out the front door.

"Jeb's tray is ready, hon," Rosie said, wiping off the cabinet with a clean towel. "If you don't think you'll be needing me anymore this evening, I'm going to retire. My old arthritic knees are giving me a fit."

McKenzie walked over and gave her a hug before picking up the tray. "Scoot," she ordered, smiling. "I don't want to see your bright and shining face until morning."

Rosie's round face puckered. "All right, but only if you promise to call me if you need me."

"I promise. Now go."

Knowing that Jeb was more than likely wondering what had happened to delay her so, McKenzie balanced the tray with adept fingers and made her way very gingerly toward the stairs.

Suddenly, the sharp peal of the phone stilled her actions. "Damn!" she muttered, doing an about-face and lowering the tray to the hall table. She lifted the phone to her ear, snuggling it against her shoulder. At this rate, she'd never make it back to Jeb, she thought irritably.

"Yes," she said without frills.

"McKenzie?"

She clung to the edge of the table to steady herself as Daniel's sober voice sent shock waves rushing through her. Daniel. Dear God, much to her shame, he had fled her mind, as her every waking thought had been on Jeb and her love for him. Hurting Daniel was inevitable.

"McKenzie, how's Jeb?"

She knew how much it must have cost him to ask that question. There was certainly no love lost between the two. "He's . . . he's much better," she said, then rushed to add, "I brought him home from the hospital this afternoon."

"Are you sure you're okay?"

"I'm fine. Just bruised a bit, that's all."

"That's good." The wistful note in his voice was followed by a short pause. "I guess flying with me to my parents' for Christmas and joining in on their fiftieth wedding anniversary is out?"

Strike two, McKenzie! It had completely slipped her mind that she had halfway promised to accompany him to Missouri to, as he'd put it, "celebrate an old-fashioned white Christmas." Of course, that was impossible now. She could not, would not, leave Jeb or her stepfather. Not now.

"McKenzie?" he asked again, making an effort to trap her wandering mind.

"You're right, there's no way I can leave now," she said, letting him down as gently as possible.

His rough sigh filtered through the line. "I was afraid you'd say that." He paused. "But I really think you should reconsider. What if there's another attempt on your life?"

"Oh, Daniel, please," she said, alarmed, "I don't think it was that. I think they were just out to scare me—us. But murder..." She shivered. "No, I don't think so."

"Well, I sure as hell do," he charged stoutly. "And that's all the more reason for you to get out of town for a few days."

She heard the pleading in his voice, and she hated to hear it, but more than that, she hated what she was doing to him.

"I'm sorry, but I can't."

There was a moment of strained silence.

"My plane leaves tomorrow night," he said at length. "Will I see you before I go?"

She toyed with her lower lip. "Oh, Daniel, I don't know. Right now, though, I need to get off the phone. I promise I'll call you later." Her tone was firm yet gentle.

"McKenzie, let's get married. Tomorrow."

His words crackling through the telephone line felt like lightning splitting a tree. For a moment, she felt dazed, incapacitated, unable to think clearly. Then, slowly, the shorted-out segments of her brain fused back together, and she realized what she must do. She had to tell him about her and Jeb. She had no choice; she owed him that. But there was a time and place for everything. And to tell him now, on the phone, was not the time or the place.

"McKenzie, will you?"

"Daniel, please, not now. I...I don't...can't talk about us now. I must go. I'll talk to you later. Goodbye."

Daniel's forlorn, "Have a merry Christmas," barely registered as she placed the receiver back in its cradle, snatched up the tray and headed for Jeb's room.

"I thought for sure you'd run away and left me," Jeb murmured as she nudged the door open with the toe of her shoe and walked into the shadowed room. Although still sitting propped up in the bed, he was taking long puffs of a cigarette, his eyes squinting against the curls of gray smoke before his face.

McKenzie frowned as she set the cumbersome tray on the bedside table. "You know, you really should stop punishing your body with those foul things," she said without censure, though her tone was serious.

Jeb gave her a lopsided grin and, leaning over, crushed out the cigarette in the ashtray. "You're right. It's a nasty habit that I wish I could break."

She smiled fetchingly. "Well, I'll have to see what I can do to help you do just that. But now first things first." She sat down beside him on the bed and removed the lid from the container of soup. "Mmmm," she said, "smell that. If this rich stuff won't give you vim and vigor, nothing will." She laughed, twisting back toward him, suddenly fighting the urge to run her fingers through his mussed-up hair.

He stared at her, his own thoughts equally chaotic, imagining her on the bed with him, resting on top of him. Flesh against flesh. Abruptly, he took a sip of the broth, almost scalding his tongue in the process.

Then stifling an oath, he forced a smile to his lips. "If you don't watch out, you'll spoil me, waiting on me like this."

"Well, that's the least I can do, since I feel responsible..." Her voice suddenly faded, and she watched the movement of his hand as he set the bowl back on the tray;

t was as though she were momentarily hypnotized by this
insignificant action.

"Stop it," he scolded gently. "I thought we had already
reached an understanding about that." His eyes were on her
now, delving into hers, the warmth from his voice spilling
over into his eyes while a questing finger explored her lips,
parting them, inching at a snail's pace along the moist
sweetness within.

"Oh, McKenzie," he whispered thickly, his hand slipping to the back of her neck and slowly pulling her forward, his eyes on her mouth, anticipating the taste of her.

Their lips met and clung as he drew her into his arms and
held her tightly against him. Then he began to edge down
into the bed, taking her with him, the descent slow, achingly slow. Belly to belly, he was hard against her and the
pleasure was dizzying, the response within her making it
difficult to breathe. She let her head rest against his shoulder and moved still closer.

He could scarcely believe what was happening. This woman. This woman who, when he held her, always made him
fear it would be his last time, was all at once very present,
very real, exquisitely acquiescent. Her scent mesmerizing,
her softness compelling, her breasts pressing against his
chest.

"Stay with me," he pressed urgently, pulling back and
looking into her eyes. "I want to hold you, to love you."

"Yes, oh, yes," McKenzie whispered, knowing that for
these precious moments she was his for the taking. Her
flesh, with a mind of its own, was offering itself to him. He
was free to do as he liked with it. It was with a feeling not
unlike terror that she realized anew just how utterly vulnerable she was to him. Love. Love had rendered her useless.

With a soft groan, he pressed his lips to hers once again
while his hand closed firmly around an already swollen
breast. He drank her in, kissing her a full minute.

McKenzie could feel her nipples hardening as he tweakeo
one, then the other, with his talented fingers. She wanted to
be free of the confining garments, needed to feel the touch
of his calloused hands on her bare skin.

McKenzie squirmed, burrowing closer. She heard another sigh slip through his lips as he moved back and then
slowly began easing her caftan down around her waist and
over her hips, finally flinging it over the side of the bed.

In one agile move, he rolled over and off the bed to shed
his briefs, and with eager quickness, McKenzie was against
his nakedness, feeling warm, deliciously warm as his fingers stroked her breasts.

"If I lived forever, I could never get enough of you," he
whispered, going round and round her breasts.

She could scarcely breathe for the heat. Her body was on
fire, her throat pulsing. "You're wonderful," she murmured, drawing his mouth to hers. She was hungry, made
so by his tongue coaxing hers to respond. Her breathing was
as labored as a small puppy's.

His hand slid up the length of her inner thigh and she
went limp. Her belly trembled as he pressed kisses on her
navel, moving down.

"Love your long, beautiful legs." He smiled, then eased
her thighs open and put his mouth to her.

His tongue striking at her drew a mewing sound from her
throat, causing her hips to roll, her insides to twist. It was
as if he'd peeled away her flesh, like an invisible protective
skin and was making love to her exposed nerve endings. She
clenched her fists against the pleasure, moving steadily toward completion.

Then he paused and lay atop her, his mouth at her neck,
his legs nudging hers apart.

She started to say something, but he whispered, "Shhh,
don't talk, just feel. Feel how much I want you...need
you...love you."

McKenzie read his message and answered him with one of her own. Wordlessly, she wedged a hand between them and closed it around him.

A guttural sound broke from his throat as his mouth pressed to hers, his hands on her breasts, then sliding down, down, the pleasure building inside them both as the delicate stabbing of his tongue made her want to scream, taking her deeper and deeper, closer and closer to the edge.

"Now...now," she cried into his mouth, experiencing ecstasy that was more than ecstasy, blindly reaching to lead him in, to fill the emptiness.

His control snapped. He moved swiftly into her warmth, listening to the little cries she uttered as her hands dug into his flesh.

Each moving thrust, each return saw her legs fall open and then close back against him like the petal of a flower unfolding itself to the sun.

Together their cries grew louder, deeper, each one rising from new wellsprings of pleasure as he stayed poised at the very edge of her and she arched beneath him.

"Jeb, oh, Jeb, please don't stop," she half sobbed as her hands pulled at him, drawing him to her.

He touched deeper into her as together, flesh into flesh, they reached a pinnacle never to be returned to in exactly the same way, but forever renewed, forever different.

She clung to him as a tiny wave clings to a rock, trembling, shimmering, then finally slipping away.

He moved slowly again inside her and she moaned softly until he lay still beside her....

Afterward they lay curled together, she kittenlike, almost in a ball in the circle of his arms. Finally, he stirred and lifted her face, kissing her eyes open.

Then, like rich, warm honey, the words flowed from his lips. "I love you," he said softly.

Turning, she gazed up at him, her soul shining through her eyes. "And I love you."

"My darling...my darling," he moaned, rocking her against him, inhaling her smooth, scented flesh, cherishing her, knowing that he could never let her go.

As the early sun flooded the room, they came together again and still again until once more she knew that single moment when there was neither yesterday nor tomorrow, beginning nor end, but only that burning instant.

His love lay like silk upon her skin; she felt cloaked in it, secure.

That night of love set the precedent for the next few days. Christmas passed in a blissful blur, McKenzie thinking she had never been so happy. The special day was spent at home, with Rosie again preparing a huge dinner.

There was laughter aplenty as McKenzie, Jeb and Rachel exchanged presents under the tree while Jeb enlightened Rachel as to how the tree had gotten decorated. Rachel laughed until tears came to her eyes. She was still chuckling later when they all went into the dining room to consume huge portions of Rosie's turkey and dressing. Later that evening they visited the hospital and, one by one, went in to visit with Carson, who was beginning to show a marked improvement.

The daylight hours found McKenzie working like a Trojan, preparing the article that would hang the mayor and his cronies. Careful not to destroy the evidence, she had placed the tape in the safe at home. Before the article ran in the paper, she planned to confront Witherspoon with it. So far the two men that had tried to run her and Jeb off the road had not been taken into custody, so no matter where she went, she found herself looking over her shoulder.

But once the sunlight waned, the nights belonged exclusively to Jeb. Their evenings were filled with a special kind of magic. They could not get enough of each other.

This evening was no exception. It was New Year's Eve, and they were sitting in front of the fireplace after having been out to dinner and dancing. But the outing had been short-lived; they had decided to come home, wanting to be alone.

"Happy New Year, my love," Jeb said, raising his champagne glass and clinking it against hers.

McKenzie smiled her satisfaction. "Happy New Year," she echoed in perfect harmony with the grandfather clock as it, too, rang in the New Year.

With their eyes fastened on each other over the rims of their glasses, they sipped the bubbly liquid. Then slowly, as though mesmerized by McKenzie's bewitching presence, Jeb removed the crystal from her fingers and, without taking his eyes from her, set it on the hearth.

Still trancelike, he leaned across and paused within a hairsbreadth of her mouth. "I love you," he said thickly.

"Oh, Jeb..." Suddenly, her throat squeezed shut with such sweet emotion that all she could do was lay her quivering lips against the firmness of his.

For the longest of moments their lips melted as one, the depth of the kiss reaching, delving, searching their very souls.

Jeb was the first to draw back, the harsh intake of his breath the only sound in the room. McKenzie's head was buried in the crook of his neck; his hand gently cupped her breast.

Although still dressed in their evening finery, they were stretched out comfortably on the floor, the front of the couch their cushion. The flames leaping from the fireplace added a cozy warmth, as did the lights on the Christmas tree, now looking a little sad with the presents gone.

Finally McKenzie spoke, conscious of Jeb's probing fin
gers. "I feel like I've just been given a glimpse of para
dise."

"Mmmm, me too," Jeb murmured, concentrating, never
missing a stroke.

"That feels good."

"It's meant to," he whispered.

"I'm sleepy."

"Sleep wasn't what I had in mind."

"Oh."

"Is that by any chance an invitation?"

"Yes."

"You're a lady after my own heart."

"What are we waiting for?"

"I want you to promise me something first."

"Anything," she said, her voice purring with content
ment.

His warm breath fanned across her cheek. "Promise me
you'll marry me. Soon."

McKenzie's heart skipped like a mountain creek on a
spring day. Marry him! She never thought she would hear
those words pass his lips. Even now she wasn't sure she had
heard him right. This was what she'd been waiting for all her
life. The culmination of all her hopes, her dreams . . .

Jeb saw first the shock, then the surprise, then the de
light register on her face. He had been so afraid to ask that
question, totally unsure of the answer he would receive. But
he had given her all the time and space he could. He wanted
her to share his life. Now. Every part of it.

"I've dreamed of this moment," she whispered huskily,
looking up at him. "But I . . ."

Her eyes were shimmering pools as he peered into them;
now he knew what the poet meant about the depths where
a man could lose himself.

"Shhh. Don't even think it," he warned, lifting her hand and kissing the tip of each finger in turn, sending electrifying surges to the center of her feminity. "I won't take no for an answer. Our fate, my darling, was sealed a long time ago."

Silently, she buried her face against him. "Oh, Jeb, I do love you."

His heart stirred. "What do you say we celebrate and start the New Year off the right way?" he offered, standing up and sweeping her up in his arms, then making his way toward the bedroom.

She wrapped her arms around his neck and whispered, "Well, it's about time."

Chapter 12

The north wind blustered around McKenzie, threatening to lift her off her feet, pricking her skin like tiny chips of sharp ice.

"Brrr," she said aloud, visibly shivering, before locking the car and making her way across the hospital parking lot and into the main building. Again she shivered, the smell slapping her in the face as she crossed the lobby toward the elevator.

But in spite of the weather and her distaste for hospitals, she felt on top of the world. Her smile was genuine and sparkling and many a head turned her way, taking in the striking figure she made in a soft wool dress the color of ripe field corn. It clung to her willowy silhouette, giving a hint of hidden allure. And her cap of honeyed curls called attention to her golden skin and soft, expressive eyes. She seemed to radiate an inner blush of confidence and a vibrant but subtle sensuality.

McKenzie was in love, and from that pedestal on high everything looked rosy. From the moment Jeb had asked her to marry him, she had been walking on this same cloud. When fear and guilt tried to nudge their way into her conscious mind, she shunned them, fought them, refusing to let them intrude to mar her happiness.

She had not seen Jeb since that night, three days ago now, except in passing. He made a point to stay out of her way, and she knew the reason why. He was giving her time, time to adjust to the idea of marriage with him and time to tell Daniel and Carson.

To date, she had told neither. Where Daniel was concerned, she had a good reason; he was still out of town. But her stepfather was another matter.

Jeb's last words continued to plague her: "McKenzie, shall we tell Carson together?"

For a second her insides had twisted in panic. "No...no," she'd whispered, averting her eyes. "I'll tell him. Alone."

Jeb had appeared dissatisfied with her answer, but much to her relief, he'd refrained from saying anything to the contrary.

And why had she hesitated? Carson's health had certainly improved enough that she could have told him the truth. So why hadn't she just taken the plunge and spilled her heart?

She honestly did not know the answer. But one thing she did know: she could not give up Jeb. Not again. Being in love was the most wonderful feeling in the world, and she was making the most of every precious moment.

It never entered her mind that once they were married, Jeb wouldn't want to settle down. She assumed his days of constant travel to foreign countries were over. They might take pleasure trips, of course, but certainly not to countries that lived and died by the gun. Even though he had not mentioned giving up his life as a foreign reporter—in fact, he had said just the opposite after he'd first come home—she knew he would be willing to make the sacrifice. He knew how important settling down to a real home and family was to her.

Anyway, hadn't he proved that he could make it on his own, that he didn't need his father's approval, nor his wealth, nor his influence to make it in the field of journalism? He had proven his worth in more ways than one, having already won the distinguished Pulitzer Prize in journalism. And hadn't he shown as well his expertise in taking over the newspaper and running it successfully in Carson's absence? Yes, she was positive his goals had been realized.

Now that he'd reached a comfortable plane of success, wouldn't he be content to go into newspaper work full-time? If not that, then maybe write for a magazine and forget the dangers of following stories around the globe.

Yes, of course he would, she told herself. Then together they could build a future with love and devotion and trust as its foundation. What could be more rewarding or promising?

And because of this hope, she knew she could not prolong telling her beloved stepfather about her and Jeb. The deceit had gone on long enough.

To add icing on the cake, her stepfather had taken a ninety-degree turn for the better. His speech and muscular coordination were much improved. The daily trips to the physical therapy room and to the speech therapist had paid off. McKenzie was ecstatic, as were Jeb and Rachel. Times had been tough, but now they were seeing the light at the end of the tunnel.

As McKenzie stepped off the elevator and began her trek down the hall to Carson's room, it was as though she had springs on her feet.

The first order of the day was to inform her stepfather about the Cedar Plaza investigation and the mayor's part in it. If he needed a tonic to spur on his recovery, this would be it. She could see his face now, she told herself, quickening her pace. He would be beside himself with excitement. She also intended to show him the article she had so carefully written. She had spent two days and two nights of drudgery just so every word, every phrase, was to the point and carried a punch aimed at the belly of Jackson Witherspoon.

Then she would tell him about her and Jeb. Save the best for last, she thought.

McKenzie was trying to hold her eagerness in check as she paused outside her stepfather's door and knocked. Then, not waiting for an answer, she pushed open the heavy door and crossed the threshold, a smile on her face.

"Good morning," she chirped, eying Carson Langley sitting up in bed, a breakfast cart in front of him. He stared at her from under bushy brows while carefully stirring his coffee with his good hand.

"Well, it's about time you showed up, girl," he said gruffly, though his words were softened by the smile that showed a row of perfect white teeth.

McKenzie was delighted to find that the raspy slur was practically nonexistent. The only visible and lingering symptom of his stroke was the slight paralysis of his left side.

This morning Carson was more like his old self, though his long bout of sickness was evident. There was a gauntness about him, and a sunken hollowness to his cheeks. Gone was the hardy, robust look that was his trademark, but the sharp shrewdness had returned to his vivid blue eyes, and for that she gave a simple prayer of thanks.

And there was something else, but McKenzie could not quite put her finger on it. Maybe an underlying sense of excitement. She couldn't be sure. Suddenly, she felt her heart shudder as she looked at him. She had come so close to losing him.

It wouldn't be long now, she hoped, before he would be back in command of his life and of the newspaper. What of Jeb? Would Carson continue to let him handle some of the responsibilities of the paper? She was convinced her stepfather would be proud of the job Jeb had done in the day-to-day business of operating the *Tribune*. Who could predict the future—maybe they could even work together. She smiled. Stranger things had happened....

"What's the matter, girl, cat got your tongue? Besides that, you have a weird expression on your face. Been keeping too many late hours, huh?" A peevish edge had crept into his voice, giving it a weak sound.

With a vigorous shake of her head, McKenzie laughed. "Huh yourself! This is the first morning lately that I haven't been here at the crack of dawn, and you know that." She laughed again while rolling the tray off to the side, noticing that he had eaten almost everything on his plate. That, too, was a sure sign he was improving, she thought, sinking down into the chair beside his bed.

Then McKenzie reached out and clasped his hand in hers. "Everything's fine, Dad," she said. "But you're right, I've been working long and late."

Carson shoved his glasses back on his nose with his free hand before saying, "I want to hear what you've been working on—I know it must be big—but first I want to know how things are at the paper. It's been so long...." Suddenly, his voice cracked and he was unable to continue.

McKenzie's hold on his hand tightened as she felt pity surge through her. But for his own good, she couldn't let him see it, so she immediately schooled her features to show none of her inner emotions.

"It's not the same without you, of course," she assured him gently. "I'd be lying if I said otherwise, but you had us all whipped into such good shape that we're managing." Which was the truth, she added silently. Even if Jeb hadn't appeared on the scene and taken over, the paper would have survived. It was impossible to work for Carson Langley and not learn the art of survival.

A short silence followed, and then Carson spoke again, his good humor having resurfaced. "Now suppose you tell me what you've been up to since your old man has been lying on his duff being punctured, poked, prodded and hassled in general." He laughed. "And don't leave out a thing, either, you hear?"

McKenzie settled back in her chair while opening the leather carryall on her lap. Her grin was enchanting. "Are you sure you're ready for this, Dad?" she asked.

Carson glared at her. "How the hell can you ask me a thing like that when the most exciting thing that happens around here is the change of nurses? And I wouldn't give you a plug nickel for the lot of them. They're all sour-faced and think my body is nothing but a damned pincushion."

McKenzie giggled, unable to help herself. If there had been any doubt that her stepfather was returning to full form, there was none now, after that outburst. "Well, maybe what I have to tell you will ease a few of those moments of discomfort and pain," she said, the grin maintaining a hold on her lips. Then, suddenly, she became serious. "I've finally done something to make you proud, Dad," she added confidently.

He gave her an odd look before saying roughly, "I've always been proud of you, girl. But go on," he said, waving his hand. "You've got my curiosity aroused."

"We've got Jackson Witherspoon exactly where we want him." McKenzie scooted to the edge of the chair, her eyes animated. "And that's precisely between a rock and a hard place."

Carson threw her an astonished look. "Oh, and how did you manage to accomplish that feat?" he asked with admiration, though his tone held a tinge of disbelief and something else. Was it bitterness? Regret? Then, before she could answer, he went on, "As you well know, I've been after that bastard for years, and like most sleaze balls, he's slipped through the net every time."

"But not this time," McKenzie ground out with conviction.

"You're really serious, aren't you?"

"As serious as death and taxes."

"Then for heaven's sakes, girl, spit it out! Don't keep me in suspense a second longer."

McKenzie couldn't help but smile at his childish eagerness; in this mood, his resemblance to Jeb was shocking. She shook herself mentally, refusing to think about Jeb now. Their turn would come soon enough.

"All right," she said. "Here goes—and a detailed accounting, too."

Approximately thirty minutes later, McKenzie had told him everything—everything, that is, except the attack on her and Jeb. At this point, she saw no reason to tell him that. It would serve only to upset him, and according to the doctor, that was a no-no.

Then before her courage deserted her, McKenzie handed him the article. She gnawed the inside of her lips until they were raw, watching his eyes scan the pages. Both she and Jeb thought it was an excellent piece of journalism, perhaps the best she'd ever done—of course, her stepfather would be the final judge of that—and she was sitting on pins and needles until she heard his verdict.

Eventually, Carson removed his glasses and simply stared at McKenzie, an unreadable expression on his face for what seemed like forever.

"Well?" The sound of her own voice made her wince; she was reminded of a croaking bullfrog.

"You're right, my dear," Carson confirmed, "you have given me something to be proud of. This is a remarkable piece of work." Suddenly, he seemed overcome with emotion, his mouth working as though he wanted to say something else but couldn't. McKenzie watched as his Adam's apple bobbed up and down.

"Oh, Dad," she cried, jumping up and bridging the distance between them. Sinking down onto the side of the bed, she was immediately enclosed within the circle of his arms, feeling the trembling in his weakened limbs, her eyes filling with tears.

Carson held her close for a moment, and then McKenzie pulled back, grinning through the steady stream of tears flowing down her face. "We're acting rather foolishly, aren't we?" she whispered, dabbing at the tears with the back of her hand.

Carson cleared his throat. "Well, as the old saying goes, There's no fool like an old fool." He grinned. "But what's your excuse?"

"I have none, except that it means so much to me to have your approval," McKenzie said, having gotten herself under control.

"Hellfire!" he exclaimed, lifting the sheaf of papers and thrusting them toward her. "This is not only damned fine work, but you've got that creep in a vise. I can't wait to see him try to weasel out of it. That's when you plan to show Witherspoon the tapes, right?"

"You got it!"

Carson's laughter ran around the room as he gave McKenzie another spontaneous hug. "What about his cronies, this Dillard and Rollins, who helped him pull off the swindle? Surely they won't get off scot-free."

Remember, nothing's wrong with his mind, McKenzie cautioned herself sharply. She'd have to be careful or he'd figure out a way to manipulate her, and before she would realize what was happening, she'd be telling him all about the accident. Heaven forbid!

"Actually, I think the police are already on to them," she said at last. *Play it cool, McKenzie. Don't forget, he can read you like a book.*

"Great! And was that your doing as well?"

McKenzie shifted her gaze. "Actually, no. It...it was Jeb who took care of that." *Smooth, McKenzie. You're becoming quite an accomplished liar.*

"Ah, Jeb," he said, inching backward into the pillow, a look of relief highlighting his features. "So he was involved in this, too, huh?"

Again McKenzie hedged, uncertain of what to say next. "Yes...but only up to a point," she qualified.

"Well, I'm glad. Knowing Witherspoon as I do, your investigation could have turned rather nasty, and still could." His lips thinned. "I don't want you confronting Witherspoon alone, either. When you go to him with your charges, be sure Jeb or Daniel goes with you. Promise?"

McKenzie nodded stiffly, the mere mention of Daniel's name in the same breath's with Jeb's suddenly throwing her off key. She was surprised that Carson hadn't already asked about Daniel. But now that Jeb was back and they had reached an understanding... She shrugged inwardly. Who could guess? Anything was possible, wasn't it?

"You're right, of course, it would be foolish to go alone." McKenzie swung her gaze back to him, her eyes soft. "I wish *you* could go with me, Dad. After all, this is more your triumph than mine." She paused with a sigh. "But I realize that's like asking for the moon."

Suddenly, his hand popped up in front of McKenzie's face. "Hold it right there, girl. I've been saving my own ace in the hole until I heard what you had to tell me. Now it's my turn."

McKenzie was puzzled and it showed. "I . . . I don't understand."

"Course you don't," he said in a clipped, impatient tone. "But it's simple. I'm getting out of this hellhole this coming weekend. How 'bout that!"

For several seconds, McKenzie was too stunned to utter a sound. Finally, though, his words sank into her befuddled brain and she squealed, flinging her arms around his neck. "Why didn't you tell me?"

"Why, I just did!"

McKenzie leaned back to look at him, her eyes sparkling. "Don't you dare play the innocent with me. You know very well what I mean. You waited all this time to tell me, and you did it on purpose, too, didn't you?"

He gave her a sheepish grin. "Well, I couldn't steal your thunder, now could I?" he said. "I knew you had something important to tell me, so I figured my announcement could take a backseat."

"Oh, Dad, I still can't believe you're finally going to come home. It's been so long."

"Tell me about it," he grumbled good-naturedly. But then his expression sobered. "No one had to tell me; I knew I was a sick man."

You'll never know just how sick. She patted his arm. "But that's all in the past now. We have only the future to look forward to. No looking back." She laughed with pure enjoyment. "Why don't I go down to the machine and get us two Cokes and we'll celebrate in style." She twisted her head impishly and shrugged. "Too bad it can't be champagne, but beggars can't be choosers."

Carson screwed his face into a frown. "God! Coke! That sounds awful. Sorry, hon, thanks but no thanks. Now, if you offered to sneak me in a cold can of beer, I'd be de-

lighted to have a party." He laughed. "But then, it won't b
long till I can have that beer, and in my own house to boot!"

McKenzie impulsively hugged him again. "You're im
possible, did you know that?"

He played along with her. "I can't imagine where you go
an idea like that."

"Huh! I just bet you can't," she retaliated, then sud
denly changed the subject, asking eagerly, "Does Aunt Ra
chel know?"

"Nope. Not yet. Just found out myself this morning
Actually, the doc had just told me when you came in look
ing like the cat that swallowed the canary."

McKenzie wrinkled her nose. "I've been waiting a long
time to share my coup with you, and I felt I'd burst if I had
to wait much longer."

"Well, by the time I get out of here, maybe the whole case
will be tied up in a neat package, and Witherspoon will have
cleaned out his desk drawer and be standing in the unem
ployment line." His chin suddenly jutted menacingly. "By
damn, it'd be just like him to file for unemployment and ge
it."

McKenzie laughed outright again. Leave it to her step
father to think of something like that. He was definitely one
of a kind.

Suddenly, a knowing smile thinned his lips. "Okay, I'm
indulging myself, so now I'll get off my soapbox. Anyway
I have something else important to discuss with you."

McKenzie arched a perfect brow. "Oh, and what is that?"

"Why, your wedding, of course. What else?"

So shocked was McKenzie by his statement that if she
hadn't been sitting down, her legs would have caved in un
der her. As it was, she fought for her next breath.

"What . . . what did you say?" McKenzie managed,
knowing very well what he'd said, yet unwilling to face the
truth.

"You heard what I said," Carson replied testily, cognizant of the fact that McKenzie's face had lost its color and that a look of pain had invaded her blue eyes. "And why are you staring at me as though I had suddenly sprouted two heads?"

A note of concern had suddenly seeped into Carson's voice, but McKenzie was oblivious to it as she continued to struggle to get her thoughts organized.

She fought to swallow the bile that rose to the back of her throat as she stood up on jellied legs and turned around. With her back to Carson, she sagged inwardly.

Tell him! Now, her conscience shrieked. *Tell him you can't marry Daniel, that you're going to marry his son instead. What's the matter with you? Don't just stand here like a zombie!*

But with each second that ticked by, time became her enemy, the road to the truth narrower, impossible to tread.

"McKenzie, turn around, please," Carson ordered, a pleading note softening the harsh edge of his command, "and tell me you haven't changed your mind about marrying Daniel. Put my mind to rest."

From behind her came a rustling sound....What was it? Was her stepfather making an effort to get out of bed? Whipping around, her question was answered with a dose of reality. Carson had slid to the side of the bed, teetering on the edge, with his bare feet dangling, almost touching the cold tiled floor. His head was lowered, the movement obviously taking all of his energy.

"No! Wait!" McKenzie cried, swiftly crossing to the bed and clamping a hand down on his shoulder to halt his action. He stared up at her as she loomed over him. For a moment it was a battle of wills.

"Just where do you think you're going?" McKenzie demanded, trying to inject a little humor into her voice, but

from the grim look on Carson's face, she knew she had
failed.

"Nowhere, if you'll quit stalling."

McKenzie ran the tip of her tongue across dry lips.
"Dad...I—"

He interrupted. "Oh, hell, I guess what I'm trying to say
is that I want you to humor me and marry Daniel immediately, push the wedding forward, like the day after I get
home from the hospital." He paused, giving into her urging hand and falling back against the pillow, a white line
around his mouth, his body visibly shaking.

Yet he continued to scrutinize McKenzie closely, while she
busied her own trembling hands by yanking the sheet up and
under his chin, forcing him to stay put.

"Well, what's it gonna be? Are you willing to placate this
sick old man and do as I ask? I know Daniel would be all for
it." There was a desperate note in his voice now.

Trying to pretend her heart wasn't somewhere in the vi-
cinity of her toes was one of the hardest things McKenzie
had ever pulled off in her life. It was by sheer force of will
that she kept her facial features from reflecting the battle
raging within her. Oh, God, what was she going to do?

The truth, McKenzie! For God's sakes, tell him the truth.

Seeing the silence as a chance to press on, Carson stilled
her hand by clasping it tightly in his. "While I've been
chained to this damned bed, I've had plenty of time to
think. In fact, my whole life has flashed before my eyes
several times. I've made a lot of mistakes, with Jeb, with
you—mistakes that I'm not proud of, mind you. But now
I've been given a second chance, a chance to rectify those
mistakes."

He paused, putting more pressure on her hand, his voice
rising an octave, color rushing to his cheeks. "I guess what
I'm trying to tell you is that I'm scared, really scared that my

days are numbered and . . . that I won't be around to rectify those mistakes."

"Oh, Dad," McKenzie cried, damming up his flow of words with her plea. "Don't say that. You're upsetting yourself for no reason. How about if we talk later? Right now, you need to rest. You're wearing yourself out."

McKenzie's heart constricted, for she was positive that she spoke the truth. He had overexerted himself. And following on the heels of that deduction came another: even though the doctor had agreed to release him, he was still far from being a well man. Seeing his heightened color and feeling the clammy texture of his skin, she now understood more than ever what the doctor meant when he said not to upset him.

"Hell, that's the last thing I need to do," Carson snapped waspishly, pinning her with his eyes. "I want to see you settled down with a home and family. And dammit, I want to hold my grandchild in my arms before they throw dirt in my face."

Stop it! Don't do this to me! "If you don't settle down," she threatened, hating herself and her deceit more by the second, "I'm going to call the nurse." Her tone brooked no argument.

As though Carson sensed she meant what she said, the fight went out of him. He let go of her hand and closed his eyes, clearly exhausted.

With a lump the size of the Grand Canyon lodged in her throat, McKenzie leaned over and kissed his forehead and then pulled back, but not before a lone tear splashed where her lips had touched.

His eyes flew open, displaying a sense of panic. "Promise me you'll think about what I ask?"

Feeling herself dismantling on the inside, she nodded. "I . . . I promise."

It was after dark when McKenzie stopped the car in fron
of the house, her mind in an uproar. She had been drivin;
for hours, had stopped only once since leaving the hospital
and that was to force a cup of coffee into her empty stom
ach.

Giving in to the feeling of exhaustion that was over
powering, she leaned her head against the steering wheel an(
forced herself to take deep breaths. But it didn't help; he
stomach was still as twisted as a city road map.

Jeb. Would he understand why she hadn't told her step
father? She longed to be in his arms, to feel his lips agains
hers, to have his reassurance that she had indeed done th(
right thing. Yet she was afraid for the same reason. What i
he didn't understand? But she knew he would, especiall}
when she explained how Carson had worked himself into ;
frenzy. In the long run, it would be better this way, she con
soled herself, feeling herself beginning to unwind on the in
side. Carson would soon be home in comfortable an(
familiar surroundings where he would digest the news much
better. Yes, she had made the right decision. There woul(
definitely be a better time.

She had no more than slammed the front door behind he
when she heard Jeb call her name.

"McKenzie, darling, is that you?"

The sound of his voice was needed fuel for her soul. Sh(
moved toward him, loving him, wanting him with an in
tense longing that knew no boundaries.

Jeb met her halfway. "I was beginning to get worried
Surely you haven't been at the hospital all this time."

A cry rose from deep inside her as she hurled herself int(
his waiting arms. "Oh, Jeb..."

His hands roamed her body with urgent precision. "My
God, you're shaking like a leaf. Did something happen? I:
it Dad?"

"Oh, Jeb," she cried again, clinging to him, "nothing's wrong, really. It's...it's just that I love you...."

Relief made Jeb weak. "Oh, God, McKenzie," he whispered, his mouth against her neck, her body fitting against his bigness with ease and comfort. "Don't you ever do that to me again. I don't know whether to strangle you or kiss you. You scared the living hell out of me."

McKenzie pulled back and looked up at him. "I'm sorry. I didn't mean to."

Wordlessly, he drew her close again, content just to hold her.

"Does that mean I escape strangulation and get a kiss instead?" she asked, her words muffled against his chest.

He chuckled, tipping her chin up, his gaze worshipful on her face. "Although I'm tempted to do both, I believe I'll just settle for the kiss." His expression suddenly darkened and his voice became hoarse. "In fact, I can't wait another second to taste you...."

Jeb's lips crushed against hers with brutal gentleness, his hands boldly combing her lissome curves, fitting her to the answering tautness of his. McKenzie was losing herself in the burning intensity of his touch. Only when they were approaching the point of no return did Jeb release her.

"Oh, McKenzie, my darling," he rasped, "let's not wait to get married. Say you'll marry me tomorrow." His body begged for a reprieve. "Now that you've told my father about us, I don't have to wait any longer to make you mine."

"Well, perhaps a little longer," McKenzie whispered through passion-swelled lips.

"Please, no longer than nine o'clock in the morning," he teased, his hand squeezing a breast through her silk blouse.

"Jeb...I haven't told Carson about us."

Her softly spoken words burst through the air like a bul
let from a gun. It blew the peace and tranquility of the mo
ment into tiny fragments.

McKenzie felt every muscle in Jeb's body become tense
Then he slowly pushed her to arm's length and stared at he
while silence stretched between them. A silence that was a
stony as the rock-strewn desert.

She tried to return his stare, but it was hard to compet
with the knives that were neatly cutting her to shreds.

"Why?" he asked at last, that one word sounding
clipped, deadly.

McKenzie tried to ignore her heart slamming against he
ribs. "I...it...it wasn't..."

"Spit it out, McKenzie. The truth. I want the truth!"

Everything was suddenly spinning out of control
"Dad...wanted us...Daniel and me to...push our wed
ding forward. He's...so afraid he's going to die...before
he has a grandchild...." Her last words were barely audi
ble.

"Damn him to hell!" Jeb exploded.

McKenzie stepped back, looking at him round-eyed
"Oh, Jeb...don't!"

"And why the hell not!" he ranted, his words jabbing like
ice picks. "He's doing it again, McKenzie. Surely you car
see that."

McKenzie shook her head. "No, Jeb, you're wrong. It's
not like that. If you could have seen him. It's hard to ex
plain, but he was scared, really scared." She twined her fin
gers. "He's...coming home in a few days. I'll...we'll tel
him then. Don't you see it'll be better this way? He's still
awfully sick and I'm afraid—"

"That's just it, isn't it?" Jeb spat. "That's the crux of the
matter. You're afraid, have always been afraid to cross the
mighty Carson Langley. For Pete's sakes, he doesn't walk
on water." He paused, breathing heavily, his nostrils flar-

ing. "God, it's obvious that nothing has changed. The old man still has you exactly where he wants you and that's right under his thumb!"

"Now you wait just a minute," McKenzie cried, aghast, striving to hang on to her temper. "You're way off base and you know it."

"Oh, I am, am I? Well, then prove it to me by going back to the hospital right this minute and telling my father that you're going to marry *me* and not Daniel Evans!"

"Jeb...please...don't." She could hardly speak for the hot throbbing ache that was building inside her. "You're...being unreasonable," she whispered, her mouth trembling.

He prayed for a patience and tried another approach. "Oh, McKenzie, McKenzie, open your eyes. See what he's doing to you, to us. He's using his illness to tighten the screws, just like always. It's time to stand up for what you believe, for what you think, to stop letting him control your life."

Suddenly, McKenzie's eyes flashed anger. "And what if I tell him and he does have another stroke? Are you prepared to live with that on your conscience?"

"Don't you try to make me the heavy in this," he countered harshly. "What's the difference between telling him now or a few days from now? Not one goddamned thing, I'll tell you! The same thing could happen then and you know it."

McKenzie struggled to hold back the tears. "Jeb..."

He charged on as though she hadn't spoken. "Come on, McKenzie, 'fess up. That's not the real reason you didn't tell him now, is it?" He paused, closing his eyes against the hollow feeling of impending doom. "You're still afraid to trust. It's only when the surface is scratched that the truth comes out. You're nothing but a scared little girl, afraid to let go of *daddy* and take a chance with me, with our love."

Jeb paused again, his eyes looking venomous. "You're a coward, McKenzie Moore, a coward." He threw out his hands in despair. "I can see that so clearly, even if you can't."

McKenzie opened her mouth, wanting to scream at him, *No, you're wrong! No, I won't let you do this to me!* But her jaws locked before the words could pass her lips; only a deadly silence greeted his accusations.

Tears were streaming down her face. She made no attempt to control them. Her mind had splintered in a million different directions. Oh, God, was there any truth to what he said? Was she afraid to trust? To take a chance? Knowing that if they failed this time it would kill her?

No. He was wrong. She *was* willing to give up everything for him. But by the same token, he must be willing to meet her halfway. She could never forgive herself if they used her stepfather as a stepping stone to happiness. She could not live with that. She had to make him understand.

Jeb saw the warring emotions cross her face and felt a sudden chill as he held his breath, afraid to hope, afraid not to.

"I love you, Jeb, more than you'll ever know," she whispered, "but I need this extra time."

His face was drained of color, his voice empty of emotion. "Then I guess that says it all."

McKenzie clutched her stomach as though he'd just kicked her. No, this can't be happening. He won't leave me again. He can't!

"Jeb, please..."

"I'm sorry, McKenzie, but I won't play second fiddle to my father any longer." His eyes were unreadable. "Good luck and God bless."

McKenzie stood paralyzed in the middle of the room, with her heart in her throat, watching as he trudged heavily to the

oor and walked out, never to know that he took her heart
ith him.

She folded to her knees under the onslaught of pain....

Chapter 13

I can't marry you, Daniel."

Daniel's brown eyes were unreadable as he watched McKenzie from his position next to the fireplace in the Langley mansion. "Well, I can't say that I'm surprised," he said coldly.

McKenzie's nerves were frayed almost to the breaking point as she searched for the right words to get through this difficult time, to keep from hurting Daniel more than she already had. But nothing about her seemed to be functioning correctly, least of all her mind. She had been feeling this way since Jeb had stormed out of her life two weeks ago.

McKenzie forced herself to move toward the bar. She opened the small refrigerator and reached for a carafe. "Would you like a glass of wine?" she asked, avoiding his eyes.

"I'll pass on the wine, but I'll take a Scotch on the rocks instead."

McKenzie nodded mutely and set about complying with his request, thinking that suddenly they were behaving like virtual strangers. She swallowed a deep sigh and walked toward him, handing him the drink.

She hadn't wanted to go out to dinner with Daniel this evening, but she'd had no choice. She couldn't delay any longer telling him that she couldn't marry him.

He captured her eyes. "Have you told Carson?"

McKenzie's stomach turned a somersault. "No...I haven't. I wanted to tell you first. Anyway, Dad's not strong enough yet. He...he just came home from the hospital."

A taut silence hung in the air.

Then he added, "It's Langley, isn't it?" There was a snarl on his lips as he began stalking the premises like an animal on the prowl, his hand tightfisted around the glass of Scotch.

McKenzie snagged her lower lip between her teeth to keep it from trembling and remained silent. This conversation was turning out to be just as painful as she'd predicted. Unconsciously, she sank her teeth deeper into her lip. She didn't want to discuss Jeb with him, not now, not ever.

"Answer me, McKenzie," Daniel demanded. "Surely I deserve to know the truth." His last words dripped with sarcasm.

"Of...course you do," McKenzie stammered, flushing. "But first will you please sit down?" Her nerves were frayed almost to the breaking point.

Daniel paused in his pacing, his eyes becoming narrowed slits. "Sit down," he mimicked. "Is that all you have to say? Sit down? I'm tempted to wring your beautiful neck for doing this to me." He paused again. "Just exactly how long have you two been carrying on behind my back?"

The color slowly receded from her face under the cruel lash of his tongue. But she withstood the abuse, knowing it was deserved. *Oh, God, would the pain ever go away?* she cried in silent anguish.

"I'm sorry, so sorry," she whispered. "Sorry I...I betrayed you."

"Sorry," he sneered. "Is that your only explanation? You and Langley ride off into the sunset and leave me practically at the altar looking like a goddamned fool, you say, *'sorry!'*"

"Well, if it's any consolation to your battered ego," she cried, his antagonism goading her into lashing back, "Jeb and I are not riding off into the sunset, as you put it." In spite of the nearly intolerable pain, she inhaled a deep breath and plunged on. "My relationship...with...Jeb is over. I...won't be seeing him anymore."

"I don't believe you."

"I don't care what you believe."

"What happened? Did he cut out on you again? Carson always said—"

"Stop it! Don't you dare say another word!"

"Hey, wait a goddamned minute—"

"No, you wait a minute. I told you I was wrong, that I was sorry for what I've done to you, but nothing, absolutely nothing, gives you the right to pass judgment on Jeb, or me, or anyone else for that matter."

She was facing him now, fury pinching her features, but it was the coldness in her eyes that did the damage. "Please...I think you'd better leave now."

Daniel's shoulders slumped in defeat. With a muttered curse, he clawed at his tight neck muscles with his hand. "I'm sorry, McKenzie. You're right. I'm way off base here. It's just that I had so many plans...."

"And I'm sorry, too, Daniel," she said achingly, pressing her palms to her hot cheeks. "But you know, whether you want to admit it or not, that marriage between us would never have worked." Her fingers curved into a ball. "I don't think you ever really loved me—"

"You're wrong there," Daniel cut in, moving his hand from his neck to rub his forehead, his voice filled with weary dejection. "I did love you and still do." He released his breath on a ragged note. "And if you ever change your mind..."

Hot tears burned her eyes. "Thanks," she whispered, swallowing the lump in her throat. "But I...I won't change my mind."

Daniel stared at her an endless moment and then stuck out his hand. "Friends?"

McKenzie's small hand held his as she smiled through her tears. "Friends."

By the time McKenzie trudged wearily up the stairs to her room and closed the door gently behind her, the smile had completely disappeared from her lips.

The silence was almost smothering in its intensity. And the loneliness—God, that didn't even bear thinking about. Yet that devastating emotion was as much a part of her life now as breathing.

Methodically, she began shedding her clothing, an article at a time, until she was down to her bra and panties. She padded into the bathroom, turned on the shower and, after discarding those flimsy garments, merged with the hot water.

However, the water failed to buoy her sagging spirits. Once she had toweled herself dry and doused her body with powder, her mind was again churning at full force.

McKenzie slipped her arms into the robe hanging on the back of the door and made her way back into the bedroom. There she paused and stared at the bed. Should she chance it? She was dead tired. Surely she could sleep. No. Her instincts warned that sleep was still an elusive prey that she would never get this night, even though it was well after midnight.

It would have been so easy to blame her feelings of despair on her confrontation with Daniel, but she knew that wasn't what was ailing her. Oh, that had been traumatic enough all right, but nothing, no matter how terrible, could overshadow losing Jeb. Even the task ahead of telling her stepfather about her and Daniel was no longer a threat.

She felt nothing but emptiness, and when her legs suddenly threatened to buckle beneath her, she stumbled to the bed, giving in to the weak trembles of body and soul.

Hot tears stabbed at the back of her eyes as she squeezed them shut, trying to block out the image of Jeb's face.

Nothing doing. His features were imprinted indelibly on the screen of her mind, even though she had not laid eyes on him since he left. She had no idea where he was. No one did as far as she knew. The morning after their confrontation, the door to his room was wide open, but there had been no sign of Jeb. His clothes were gone, as was everything else that bore testimony to him.

If Rachel knew his whereabouts, she wasn't saying, though Rachel had managed to draw out of McKenzie some of what had taken place between them. McKenzie had cried for hours on Rachel's shoulder with Rachel rocking and soothing her like a baby.

Forget him! her heart had cried. *He's no longer part of your life.*

That ploy failed as well. She was finding it impossible to escape thoughts of Jeb. Her misery was immense. But after that first day, she showed it to no one. Not Rachel. And certainly not Carson. He did not know that she cried in her sleep, and that her spirit was as hushed as the spirit of someone in grief. Grief for what might have been. When Jeb left, part of her had died and nothing could revive it. Never had she known such agony.

How could she have misjudged him so? He hadn't loved ɛr. Nothing but lies had come from his lips. He hadn't anted to settle down. He didn't know the meaning of love ıd commitment. By her hesitation, she had handed him the cuse he needed to pursue his own goals. He had used her. was that simple. She kept telling herself that she did not ɛed Jeb, that she was better off without him, yet she had ɔt been able to convince her heart of this.

Oh, Jeb, she wept, *I thought we had it all.* But they ıdn't. It had all been a mirage. She had told herself so ɔuntless times, and so far that was the only thing that had ɛpt her sane.

That and her confrontation with Jackson Witherspoon. week ago she had pushed aside her heartache and, adrenine pumping through her body, had gone to Witherɔoon's office. The results still brought a smile to her lips....

She had sat patiently in the mayor's reception area and ʋed the hunk behind what she presumed was the secreɾy's desk. Who was he? she wondered idly. Giving him a ɔser look, she decided the hunk was more than likely ʹitherspoon's chauffeur.

The shrill sound of the phone brought McKenzie back to ality. She listened as the man spoke into the receiver. "Yes, ɾ," he said, turning his head toward McKenzie, "she's still aiting." After a few seconds of nodding his head, he put ιe receiver back on its cradle.

McKenzie stood up as the hunk came around the desk. He'll see you now, Ms. Moore."

Nodding politely and snubbing his leering gaze, Mcenzie breezed confidently through the door he held open r her. She had waited a long time for this moment, and no ɔmcat with more brawn than brains was going to rattle her.

Jackson Witherspoon met her just inside the door, his ιnd outstretched, his teeth gleaming as he smiled broadly.

"Sorry to have kept you waiting," he began uneasil
pumping her hand. "But you know how one can get i
volved in his business..." He shrugged, letting his se
tence trail off.

McKenzie's smile was cool. "No, I don't know, M
Witherspoon. Suppose you tell me about it."

Witherspoon was immediately on guard, taking a se
behind his massive desk as though it would protect hin
"What did you want to see me about, Ms. Moore?" l
asked, a hand waving McKenzie toward the empty chair. '
know you're from the *Tribune*."

God, what an accomplished liar, McKenzie thought, ey
ing him as if he had just crawled out from under a rock. Yo
know exactly why I'm here and that's why you're sweatir
like you've been running a marathon.

"Let's just cut the formalities, Witherspoon," McKenz
said, "and get to the heart of the matter."

Fear froze his eyes.

McKenzie went on, "What I have to say won't take nearl
as long as you kept me waiting."

"I beg your pardon?"

McKenzie dropped her briefcase in the chair in front c
her and, placing both her hands on the back of it, began h
rehearsed execution. "First, let me inform you that a fu
investigation of your personal and business affairs has bee
completed." Ignoring his gasp, she continued. "I have fig
ures concerning your outside income and, more impor
tantly, your expenses. I also know that your companior
Shelley Storm, costs you about half of what the taxpayer
give you in salary. To say nothing of the condo at Corpu
and the new boat and—"

Suddenly, Witherspoon jumped up and slammed his han
down on the desk, his lips tissue-paper white, his chi
shaking. "Now you wait just a damned minute, young lady

Where do you get off checking into my personal affairs? My affairs are no one's business but mine.''

"I happen to disagree," McKenzie countered, unruffled. I know for a fact the voters would be most interested in knowing just how you got the money for your 'little ex-as.'"

Droplets of pearllike sweat began their march down Witherspoon's face. He lowered himself back into the chair, his legs no longer supporting him.

Dammit, he thought, everything was coming apart at the seams, and he didn't know what to do about it. He felt like a cornered animal, with everyone out to get him. First Dillard taking off, leaving him holding the bag, and now this nosey broad with a vendetta comes in threatening to topple his empire.

Suddenly, Witherspoon bowed his shoulders. He wasn't dead yet, just temporarily wounded. "Just what the hell are you trying to say?" he demanded harshly.

McKenzie had him by the jugular and she knew it. "Ah, Mr. Mayor, you've asked, so you shall receive. Now comes the good part. How would you like to hear how you sound on tape?"

Witherspoon's face turned whiter.

With deliberate slowness, McKenzie leaned over, snapped open her case and reached for the tiny tape recorder lying on top. She flipped it on.

For several seconds there was a silence. Then came the hushed voice of Witherspoon demanding from Dillard that he damn well better deliver the promised amount of cash before he, Dillard, turned tail and ran.

"Turn it off!" Witherspoon gritted through his teeth. "Turn it off!"

"Well, how do you think you sounded?" McKenzie demanded, turning the screw just a bit tighter.

Witherspoon was trying desperately to regroup, fightin, for his lost composure. "You can't use that in a court of law and you know it."

McKenzie snapped off the machine and looked hin squarely in the eye. "We'll see about that, Mr. Mayor, we'l see about that." She watched then as he slumped over hi desk, dropping his head in his hands. "I think we both knov what the outcome will be." McKenzie pivoted on her hee and walked out the door.

Long minutes passed as the mayor sat, unmoving. Ther Jackson Witherspoon raised his head and, staring inte space, mentally began to draft a letter. "It is with regret tha I submit my resignation..."

Unfortunately, the high from bringing the mayor to hee had not lasted, had not proved to be the panacea McKenzie had hoped. She went back down to the depths of despair where she wallowed, hating herself because she could no rebound.

But then fate had intervened, perking her up consider ably. Carson was released from the hospital. The delay had been for precautionary measures, the doctors had said. I turned out that her stepfather was not quite as strong as they first had thought.

McKenzie had been tempted to throw a party for his homecoming, but was glad she had scratched the idea wher she saw how exhausted Carson was. The trip in itself was exhilarating enough. After remaining downstairs for only a short time, he'd gone straight upstairs to bed.

Now that her stepfather was home and definitely on the mend, she was anxious to tell him about her broken engagement, and then maybe, just maybe, she could pick up the pieces of her life and start anew. Was that possible?

Could she actually banish Jeb from her heart, her life? Could she survive, never again to feel his hands on her reasts? She would miss those big, strong hands that felt lightly rough against her smooth skin as he squeezed softly t first, then harder...harder, her nipples burning in his palms. What would it be like never to feel his mouth on her reasts, taking the nipples between his teeth? Never to feel im stroke them with his tongue...? Oh, God!

Suddenly, fighting off the pain, McKenzie forced her eyes open and sprang from the bed. Tightening the sash on her robe, she padded across the room, slid back the door to the patio and walked out into the cold night air.

Stars. Hundred of stars winked at her from the heavens, cutting through her tears. Were they signaling her a message? she wondered. Yes, perhaps they were. Perhaps they were saying that today is a new day, a day filled with hope and challenge.

Suddenly, McKenzie felt her heart swell, knowing that she must meet this day head-on, accept new challenges, cling to new hopes. No more wallowing in self-pity. No more tears.

She could have a full life without Jeb. She had done so in the past; she could do so again.

After all, she was a survivor, wasn't she?

"Well, Dad, what kind of day did you have?" McKenzie asked, walking into the den and tossing her purse onto the nearest chair, exhaustion etched in her finely boned face.

Carson Langley rose from his comfortable chair and moved slowly toward his stepdaughter, a smile brightening his gaunt features. After leaning over and grazing her cheek with his lips, he said, "Now that I'm home, I feel as if I've got the world by the tail."

"And you look like it, too," she said, taking his hand in hers and leading him to the couch. "A little thin perhaps, but it won't take Rosie any time to put meat back on those bones."

After they were seated, slightly apart from each other, Carson said a tad gruffly, "Unfortunately, I can't say the same for you." A frown creased his brow. "I've never seen you looking so poorly, girl. If I didn't know better, I'd think someone had punched you in both eyes."

McKenzie tossed his concern aside with a smile, though she did make a point to shift her gaze. "Just a case of insomnia," she said lightly, before standing up and moving to the bar. "I think I'll treat myself to a glass of wine. It's been a long day."

Carson ambled toward her. "Sounds good."

"What about you?" McKenzie asked. "Think the good doctor would let you have a taste of beer?" Her lips broke into a smile and her eyes took on a sparkle. "Not only do we have your homecoming to celebrate, but something else as well."

Carson's gaze was expectant. "Oh, and might that be that you and Daniel have set a wedding date?"

Both the smile and the sparkle suddenly disappeared like a flame doused with a bucket of water. "Not now, Dad. Later, please," she said, her voice strong but tense.

"McKenzie?"

"You'll be beside yourself when you hear this," she said quickly, her eyes lighting up once again.

Carson was curious in spite of himself. "Is it, by any chance, Witherspoon?"

McKenzie laughed. "That's right. He'll be resigning any day now."

"Hot damn, girl, you did it! You actually succeeded in cutting that bastard down to size." His laugh rang around the room as he grabbed her at the waist, giving her a bear hug. "Doctor or no doctor, this does indeed call for a celebration. Hand me one of those beers."

"Only a tiny sip now, Dad."

Carson frowned, then popped the top on the can and, reaching out, clanked it against her glass. With misty eyes matching his crusty voice, he said, "A job well done!"

For a second, McKenzie had trouble speaking. At last, blinking back the tears, she smiled proudly and said, "Thanks, Dad. I'm glad I made you happy."

Suddenly, an awkward silence fell between them as their emotions took over. Then, after giving McKenzie another brief hug, Carson plopped his beer down on the counter and eased himself onto a bar stool. "Let's hear it. I want you to feed this starving old man all the gory details."

She did. McKenzie entertained him with a blow-by-blow account of her interview with the mayor.

Then, determined to take advantage of his mellow mood, she took a deep breath and plunged ahead. "Dad, I'm not going to marry Daniel." There, she'd said it; she had delivered the bombshell.

A stillness descended over the room.

For a moment longer, Carson just stared at her in silence. Finally he said, "Was this a sudden decision?"

McKenzie met his gaze head on. "No...no, it wasn't. I've known for a long time that...Daniel and I weren't right for each other, but I..." Her voice trailed off.

"All right, McKenzie," he said with a weary droop of his shoulders. "I guess I have no choice but to accept your decision, though I don't have to like it. But what I can't accept is your explanation for those ungodly smudges under your eyes and the haunted look in them."

"It...it's nothing, Dad. I'm just tired, that's all."

"I bet! Something's going on; I can feel it in these old bones, but I can't get a damned thing out of anyone. That sister of mine is clammed up tighter than a widow woman's purse. And Jeb. Well, I haven't seen hide nor hair of him in over two weeks now."

"He's...not here anymore." She almost choked on the words

"I know that, dammit. I may be sick, but I'm not blind." Carson's eyes narrowed. "It's Jeb, isn't it?"

McKenzie's body froze. "No," she lied, twisting her back to him.

"I don't believe you."

She turned a deaf ear.

Carson refused to give up. "Has he hurt you again?"

McKenzie couldn't take any more, nor could she allow this conversation to go any further. She had no intention of airing her pain. It was still too fresh, exposed, raw.

Before she could lose her ongoing battle with tears, she whirled and suddenly kissed Carson on his lined cheek. "Good night, Dad," she whispered. "I'll see you in the morning." Without a backward glance, she tore from the room.

His "Dammit, girl, I'm not through talking to you" followed her all the way to her room.

McKenzie just made it to her room and closed the door before the sobs broke loose from her throat.

Spring rode in on the coattails of winter, fusing one day with another. With the coming of a new season, McKenzie made great strides in gathering the scattered pieces of her life and mending them carefully back together.

Work was again the lifeline to which she clung. She worked long hours, taking every assignment that came her way, determined to fill the hours. And it was paying off; her work had never been better.

To those on the outside looking in, McKenzie's life was one worth envying. The news media, not just the *Tribune*, had given her full credit for the dethroning the mayor. When the news of his resignation hit the television and the paɔers, McKenzie immediately became a hot item. But she shunned the publicity, wanting only to be left alone.

Following Witherspoon's resignation and subsequent arrest for fraud, Dillard and Rollins were picked up and charged with attempted murder, which added fuel to the fire. Charges of theft were brought against them also, as a cache of money was found in their possession. It was a scandal that rocked the city and would not be soon forgotten.

If it hadn't been for her stepfather, though, the victory would have meant very little to her. Carson could not have been prouder.

Yet there were still days when the memories of Jeb could not be suppressed, and today was one of them.

McKenzie had come home early from the office and had just sat down in the kitchen, toying with a bowl of fruit, when she sensed she had company. She looked quickly toward the door. Rachel was standing there watching her.

"You can't keep on pushing yourself like this, you know," her aunt said calmly, wandering farther into the kitchen and taking a chair in front of McKenzie.

"I'm . . . I'm all right," McKenzie responded softly.

"Well, Jeb's not." Her tone was flat.

McKenzie's head jerked up. "He . . . he told you that?"

"Not in so many words, no, but all I have to do is look at him." She paused. "He's been staying some with me and some at his mother's old place."

McKenzie licked her lips. "How . . . how is he?"

"Not good. Drinking, wearing his misery like a second skin."

"Oh, Aunt Rachel," McKenzie cried, her chin starting to quiver.

"Do you love him?"

For a long moment McKenzie sat silent, her forehead knitted, her fingers lacing nervously. "I . . ."

"Answer the question, please," Rachel pressed softly.

McKenzie's eyes were brimming with tears. "Of course I love him."

"Then go to him, child, and tell him."

"Oh, Auntie, if it were only that simple," McKenzie cried, feeling as if her entire life had passed from her hands. "He . . . he accused me of not loving him enough, that . . . I loved Dad more than him . . . that I was afraid . . ." Hot tears scaled her face. "I tried to tell him that wasn't so . . . that I loved him more than life itself."

Rachel grasped McKenzie's hands. "Then prove it to him," she urged again. "He's bleeding on the inside. I beg you, don't sacrifice love for pride. Haven't you learned by now that we have to reach out and grab the precious moments that life has to offer?" Rachel let go of McKenzie's hand and tried to dam the flow of tears with her warm fingertips. "You're being given a second chance; so few people get one. But in order to get that second chance you have to be willing to *take* a chance. Can't you see that?"

McKenzie sat motionless. Her heart began to pound.

Was Rachel right? Had she been afraid to take a chance for fear of being hurt again? Jeb had accused her of the same thing. And they were right.

She had been afraid. But no longer. Rachel had finally made her see the truth—that without Jeb, life had no meaning. Jeb was her life.

Suddenly, a brilliant smile changed McKenzie's features. She jumped up and dashed around the table to grab Rachel.

"Remember, I owe you one, Auntie!" she cried ecstatically.

Chapter 14

The bright sunlight of the early morning almost blinded Jeb as he drew back the curtain in his aunt's apartment. That done, he turned, his eyes sweeping the room.

His bags were packed. Again. Everything seemed in order. Nothing of importance left behind. When Rachel returned home this evening, there would be no sign that a warm body had ever occupied this room, he thought with cynical amusement.

Shifting, he stared out the window, hearing the birds chirp, the only sound able to penetrate his foggy brain. But for their cry, he might as well have been on another planet, so complete was his sense of estrangement. He felt separated from McKenzie by a whole world, a distance so far-reaching, the mind could not grasp it.

He began pacing the floor, swaying somewhat, disoriented. His head weighed a ton, at least, and yet he hadn't had a drink in over two days now.

With a disgusted sigh, Jeb stomped into the bathroom, checking one last time for articles left behind. After switching on the light, he peered at his reflection in the mirror.

Gawd! He looked as if he had one foot in the grave and the other on a banana peel. Bleary eyes, pale skin beneath the natural tan and a tongue that came complete with its own coat of fur and a slab of cement in the pit of his stomach mocked him from the mirror.

He had been like this from the moment he had lost McKenzie, feeling sorry for himself while shuffling back and forth between the Hill-Country place and here. And when he knew McKenzie would be away from the office, he'd gone to the *Tribune* and made sure things were in order, knowing his departure was imminent.

It was during this time that the news of the mayor's resignation had jumped into prime time. He couldn't have been prouder of McKenzie's accomplishment; it was a bitter pill to swallow that he hadn't been able to tell her so.

And he was damned glad that Dillard and Rollins had been arrested before he'd gotten his hands on them. If he had his way, they'd put them under the jail instead of inside it.

Now that he was actually leaving, hell-bent on taking another foreign assignment, he felt as though he were about to face a firing squad. His insides were twisted and mangled. But he had to go. He'd already said his goodbyes to Rachel, and as soon as the taxi came for him, he had one more stop to make and that was to say goodbye to his father, hoping that he wouldn't run into McKenzie.

Jeb blinked furiously into the mirror, willing his face to disappear. It did, only to have McKenzie's suddenly appear in its place. With an agonized groan, he stagged back into the bedroom and flopped down into a chair. Leaning his head back and closing his eyes, he prayed for McKenzie's image to vanish.

But it was not meant to be. McKenzie. She was everywhere he went, everywhere he smelled, everywhere he touched. He often dreamed that she was permanently mounted to the base of his spine, never to leave him. He remembered the times they made love, her body reacting so violently he thought her joints would snap in two.

Sometimes, after a climax, he was afraid she would never return to him, her chin thrown back, the tensions of painful pleasure etched in the curves of her face, her breasts high and proud, undefended on the fragile cage of her ribs....

Sweet Jesus!

In desperation, he lunged out of the chair. He was going off the deep end! Thoughts of her were driving him crazy. Why couldn't he let her go? Why was he punishing himself this way?

Fool! She doesn't love you. Why is that so hard for you to comprehend? That's life, man. You've got to roll with the punches and go on with your life.

Suddenly, the sound of the taxi's horn jolted him out of his tormenting thoughts and stilled his pacing. Wasting no time, he grabbed his duffel bag and strode out the door, kicking it closed behind him.

He had never felt more alone in his life.

McKenzie's hands were clammy as she made her way down the stairs, a new day fresh on the horizon.

Her eyes had popped open at the crack of dawn, but she had forced herself to remain in bed awhile longer, even though sleep was impossible. Over and over she had rehearsed what she would say to Jeb when she went to him this morning. She just prayed she wasn't too late, that she hadn't killed his love.

As McKenzie fastened her hand around the front doorknob, she heard a movement behind her. Slowly, she turned around.

"You're going to him, aren't you?" Carson asked, standing in the doorway to the den.

McKenzie felt the bottom drop out of her stomach as she encountered his lined features. Her eyes were as wide as saucers. "You . . . you know?"

"Yes, I know," he said softly. "Rachel told me."

"I see," McKenzie said, waiting for the brewing storm to erupt. Yet, she knew this time she would weather it. Nothing her stepfather could do or say could stop her from going to Jeb.

Then, miraculously, Carson smiled. "Go with my blessing, then, my child," he said gently, holding out his arms to her.

For a moment, McKenzie stood in stunned disbelief, positive she had not heard him correctly.

At last he spoke again, his eyes watering. "Can you . . . find it in your heart to forgive me for being an ornery old fool and interfering in your life to the point that I almost ruined it?"

"Oh, Dad," McKenzie cried, diving into his arms, sobs racking her body.

"Shhh," Carson begged, "dry up those tears before you mess up that pretty face." He patted her on the back. "Go now, go to him."

Smiling through her tears, McKenzie pulled back and whispered, "I love you."

Quickly, she retraced her steps to the door and opened it, only to have Carson's voice stop her again.

"Oh, would you please tell my son for me that if he's interested in taking over the newspaper permanently, it's his. I'm retiring so I can enjoy life and get ready to bounce my grandchild on my knee." His eyes twinkled.

Smiling tremulously, and with a heart as light as air, McKenzie blew him a kiss. "You bet I'll tell him."

Jeb had just opened the back door of the cab when he saw her. She was walking toward him. *Is she real or just a figment of my imagination!* He shut his eyes only for an instant, then opened them.

Their eyes collided.

Jeb drank in every detail of McKenzie's face, committing to memory her pale features, emphasized now by the bruised shadows under her eyes and the sunken hollows of her cheeks.

But she was no mirage and she was beautiful.

Suddenly, yesterday no longer mattered. Jeb knew in that one blinding second that he could not leave her, that his love for her was far above the price of rubies. It no longer mattered if he was second to his father; he could live with that. And it no longer mattered that she was afraid; he could handle that, too.

What he could not handle was living without her. She was the blood that flowed to his heart, and without her he could not survive.

But for the life of him, he could not move. The block of cement that was in his belly had plunged to his feet.

McKenzie swallowed, feeling her arms grow weak, her fingers tremble, her brain short out in panic and shock. Her stomach lurched, and she was afraid she might faint.

Oh, God, I'm too late! He's leaving... leaving... leaving... Her heart stopped beating. Her life would end.

The driver was waiting, leaning nonchalantly against the side of the car, taking it all in.

Suddenly, Jeb moved, swinging around to face the man.

McKenzie reeled as a pain so excruciating, so devastating, splintered through her, almost cutting her legs out from under her. *I can't stand this!* she screamed silently, squeezing her eyes shut, turning slowly, praying she could make it back to her car before she completely fell apart.

"McKenzie!"

Jeb's agonizing cry pierced her soul.

Then, like a flash of lightning on a stormy night, McKenzie whirled and stood rooted to the spot as Jeb began making his way toward her.

"Don't go," he pleaded brokenly, his voice barely above a whisper. "I love you."

McKenzie remained helpless, unable to move, to speak, to think. Only her eyes were alive, watching the taxi as it sped down the deserted street. Was she hallucinating? Had he said he loved her? For a moment she was afraid her heart would shatter with happiness.

And I love you, McKenzie wanted to say, but her lips could not form the words. They felt paralyzed.

Jeb stopped within touching distance of her, his eyes deep in their sockets, a panicked expression on his face.

Later, neither one knew who had made the first move. But it made not a whit of difference as they clung fiercely, their tears mingling, their hearts joining.

"Don't cry, my darling, don't cry," he begged raggedly, his face curved into the fragrance of her neck. "I'm sorry...so sorry."

"No," she whispered, "I'm the one who's sorry."

Suddenly, he swept her up in his arms and, leaving his bag sitting on the ground, strode up the walk and into the house, holding her as though she were made of the rarest of glass. He didn't pause until he had reached the bedroom.

"Love me," McKenzie pleaded, meeting his eyes, touching the bruised shadows on his face as if to prove to herself that he was real, achingly real.

Words, explanations, the cleansing of their souls would come later. Now all McKenzie cared about was proving her love for him, replacing the pain, the heartaches, with a magic that was born of old.

"I could never have left you," Jeb said thickly, his mouth hovering above hers. "Please believe me."

"Oh, Jeb, I love you. Love you so much."

With unsteady hands, Jeb let her down, McKenzie's body grazing the length of his, every muscle, every nerve experiencing a jolt, setting him on fire.

Then his hold tightened, his lips seeking and finding the moist sweetness of hers. He groaned, their breaths mingling. "I love you, want you..."

"Oh, yes, yes," McKenzie sighed, the tip of her tongue probing his ear. "It's been so long...."

Widening the gap between them, Jeb began inching her sweater over her head. With shaking hands he unzipped her jeans and, with her help, cast them aside. When she was standing before him naked, Jeb stood motionless, held spellbound as the sunlight played over her body.

Jeb urgently flung aside his own clothing, then lifted McKenzie again into his arms and lowered her onto the bed.

"Jeb, Jeb, you smell so good, taste so good," she crooned, nibbling at his mouth, his cheeks, his neck.

He moaned, dropping a kiss on her mouth, then another, his eyes watching her as his hand rested on her kneecap, feeling her legs relax, part slightly.

"You're beautiful," Jeb whispered, his hand moving lazily up and down the inside of her thigh now.

McKenzie's eyes grew dazed as he kissed her deeply on the mouth, the base of her throat, each nipple, her stomach. Then inching lower, he spread her legs with the palm of his hand and opened his mouth on her.

Her cry reached the heavens, the muscles in her stomach going tight under the loving assault. At last, her eyelids drooped as his hand covered her breast and stroked.

"Please...I can't take much more." Her words came in short, raspy spurts as her hands launched a counterattack, probing, seeking, touching.

"Nor I," he ground out, as she climbed on top of him easing herself down slowly.

"Oh, God, oh, yes," Jeb muttered incoherently as sh arched her back, her hands digging into his shoulders.

Then McKenzie lunged forward, her hair disheveled Their eyes locked, and her stomach quivered as she matched him thrust for thrust until his hands flew to her hips, holding her steady, reaching deep into her.

Spent and panting, Jeb drew her down on his chest, hi mouth against her ear, whispering, "I love you."

"And I love you," McKenzie said, her face hidden agains his neck.

They lay, still joined, for a long, long time.

"It's against the law, you know, to sleep during the day,' a voice drawled, nudging her back to reality.

"Mmmm." McKenzie stretched, then her eyes poppe open, remembering, remembering being carried to bed Jeb's bed, and loving the entire day away.

"What about making love during the day? Is that agains the law, too?" she asked, snuggling closer against him.

"Never, my love, never that," Jeb teased, her breast sof under his palm.

As she watched his beloved face, a silence fell betwee them. "Jeb," she began, searching for words to tell hin what was in her heart, while trying to block out the feel o his hands on her. "I just want you to know that you wer right, that I . . . I was a coward, that it was easier just to g along with Dad. It . . . it was safe that way, no chance o getting hurt. . . ."

Jeb's hand stilled. "And now?"

"I'm yours for as long as you want me."

"Forever, darling, forever," Jeb whispered, peering dow at her, devouring her with his eyes. "But the blame is not al yours."

McKenzie shook her head, trying to silence him. "No."

"Yes," Jeb countered. "I've been headstrong, pig-headed, determined to have everything my way. Will you ever forgive me for not being more patient, more under-standing?" He paused, drawing a ragged breath. "After all, you suffered at my hands...losing the baby...I should—"

This time she was successful in stopping his flow of words. Her lips slammed into his, sweetly silencing him.

After a long moment, McKenzie pulled back and smiled through misty eyes. "Let's not think about yesterday, only today and our future together."

"Speaking of the future, what do you think about my writing a book?" He grinned sheepishly. "I've always had a secret yearning to do that."

McKenzie's smile flashed like the purest sunshine. "Oh, I think that's wonderful. But you may want to change your mind when you hear what I have to tell you."

"Oh, and what might that be?" Jeb asked indulgently.

"Your father wants you to take over the paper, perma-nently."

Jeb looked stunned. "Well, what do you know about that?" There was awe in his voice. "I guess that means he approves of us."

"Yep."

"Miracles never cease."

"Will you consider it?"

"Only if you want me to."

McKenzie ran her hands down his chest. "I...I don't see why you can't do both—write a book as well as publish the paper."

"What's my father going to do?" he asked thickly.

"Retire and wait for a grandchild to bounce on his knee. And that's a direct quote."

He flashed her a leering grin. "Well, in that case, we'd better not disappoint him."

"No, I guess not."

"I warn you, there'll be no rest for the weary."

"Is that a promise?"

"Carved in stone." His hand slid down her thighs.

McKenzie sighed and closed her eyes, drowning in the sensations his hands were arousing.

"Mmmm...so warm...so perfect..." he whispered.

"You're impossible."

"I'm in love."

"It's wonderful, isn't it?" she gasped under his expert touch.

"You're wonderful."

"I love you," McKenzie said with a heavy sigh, sliding her arms around Jeb's neck, her body moving, pushing under his, her lips seeking his. They kissed deeply, urgently.

"And I love you, more than life."

A sweet smile curved McKenzie's lips as love spilled from her eyes. "Who said fairy tales don't come true?" she whispered, their bodies meshing as one.

READERS' COMMENTS ON SILHOUETTE INTIMATE MOMENTS:

"About a month ago a friend loaned me my first Silhouette. I was thoroughly surprised as well as totally addicted. Last week I read a Silhouette Intimate Moments and I was even more pleased. They are the best romance series novels I have ever read. They give much more depth to the plot, characters, and the story is fundamentally realistic. They incorporate tasteful sex scenes, which is a must, especially in the 1980's. I only hope you can publish them fast enough."

S.B.*, Lees Summit, MO

"After noticing the attractive covers on the new line of Silhouette Intimate Moments, I decided to read the inside and discovered that this new line was more in the line of books that I like to read. I do want to say I enjoyed the books because they are so realistic and a lot more truthful than so many romance books today."

J.C., Onekama, MI

"I would like to compliment you on your books. I will continue to purchase all of the Silhouette Intimate Moments. They are your best line of books that I have had the pleasure of reading."

S.M., Billings, MT

*names available on request

Take 4 Silhouette Special Edition novels
FREE

and preview future books in your home for 15 days!

When you take advantage of this offer, you get 4 Silhouette Special Edition® novels FREE and without obligation. Then you'll also have the opportunity to preview 6 brand-new books —delivered right to your door for a FREE 15-day examination period—as soon as they are published.

When you decide to keep them, you pay just $1.95 each ($2.50 each in Canada) *with no shipping, handling, or other charges of any kind!*

Romance *is* alive, well and flourishing in the moving love stories of Silhouette Special Edition novels. They'll awaken your desires, enliven your senses, and leave you tingling all over with excitement... and the first 4 novels are yours to keep. You can cancel at any time.

As an added bonus, you'll also receive a FREE subscription to the Silhouette Books Newsletter as long as you remain a member. Each issue is filled with news on upcoming books, interviews with your favorite authors, even their favorite recipes.

To get your 4 FREE books, fill out and mail the coupon today!

Silhouette Special Edition®

Silhouette Books, 120 Brighton Rd., P.O. Box 5084, Clifton, NJ 07015-5084
